# An Affair of Strangers

# *An Affair*

## A Novel by

# *of Strangers*

**JOHN CROSBY**

**STEIN AND DAY**/*Publishers*/New York

First published in 1975
Copyright © 1975 by John Crosby
All rights reserved
Designed by Ed Kaplin
Printed in the United States of America
Stein and Day/*Publishers*/ Scarborough House,
Briarcliff Manor, N.Y. 10510


*Library of Congress Cataloging in Publication Data*

Crosby, John, 1912-
    An affair of strangers.

    I.   Title.
PZ4.C9485Af  [PS3553.R55]      813'.5'4      74-30071
ISBN 0-8128-1785-0

*To Gnome*

# *An Affair of Strangers*

# CHAPTER 1

The Place de St.-Cyr on the Left Bank is the cynosure of five streets which meet at the Café des Pyramides, far too grand a name for the little zinc-barred café. The three swarthy men sat huddled to their ears in their coats. It was cold out on the pavement. They'd have been better off inside next to the zinc bar where all the other customers quite sensibly drank, but they'd been told to stay outside so as not to miss the car when it came down the Rue de Noailles. The car was to pause only momentarily, just long enough for them to jump in; then it was to disappear down the Rue de St.-Piele. That was the plan.

The girl sat apart, at a rear table, partly because she was accustomed to sitting apart, partly because she was the lookout. The men were engrossed in their talk. The girl's black eyes were never still, darting back and forth between the Rue de Noailles and the youngest of the men at the other table. He was her lover, her very first lover, and her feeling for him was one of bottomless tenderness. Not passion. Just sweetness. It was her preoccupation with her young man and with the only street she'd been told to look down that made her miss Ferenc's approach.

Ferenc came down the Rue de Grenouille, which ran along the little triangular café, very swiftly on his rubber soles, the gun already in his hand but concealed in his long sleeve. He was alone, and this was their undoing. They'd been warned of the assassination squads, even warned of the swiftness and boldness of their operation. It was eleven in the morning, and one didn't expect assassination at that hour. Still, they might have anticipated that. What they didn't anticipate was only one man, and on foot. They'd been alerted to think of squads, in cars, and there were no cars about. If a car with its premonitory noise had approached, they'd have been on their guard, but they weren't on their guard for this rubber-soled, solitary young man who walked straight to the table, poked his silenced Smith and Wesson into the chest of the young lover, and killed him with a single shot. Regretfully, as always. The next man had only time for a spasm of concern to light up his eyes, when he was extinguished with a single shot in the very center of the chest, the best place at point-blank range. The last man, who was the leader, managed only a lightning grab at the gun lying in his lap underneath *Figaro*, which would report the happening the next morning on page 2. He never made it. *Figaro* got in the way for half a second, and Ferenc killed him, the gun barely three inches from his chest. It was all over in a total elapsed time of 1.5 seconds. Impossible, you say, and it is impossible to rehearse three shots at such speed, but Ferenc had discovered time and again that his actual performance under stress —with that extra adrenaline to spur the muscles—was faster than possibility.

Ferenc hadn't expected the girl, and even under the pressure of events he felt a twinge of annoyance. Intelligence always missed one thing, and it threw you off. He'd seen the girl only as he rounded the building, and with two seconds to make up his mind, never slowing the rapid, noiseless stride because speed was essential when it was three against one, he'd decided he'd have to leave her till afterward. It was risky because his back was to her and if she had a gun, he'd be in for it.

He swung the gun around to the girl before the last of the Arabs had slid to the ground. She was gone. The gun was out now, naked for all to see, especially the drinkers in the bar, and he stubbed it away in his pocket. He could hear the light footsteps now, clacking down the Rue de Grenouille. She'd picked the closest cover—the side of the café blocked his aim—and she must have taken off with the first shot to have made even that shelter because it was thirty feet away. Well-trained, thought Ferenc, and took off after her, leaping over the rivulets of blood on the flagstone.

He rounded the café, gun out again to get a quick shot, but the young girl, running like an antelope, turned instantly into the Rue Descartes and vanished from his sight. Even as he pounded after, he was considering the alternative. Already he was off course. The plan had been to walk directly across the little five-pointed square, even though it meant exposing himself for a few seconds, to the Rue des Lignes, the quickest way to the underground, where he'd be lost in the crowd.

Now he was pelting down a street in the open, the nearest underground station on this course was—he calculated—a good seven blocks. *Merde!* He shot around the corner of the Rue Descartes. The girl was far down the block—she was fast, this one—running straight to the Boulevard des Capucines. Smart girl. Once on the boulevard she'd be safe enough. You couldn't go shooting girls on Paris boulevards at 11:00 A.M. Ferenc steadied his arm on the edge of the building and squeezed off a forlorn shot, but it was hopeless. The gun was no good over fifteen feet, not with that silencer on it. The girl never stopped running, turning off the boulevard and slowing to a jaunty walk as she disappeared around the corner.

It was Ferenc's turn to take to his heels. He was around two corners from the Café des Pyramides, but already the place was in uproar. He heard the sound of running feet coming down all five of the streets. No police sounds yet, thank God. Ferenc darted across the Rue Descartes, the gun in his pocket, and ran full out; speed attracted attention, but it was of the essence. There were only four people on the street, and they stared, but stares didn't bother him. They had nothing to go on so they wouldn't do anything.

At the next intersection he turned down the Avenue Brussic. It was risky because it was a big broad street, full of people, but Ferenc always felt it was best to flee in a crowd. It inhibited individualism. Anyway, he was on the Avenue Brussic for only one full block, pushing the pedestrians roughly out of his way; then he darted down the Rue d'Anthieu, a serpentine alley of Byzantine complexity that he knew like the back of his hand. He ran flat out down the dark, narrow street which was choked with parked cars, and took the first right turn into an even narrower alleyway, where he slowed to a walk. It was a rabbit warren from here on, and he turned and twisted through it, heading always in the direction of the Seine where the car was. A covey of garbage cans stood at the doorway of a little restaurant, and in one he dropped the gun, which sank instantly into an extravagance of pigs' entrails.

On the Boulevard des Capucines, the black-eyed girl walked swiftly, dry-eyed, the muscles of her face held in a vise of concentration which, she'd been taught, was the best way to fight back tears. That was the trouble with being an Arab. You burst into tears at every juncture. It was the Arab curse, these damned waterworks. So she kept her face taut as a bowstring and her mind a total blank, a sort of white wall against which the dead face of Abou, eyes open, only occasionally jumped up to be instantly suppressed. She walked next to the wall, keeping the rest of the pedestrians between her and any gunman on the other side of the street, as she'd been taught. She walked fast but not fast enough to attract attention. Just a beautiful black-eyed, brown-skinned, very chic girl. Paris was full of them.

At the corner of the boulevard and the Rue Général Férand she casually stepped into a taxi and gave the name of her hotel. You never took taxis to your hotel—always to someplace three blocks away so you couldn't be traced—unless you were in a very great hurry and you were about to leave the city. Chantal was in a very great hurry, and she was leaving not only the city but the country. But how?

"What did she look like?"

"Beautiful," said Ferenc. "They all are. It's easier to get them on the planes."

"And sympathy," said Jepthah dryly. "Everyone hates Arab men—and loves the girls."

Ferenc was packing swiftly. There wasn't much. "They don't stay beautiful long," he observed. "Arab girls, they blow up like balloons before thirty."

"They don't live that long. Not in this kind of work. How old was she?" Jepthah was leaning against the dresser. He'd already packed, and the slim case was at his feet, his coat over his arm.

"Eighteen, I'd say. Damn intelligence. Why don't they get it right once?"

"They got most of it right. Were the rest of them right? Abou, Ali, and Muhammad?"

Ferenc grinned. He'd been tight as a fiddle string, always was after one of these affairs, and now he was beginning to unwind. Abou, Ali, and Muhammad was one of their jokes. Ferenc had already killed six Abous and four Muhammads. The Arabs seemed to have only about three *prénoms*. It made identification difficult.

"Someday we'll get a job to do three Abous!" said Ferenc. "Have you wiped up?"

"Everything except these dresser drawers you've been opening."

Ferenc took the towel and carefully wiped the dresser from top to bottom, especially the knobs.

"Come on," he said. They left the room in the little hotel on the Rue de Seine neither more nor less grubby than when they entered it. They changed cabs twice before they took one to the airport, and at the airport the tickets read not Tel Aviv but Rome. They used to go via Zurich, but the Swiss had got awfully nosey lately. The Italians, on the other hand, were as slaphappy and inefficient and corrupt as ever. A convenience for an Israeli gunman but, unfortunately, equally convenient for Arab gunmen, who used Rome all the time. Sometimes they saw each other at Fiumicino, both Arab and Israeli well-heeled, well-dressed, each fully conscious the other was off to do a job on somebody. But whom?

They were in Tel Aviv by midnight.

The girl's face was a mask as she got her key, as she rose in the tiny lift that barely held two persons, as she slipped the key into the lock of the threadbare, grimy room, even up to the very point when she pulled the key from the lock and closed the door. Then she flung herself into a paroxysm of grief—arms outspread, mouth wide open, eyes gushing tears. But nothing came out of the mouth, no sound at all. She mouthed grief in silence, back arched, streaming eyes cast up to heaven, as much of an indulgence as she permitted. She would have liked, of course, to lie on the floor and howl like a dog in the good old Arab way, but you couldn't do that in a Paris hotel.

Besides, there wasn't much time. Even while she was silently howling her very Arab grief, she was moving across to the closet, pulling out two dresses, her wool suit, packing them neatly—not flinging them—because they'd look into her cases.

Where was the money?

If Ali had it on him, she was done. She had barely twenty francs in her purse after the taxi ride. Ali wouldn't have all that money on him. Would he? She didn't really know the drill that well because she was very new at this and very young (only seventeen, not eighteen, as Ferenc had guessed). She was fully packed in two minutes, and only then did she clamp down on the extravagance of grief. Two full minutes. That was all the grief a girl was allowed in this business. Then, in front of the little square mirror over the washstand, she made up her face—taking a full three minutes because it was important. She was very good at it.

Where would the money be? She would need money because they had not entrusted her with her ticket, thinking she'd run away, the fools! The idiots! This was why they got bested every time—they didn't think things through. The face in the mirror was a mask again, and under the Revlon and the pancake number 3, it was becoming a much older face, much older than seventeen. Chantal had discovered it was the only way to keep the men off her, to look older than time and harder than diamonds.

Where would Ali keep the money? On him, probably.

The face was finished. It could be anything up to forty years old now. Very white. The Arab had disappeared. She snapped open the case again and took out the switchblade—the only weapon they'd allowed her—and dropped it in her handbag, a contingency plan already beginning to form. In case the money wasn't in Ali's room. The room was on the *étage* just below.

Chantal took the stairs and picked the lock with a hairpin (she'd been very good at that at terror school at Der'a in Syria). Inside, she looked at her watch and was stunned to see how little time had elapsed since the shooting. Barely ten minutes. It seemed years ago. All the cases were piled on the bed, packed—Ali was a fanatic about being ready to vanish in seconds. Locked, damn it. It would take precious minutes to pick the lock, so Chantal took the knife and ripped them open, one after another, scattering the clothing everywhere. In the second one she found Ali's precious Zimba .25, the stubby little gun that he always claimed was the best in the world for close work. Why wasn't it on him? Because he'd had the .45 on him, that's why. Chantal flipped out the magazine, saw it was fully loaded, and dropped it into her handbag. She knew it had a silencer, and she searched the bag until she found it and dropped that, too, into her handbag. It couldn't stay there, of course. They were looking at handbags now at airports, but there were places on you they didn't look where you could put a little gun like that.

No money anywhere. After searching the cases, including the secret parts—which were empty—she went through the clothes, felt the seams for telltale bulges. Nothing.

She sat on the bed and thought. There was no point in searching the others' rooms. If anyone had the money—and there had been a very great deal of it—it was Ali. She seethed with rage. The police were probably counting it at that very moment. And the next thing they'd be doing would be closing in on that hotel because the drinkers would have told them there was a girl in the party, and they would soon be at the hotel looking for explanations because Ali, the idiot, had dropped the key to his room in his pocket. She had seen him and had tried to protest but had been hushed like a child. What was the point of false passports, false identity, all that subterfuge, if you did stupid things like that? It was unfair being an Arab.

No money. That meant she'd have to leave the suitcase behind because she couldn't pay the bill. And the wool suit. She opened the case and looked regretfully at it. She'd never had a wool suit before, especially one from Paris. She retrieved her toothbrush, comb and brush, and makeup kit, and dropped them in her handbag. All a girl needed really.

*Wee-yu. WEEE-yu.* She heard the French police car siren very far away because she was listening for it. They would have to use their sirens to get through the choked street, which was one of the reasons Ali had picked that hotel on the Rue de Tuffe, very hard for police cars to get through. The other virtue of cheap hotels is that they are built cheek by jowl next to other buildings, and there was always the roof. That was also the reason they were on the top floors. Chantal had no clear reason for thinking those sirens meant they were after her, but she was an underground girl and when sirens howled she took cover by instinct. Three dead Arabs was quite a score. She'd be top priorty.

In the corridor she looked carefully for chambermaids or other residents. Then she ran like a rabbit for the stairs and back to her own room. There was a fire escape in her room, and they'd rehearsed this very thing. The idea Ali had taught her was not to go down it but up to the roof, then over to the neighboring roof, and straight across the roofs of the next two buildings. At the rear of the second one was another fire escape. That one you took to the street, Ali had told her. Police might close in on one building, back to front, but never on another one, clear down the street.

Five minutes later she was on the Rue de la Douane, a white-faced, late-thirtyish, very chic figure with smoldering black eyes. She walked fifteen blocks briskly but not so briskly as to attract attention before she hailed a cab.

"Mont Blanc," she said to the taximan, a mustached old one with fierce eyes, which got even fiercer when she named Mont Blanc. It was a very expensive restaurant where the headwaiter, an immense Arab, Hassim Hakkim, was said to have at his beck and call the most beautiful and expensive call girls in Paris. Especially if you wanted brown-skinned ones. He specialized in brown-skinned ones.

# CHAPTER 2

Ferenc rolled over and over and over again in the blue water, luxuriating in the feel of it on his skin. He was a very French Jew, his Frenchness and his Jewishness at fairly constant war in him. Now he was being French, and the French were the most immediate of people. When a Frenchman ate a peach, he ate a peach—everything else dropped out of his mind—the rent, the problems with a girl, the Arab wars, every little thing—he savored the peachness of a peach, and that was it. When Ferenc swam, he turned his whole attention to it, experienced it to the very bottom of his French-Jewish toes. He swam a half mile straight out from the warm, sunny beach and then rolled over and looked back at the shore. What a delicious sea the Mediterranean was! What a heavenly bit of beach with its warm, brown, golden sand framed in those dark green cedars! And what an aesthetic atrocity that hotel was! My God, why did the Israelis disfigure such a beautiful beach with such an ugliness of a hotel? Were there any good Israeli architects? Or for that matter any good

Jewish architects? Architecture was not a Jewish virtue. He lay in the warm Mediterranean Sea and became very French.

The girl came out on the balcony of the ugly hotel, cupped her mouth in her two hands, and shouted something. He couldn't hear it over the wind, but it had a compelling look, and she was waving him back. A Swissair girl. Ferenc had picked her up on the plane, and since they both had a night off from their strenuous lives, they had spent the night together. She had plied him with questions, and he had told a great many lies. He was enormously gifted at lying, and his lies were extravagantly baroque and imaginative—too much so, they had told him at intelligence school.

She waved from the balcony again, urgently. He'd better go, he thought regretfully, and he swam back slowly, the magic of the sea already gone. She was in her Swissair costume already, the only costume she had. "He said it was important, Saul," she said. Saul. The name he'd given her. He kissed her absently and took the phone.

"Hello there," he said, which meant "I'm not alone. Be careful."

"We must have lunch," said Jepthah.

"Today?" said Ferenc. He felt outraged. Three Arabs, after all. He was entitled to a little more time off than that.

The stewardess stood there, the light of love in her eyes. Was she Swiss? Ariadne. It sounded more French. Last night when the nightmares had wakened him he had, almost absently, examined her passport and found she, too, had given a false name. It didn't mean anything. They frequently gave false names because they were married. Still, he had written the real name down, and he'd have it checked out by intelligence. He was being overly suspicious, of course, but then, there was no such thing as being overly suspicious in his line of work. She'd been full of questions, but all girls in bed were full of curiosity about the fellow they were in bed with. Still, here he was turning her into an enemy—or trying to. What a business!

"The usual place," Jepthah was saying just in case anyone was listening. It meant headquarters, and it meant serious business.

"Who's paying this time?" he asked.

"You," said Jepthah.

Oh, hell! That meant a solitary job. It was more fun with Jepthah. Solitary jobs were given when there was no way two could be fitted in. That usually meant terrible danger. There was one huge advantage. Ferenc rarely had his nightmares on solitary jobs. Too much occupied by the job. The Frenchman in him ferociously resented the danger, the discomfort, the terrible loneliness of the solitary jobs. The Israeli in him exulted in the risk and thrived on the solitude. What an abysmal ass is the Israeli in me, said the Frenchman in him.

"Can I come to lunch, too?" said the pretty Swiss eagerly.

"No," said Ferenc.

Lunch was peanut butter sandwiches. The American Jews had provided Israel with most of the money to go on with. They had also introduced the peanut butter sandwich to the Middle East. Money and peanut butter sandwiches. Ferenc ate his impassively, there were things one had to do for one's country. Laying down one's life, eating peanut butter sandwiches. O Israel!

"Competitive subversion," Tilsit was saying, mouthing the words with his ruin of a mouth in his ruin of a face. The face was the history of Israel. German death camps, the Stern Gang, the 1948 war, all of it. He'd been there, and each event had graveled a little more into that face until it looked now like a battlefield. Tilsit was chief of the Institute of Special Tasks, Hamossad 'Tafkidim M'yuchadim. Very secret, these tasks. Blowing people up. Sometimes poisoning them. Sometimes shooting them.

"Each one is trying to outhorrible the other," said Tilsit. "Palestine Liberation is for kidnapping. Fatah likes skyjacking. Black September—well, we know about them. Selima is a Maoist Syrian group, a splinter of RASD. It favors sending ears through the mail, followed by other choice bits of the anatomy of Israeli dignitaries." Tilsit smiled with the few rictal muscles the Germans had left him. "It's electioneering in terrorist terms. Our terror is better than *your* terror, that kind of appeal. We hurt more than they do. All these splinter groups are trying to get support and money." He sipped his coffee, looking at the handsome French Jew reflectively. "And that is our opportunity. Terror has moved to the world stage, as we all know, and this has led to cracking down on Arabs, tightening security at all the airports for anyone who even remotely resembles an Arab. Now they are recruiting outside the ranks. We know, of course, of those two French girls smuggling hand grenades in their bras, strapping guns on their thighs. All that means is we caught two. God knows how many we didn't catch."

He was silent, sipping his coffee. Ferenc waited. Tilsit had never taken so long to get to the point, which meant this was going to be a nasty one. He examined the dust on the desk. The headquarters were deep in the warehouse district; the office they were in was bare boards, a pine table and a few chairs were the furniture. The filing cabinet was full of dusty figures about freight shipment in case anyone was curious—and the Institute was so secret Tilsit didn't even want Israelis to know. The real file that contained all the names, identifying characteristics, case histories of both Israeli and Arab agents was an electronic memory bank. Tilsit kept it in his home, and only he knew how to run it. If anything happens to Tilsit, we'll be in a terrible fix, thought Ferenc.

"The minute they got in the non-Arabs they opened the door. We've never managed to penetrate Selima. Palestine Liberation, yes. Black September, yes—although they don't suspect it even now. But Selima, no. They blew up the Iranian Ambassador to Paris, they killed two of our best people in Rome by poison. We don't even know how they did it, much less who they are. They are very well heeled, but what's ominous—very non-Arab. If there were any Arab antennae on this, we'd know. We have been forced to conclude they are so non-Arab that they elude all our procedures. We're not looking in the right direction. That's where you come in."

Finally, thought Ferenc.

Tilsit rose and strolled to the lone window and looked out over the depressing rooftops. They were on the top floor, and the view commanded the whole street.

"Do you know anything about the Hassimi family?" he asked.

"Grand Muftis, weren't they?" asked Ferenc.

"Some of them were—the last of the Grand Muftis, really. Tied up with the Nazis in World War Two. Among other things, the Mufti advised killing all Jewish children. Nice man. But that's just one aspect of the family. There are thousands of Hassimis, all very rich —some branches have spread all over Islam, but others have spread all over Europe, taken new identities and new names. The names have got changed by marriage, sometimes by deed poll. Sometimes sheer snobbery. There is a French branch. Have you ever heard of the Duvillard family?"

"Of course. Everyone has heard of the Duvillards. Bankers.

French Jockey Club. I went to school with one. André. They're not Arabs, certainly."

"Not very Arab anymore. But they're Hassimis way back. And they keep in touch. The Hassimi family are at the center of Arab terror movements. You'll find a Hassimi in all these various groups, many times at the head of it. Four of the Hassimi family ran RASD, which we all know was the intelligence wing of Fatah. Fatah itself was led by a member of the Hassimi family, Hadash Ali. Palestine Liberation has three Hassimis in key positions. Twelve other Hassimis by marriage are in Black September and Fatah. It's a very large family, very rich, and one of its weaknesses is that no one knows how many Hassimis there are. We thought of creating a fictional one, inventing all sorts of links back to the family in Damascus—but it's too difficult and dangerous.

"No, the only thing to do is to supplant a real Hassimi with one of us. That's where you come in."

# CHAPTER 3

Chantal lay naked on her back, legs spread, eyes closed, emitting little moans of spurious ecstasy for the benefit of the fat Greek committing indecencies on her. She felt nothing at all. She was thinking: Security is all very well. We are enormously proud that Selima has never been penetrated—although the fat Greek was rather thoroughly penetrating her at that very moment, she thought—but this total security of which they had been so very proud had been bought at very great cost. The Israelis knew nothing at all about Selima, or its higher-ups or even lower-downs. But then neither did she. Here she was, stranded in Paris, friendless and alone, and yet Paris was swarming with other Selima operatives whose names she didn't know. Ali had entrusted her with nothing, not even the names of the restaurants where they were to take their meals one minute in advance. Even Abou, her lover—the twinges of regret over Abou were becoming very faint indeed—had told her nothing. This was excellent security all right, but someone should have thought the thing through. Someone should have considered what to do when something went wrong. Nobody had.

The Greek finished that particular exercise and was embarking on a wholly new adventure that involved her hind end. Chantal rolled over dutifully and submitted, this time uttering little gasps of pain, the proper response to this aberration, though she felt very little. What she was thinking was: This was the Arab curse. They were very good when things went well but they were totally unprepared for anything going wrong. If she had just been provided with a letter drop—or some money for emergencies—she would have been back with her unit in Syria a week ago.

Instead, here she was underneath this disgusting Greek, wasting time. Well, it had not been entirely wasted. She had felt herself toughening, growing more resilient. She had not, even with the first customer, dissolved into the tears and entreaties which came so naturally to her. She had learned to keep her mind operating under the most gruesome circumstances.

The Greek rolled her over now and kissed her with fat lips. She opened her eyes and smiled right into his eyes lazily and then closed them again and pressed his fat bald skull to her. It did not take much effort, a little show of synthetic affection—and it sometimes meant a 500-franc tip. Why were all Greeks so rich? No, that wasn't right at all. She was a true revolutionary, and she knew very well that most Greeks were groaning under a capitalist tyranny as oppressive as any on earth. It was only these expatriate Greeks, living off the sweat of the oppressed masses back in Greece, who were rich. And very lustful. Of the twelve customers she had entertained since she had gone to Hassim Hakkim, nine had been Greeks, any one of which she could quite cheerfully have strangled—and quite easily, for that matter, having learned her lessons very well in terror camp—but that would have been killing the goose that laid the golden eggs, wouldn't it? She opened her eyes again and smiled expertly into his disgusting eyes, drew a finger up his fat, disgusting back, closed her eyes again, and fell to thinking about her money.

With the 500 francs she'd get from Hassim for this one, plus what she devoutly hoped was a 500-franc tip, she'd have enough for the forged passport, for the air fare, for her hotel, for a new suit she'd set her heart on, and for a pair of shoes she badly needed. The passport had cost 5,000 francs alone (500-franc tips from ten satisfied customers). Not bad for a little Arab girl just turned seventeen. Hassim had got her the passport, very reluctantly. She'd had to sleep with him and also—a far more cogent argument—threaten to withhold her services before he did it.

She wondered—the Greek was now doing some rather ridiculous things with her toes—about Hassim. It was hard to know what he was about, that man. Years of fake servility in pursuit of fat tips from all these revolting Greeks had buried the real man under such layers of false meekness that it was hard to tell where the headwaiter ended and the Arab began. She'd wanted to find out if he was involved or even sympathetic with the Arab cause. She didn't dare. It would have invited too many questions to have shown the slightest interest. No, much better he take her for just another whore. It made life less complicated.

The Greek had tired himself out and fallen asleep. Chantal got out of bed quietly and examined her body in the long mirror. Such an un-Arab body. She smiled. Her mother would have been horrified to see so skinny a daughter. By Arab standards she was a beanpole. But she had slimmed down to look like the advertisements of the West in the magazines. She'd learned much from the ads. How to smile, how to stand straight. She looked at the sleeping Greek and made a little moue. It would have been very easy to slit his throat, take his entire wallet, which was, she knew, stuffed with 500-franc notes, and take to her heels. After all, he was her last customer. But she had learned a great many things in that one week, and one of them was not to go killing people just for a little extra money she didn't really need.

Instead, she lay next to the Greek and had a nap. She'd need to look fresh and rested for the plane. The police might, after all, be still looking. There had been two reasons she had gone to Hassim: To make money to get back to Damascus had been the most important. The other was to lie low. The murder of three Arabs had not gone down well with the Paris police. They didn't like corpses from somebody else's war all over their pavements, and they were looking for her to explain things. But she knew that a week made all the difference in police routine. The day of the murder she had undoubtedly been the hottest person in Paris, but each succeeding day brought fresh holdups, murders, drug-peddling operations in a big city like Paris—and police priorities changed by the minute. After a week she would be just another name on a list. The new name on the passport was not an Arab name at all. She knew very well how to take the Arabness out of her face.

Lying in the cool dimness of the baroque and very expensive hotel, she swelled with rage that she had had to take the Arab out of her name and face. For just thirty seconds she allowed herself the luxury of anger—then she suppressed it. Giving vent to impotent rage was an Arab weakness she had sworn to overcome. And had overcome.

She fell asleep.

That night, after Hassim paid her, she showed him her new coat and then—having weighed the odds very carefully—she told him she was taking a holiday. He could make trouble, lots of trouble, get her arrested, slash her face. He wouldn't give up easily so popular a hustler as she. But her instinct told her Hassim was no ordinary pimp. He couldn't afford to be as rough on his girls as the others—and still maintain his job at Mont Blanc, which was where the customers were.

He was furious, of course. She calmed him skillfully. If she didn't have a rest, she'd be ill, she told him, and he wouldn't like that, would he? Anyway, they had been good friends. He must allow her to rest. No, she didn't know when she'd be back. (If ever, but she didn't tell him that.) She didn't even know why she was telling him anything at all, since it would have been very easy to simply take off. But with her new wisdom, and her new discipline, she knew it was not wise to make an enemy of Hassim Hakkim. A girl never knew when she would need a hideout in Paris, or a job, for that matter. She kissed him tenderly, ran her fingers down the huge fierce contemptuous face, softening its line a little bit. Not much, though. He was a very tough Arab indeed.

At the airport, Chantal wore only light pancake, dimming but not obliterating the brown skin. Brown skin was very in that year. She did change the shape of her round face, elongating it, adding fashionable pouches in the cheeks. She looked much older, at least thirty, and very worldly-wise, which, she reflected, she was. Or anyway, more worldly-wise than when she had come.

She passed a flic, head high, looking absently right through him. He looked at her admiringly.

She handed the new passport to the bored immigration man and pressed her thighs together, feeling the little gun between them. She'd heard they had a gadget that detected metal—but not through thighs. Immigration looked long at the picture in the passport—and then at the girl. Then he put his stamp on it—but he didn't hand it back. Instead, he handed it to a policeman standing next to him in the little cubicle. What was he doing there? That was not police territory.

The flic looked hard at the photograph, then at her.

"Madame Ferrand," he said, like a question.

"Monsieur?" she murmured, also a question.

He handed the passport to her and smiled. He had just wanted to see her respond to her name. People responded to false names much differently from the way they responded to their real names. He had discovered this in twenty years on the force, and he was willing to swear that he could tell instantly when you threw a phony name at a person quickly enough; there was a tremor of the countenance, a tiny pause. He could tell. He was looking for an Arab girl named Chantal—where did she get that French name? he wondered—and this clearly wasn't an Arab girl, and anyway he'd been there a week and he was bored to the marrow.

He waved her through to the Rome plane. She had more sense than to buy a ticket to Damascus in Paris.

# CHAPTER 4

Insanity. The thought made the rubberized lips smile into the mirror. Grotesquely. The rubber, which thickened his features into a likeness of François Duvillard, pulled the left side down into an approximation of a sneer. The Duvillards went through life sneering at their inferiors—but they did it much better than that. One had, above all things in this masquerade, to learn to sneer properly.

The thought made Ferenc laugh outright, a facial explosion he watched with interest. No doubt about it. He was an extraordinary aristocrat. A devilish character—and he'd have been a wow back on the French stage. He felt a little twinge of regret at the thought of the notices he might have got playing this character, if he'd stuck to acting. But that was not the game. The game was playing François Duvillard, not creating a character, not interpreting a character in a new and—to the critics—interesting way. It was passing himself off as the real thing. A much more formidable job of acting.

"Lunacy," he muttered. Take the place of a French aristocrat.

Mingle with his friends! And relatives! One of them André de Quielle, who had been Ferenc's closest friend at school. "Madness!" he said to Jepthah.

"Yes," said Jepthah. "Hold still." Jepthah held his chin firmly in his left forefinger and thumb and with red chalk marked two lines that would have to be corrected. Then he slipped the chin off and turned to the cheekbones, which needed a great deal of work. He compared them to the photograph of François Duvillard and made two marks with the red chalk.

He pulled off the rubber cheekbones and held them up to the light with a ferocity of concentration. Jepthah was a Sabra, a native-born Israeli. He was far more pragmatic than Ferenc, who, he thought, harbored a dangerous streak of romanticism under his toughness. Jepthah was totally opposed to this adventure, which he thought far too risky for any conceivable return.

"You don't have to do this, you know," said Jepthah soberly. "If you said no, they'd call it off. They haven't any other French aristocrats in the unit."

"I'm *not* a French aristocrat," said Ferenc coldly. He was affronted by the very suggestion.

"You've been to the right schools. You've been to their homes. You know the drill."

"I know *some* of the drill. Very little, really. No one who is not born one of those bastards and whose father and mother and grandmother and grandfather were not born among them can really know the drill. It's madness, this caper."

"Then why do you do it?"

"Patriotism," said Ferenc cynically. "I like to die for my country over and over and over again. Except I do think I should get a little rest between deaths. And the pay should be better." He looked at himself in the mirror and made a proper patriotic face. "What am I doing in this *bétise* of a country where the food is unspeakable, the architecture a horror, the conversation rudimentary—and only the climate marginally superior to France? It must be patriotism because I can't think of any other reasons."

"You shouldn't die for your country," said Jepthah practically. "You should live for your country. It would cost more than a million francs to replace you."

"It isn't my country," said Ferenc. "France is my country.

France is full of Jews—Rothschilds, Ferriers, Blums—most of them rich, civilized, and intensely pro-Israeli. They give money, they are on committees, they give hours of their time and millions of their money. They will do anything for Israel—except live here. What am I doing here?"

He picked up the photograph of François Duvillard in his left hand, then the photograph of himself in his right, and looked at first one then the other. They looked not at all unlike. But the difference —aah, *la différence*—was all. Those thin, contemptuous lips, a contempt that seemed to blaze from the very soul. That would take some doing. He sighed. Why was he here? And why had he taken on this lunacy of an assignment? The answers to the two questions were closely tied. He'd been an actor in Paris, and a good one. He might have gone far, but it was not emotionally fulfilling enough. He was too intelligent to settle down to a run in a play. Once he'd solved the problem of performance, he got very restless. It was one of the reasons he'd got into Hamossad l'Tafkidim M'yuchadim. All of his assignments had involved performance, some of them acting of a very high degree, but just *one* performance. Then back home.

He'd never admit it to Jepthah, but it was the challenge to his acting that had made him say yes to Tilsit. The very difficulty, almost the impossibility of this assignment, drew him. Had anything more ever been asked of an actor than an impersonation of such monstrous complexity?

Aloud, he said: "I was reading Graham Greene last night. One of his prefaces. He said he started writing thrillers because he liked to read John Buchan's. But it occurred to him that Buchan was out-of-date. All that posturing about patriotism. Greene invented the other kind of agent—doing dirty jobs for degrading reasons, rotten jobs for corrupt motives." He chuckled cynically. "But now, Jepthah, Mr. Graham Greene is out of date. I am the new-style agent. We are in the game for the highest motives. We are noble savages driven by higher impulses not felt in any human breast since Stendhal's."

He bit into an apple, one of the few things in Tel Aviv worth eating. "Patriotism is back in style," he said wryly. "Look at the Arabs. Laying down their lives—throwing them away, really—very noisily and vulgarly by our standards. Yelling their selflessness from the rooftops, which we consider an indecency. That's what makes them so damned dangerous. That Arab girl who got plucked off an airplane at Lod the other day and got sent to jail for life. 'This is how I knew it would end,' she said. Nineteen years old—and a lifetime in an Israeli prison, which, believe me, is not very nice and the only prison in the world which will *not* yield her up to Arab terror. She knew how it would end and did it anyway. Oh yes, patriotism is back again, God help us."

"Hold still," commanded Jepthah. He was comparing eye colors—holding up a strip of colored plastic on which was reproduced François Duvillard's eye shade. Ferenc's eyes were Butterfly Blue 106B, François Duvillard's, Butterfly Blue 106C, a difference in dominant wavelength of 14.3 millimicrons. "Raphael would spot the difference," observed Jepthah, "but I don't think anyone else would, not even Michelangelo, who was not bad at color." Ferenc sighed with relief. It meant no contact lenses, which, besides being a nuisance, could alter the contour of the face to an alarming degree.

Tilsit came in and eased himself into a chair, groaning a little. Every movement he made hurt a little somewhere. He handed Ferenc a manuscript. "Marvelous reading," said Tilsit. "Benedict Hermann wrote that himself. It's a great story." Benedict Hermann had been the greatest impersonator of them all—a German who had taken the place of a Russian prince in the Imperial Guard in 1773, even in Catherine the Great's bed. "Truly the master," said Tilsit ironically. Hermann had carried it off for almost ten years, sending back reports to Prussia not only about the composition of Russian arms but, above all, its intentions, which could be gained only from the great Queen.

Ferenc was studying all the great impersonations of the past—not least Raphael Smith's in the American Civil War, because there were strong similarities between the Northern banker Smith had impersonated and François Duvillard. Like Duvillard, Smith's banker had been a great eccentric whose behavior was so peculiar that oddness passed almost unnoticed. They weren't all successful. Arthur Toms, the English agent in World War II who had made the immensely ingenious effort to take the place of S.S. Captain Hans Wohl, had been caught and tortured and killed in spite of the most elaborate training and painstaking intelligence. Oh, there'd been failures all right. That's what made the game so piquant.

Tilsit tapped the manuscript: "Hermann says the voice is everything."

But Ferenc already knew that. The voice was the root of personality, the wellspring of identity. He remembered early rehearsals of plays when the actors simply sat on chairs and read, gradually firming out the characters of the people they played—the voices gathering individuality as they went.

"Put on the record," commanded Ferenc. "We'll try it out on Tilsit and see if he can tell the difference."

Jepthah put the record on the phonograph and started it. The voice filled the air with Duvillard's piercing personality, reveling in his own idiosyncrasy. "Hegel perverted the word *freedom* to its very opposite." The voice high and deeply stressed. Stressed tones were the very bones of firm character, Ferenc felt. "History was its own justification because it happened. Hegel is God's apologist, unlike most historians, who find the workings of Providence deplorable." Not only the thought but the tone was deeply ironic.

"He'd been reading Karl Popper," said Ferenc. He turned over the record and played the other side. Same message. "Hegel is God's apologist. . . ."

"Brilliant," said Tilsit, his one good eye gleaming. "Yours was the first voice," he guessed, "Duvillard's the second."

"No, the other way around," said Ferenc dryly. Voices were his specialty, his hobby, his curse. He could do statesmen, singers, anyone. Just for the hell of it, he sang a phrase or two of Maurice Chevalier singing "Louise," switched to an early Bing Crosby boop-boop-a-doing an old song, "Ho Hum," then straight into François Duvillard spouting Karl Popper.

"Marvelous," applauded Tilsit. "Now if we could just do something about your handwriting."

Ferenc had tried imitating Duvillard's handwriting, but it was hopeless. Ferenc's handwriting slanted to the right, though not much; Duvillard's slanted vertiginously to the left. Graphologists would say this indicated intense emotional repression, but neither Tilsit nor Ferenc put much store in graphology. All they knew was that Duvillard's handwriting was a bewilderment—a backward-leaning scrawl that contradicted all theories on handwriting—impossible to reproduce.

"Write nothing," commanded Tilsit. "Everything must be done by telephone. You're great with the voice, terrible with the handwriting."

"Suppose I have to sign a check?"

"We've thought of that." Tilsit pulled a rubber stamp out of his shapeless clothing and handed it to Ferenc. "It's a perfect reproduction. If you have to write a letter—God forbid—have it typed and sign it with that. It'll stand cursory inspection even at a bank."

"Cursory inspection is all this masquerade will stand, anyway," muttered Ferenc gloomily.

Tilsit brushed aside the pessimism lightly. "I don't think so. Oh, it's risky, but then what in the Israeli situation is not a risk? You're playing for very large stakes, and like all missions, you have a short-term objective—to find out the real reason behind the anti-Israeli slant in French foreign policy—and a very long-range objective—to change it." Privately, Tilsit gave Ferenc's impersonation a duration of four days—but he wasn't going to tell Ferenc that. "Maybe you'll get lucky and become another Benedict Hermann," he smiled.

"Maybe I'll get spotted in the first five minutes," grated Ferenc. "What do I do then?"

Tilsit shrugged. "Shoot your way out and take to your heels. You've done it before."

Ferenc laughed. A very phony laugh. Inside he was cold as ice. It was going to end badly; he felt it in his bones.

That evening Ferenc and Tilsit reviewed the family ties—an enormous filigree of relationships that went spiraling clear back to the fifteenth century when it disappeared into the mists of legend. "Most of them are in the bank," said Ferenc. "I don't know them, thank God. And neither did André. At least not much more than to nod to. There was great hostility between André's branch of the family and the bankers. I don't know about François because I never knew him."

"François is not so much hostile to the banking side of his family as just plain indifferent to them," said Tilsit. "He's very rich and therefore he doesn't need them. The banking side of the family is hostile to *him* because he has, among other things, a great many shares in the bank. He spends the money, he does little to earn it. That is resented."

Ferenc picked up a three-foot sheet of paper covered with Duvillard genealogy. "You don't really expect me to memorize all this?"

32 ·

"No," said Tilsit, "I want you to study it and then try to forget it—just like a Duvillard. After all, except for a few genealogical nuts in the family, the Duvillards don't know their own family tree that well—or their own relatives. François hates most of his relatives and makes fun of them—that's why we picked him and not some other Duvillard. Because he's such a loner, such an individualist, and such an eccentric—you can get away with a lot of strange behavior playing him."

"And such a son of a bitch," murmured Ferenc.

"That, too." said Tilsit. "That's the rub, really, because we want you to go against his character, to operate against his grain—but François is such a queer one he might even do that. We want you suddenly to take your rightful place in the bank. Not because you have suddenly felt a twinge of conscience. God forbid. François would never feel any such thing. No, we want you—as François—to present the banking Duvillards with an imperious demand to be given a place on the board to look after your—his—own money."

"You can't really believe that the Duvillards, who are as French as Louis the Fourteenth, are really backing Arab terrorists," said Ferenc. "I don't believe it."

Tilsit rubbed his hands over his ruin of a face. "All I know is, French policy, even by pragmatic standards—a hundred million customers of French arms, easier access to the Arab oil, all that—is far more pro-Arab than the French people are. The French people, given any say in the matter—and your citadel of foreign affairs, the Quai d'Orsay, has never given the French people much say in French foreign policy—would be pro-Israeli. Instead, it's very pro-Arab. Why?"

"Why do you think bankers would know?"

"Bankers have access, they have ears." Tilsit leaned back and fixed Ferenc with his one good eye. "Bankers know what other bankers are up to. And don't forget the Duvillards are Hassimis—maybe only ten percent Arab Hassimis—but François Duvillard could use both his connections as a banker and as a cousin to find out who is providing the money to keep half a dozen Arab terrorist organizations in funds killing our people."

Ferenc yawned. Idiocy, the whole thing. He'd be dead or arrested in a week. He didn't know which was preferable. The French police were beginning to be as bad as Moroccans in their torture.

"And what do we do with the real François Duvillard when we pick him up?"

"Kill him," said Tilsit.

Now we're killing a man who is only ten percent Arab, thought Ferenc, examining his feelings about that like a surgeon probing an area for infected flesh. A ten percent Arab who hadn't, in fact, done any harm to Israel. He hadn't even gotten in the way. Ferenc had long since become accustomed to mowing down innocents who had blundered into the way of Israel, had somehow inadvertently made nuisances of themselves and had to be eliminated. But this son of a bitch hadn't even become a nuisance. They needed his position, his name, so they grabbed them. And eliminated the man. Like that.

He was staring at his shoes silently. Tilsit let him stare. He didn't know what was going through Ferenc's mind, but he'd grown accustomed to these long silences. Every time he had given Ferenc a job Ferenc had required a good long frowning silence. He needed to digest the job, let it become part of his flesh.

This was a whole new area of ethics, wasn't it? Ferenc was thinking. Erasing ten percent enemies who had done you no harm because by such erasure Israel stood to profit. The terrible thing was that it didn't bother him a bit. This was the climate of acceptance in the modern world. The new barbarism which had spread its smiling face over his generation. He collected little oddments of it for his private collection as a lepidopterist collects butterflies. Those little bits of dismembered people found in a North Dakota lake. The torture chambers of Brazil, until his generation one of the gentlest nations, the only nation which had hitherto had bloodless revolutions. His own country, once the most civilized in the world, engaging in the most sophisticated torture in Algeria as a matter of state policy. The Americans—the last, best hope of mankind, they had been called—wiping out whole villages in Vietnam, almost casually, disdainfully. The new barbarism, ethics of. He was a very ethical killer. He would not voice these objectives aloud, if they were indeed objections at all, but he must have time to think them out. Otherwise they would bother him in the middle of the operation. He frowned at his shoes.

Aloud he said: "Why can't you find out about the pro-Arab policy from your Jewish friends in France? The French government is full of

French Jews in very high places, and French banks are full of Jews who have their ears wide open."

"We have explored all those areas," said Tilsit. "Something is going on that is not vouchsafed to French-Jewish bankers or diplomats. As a Duvillard, and a member of the Hassimi family, they might let you in on it. They might even ask you to be part of the operation in exchange for a little financial consideration. It would be very nice if they did that."

# CHAPTER 5

Chantal took her naked face straight through the hordes of staring children, fixing her gaze on the water wheel on the rocky desert hill, watching the donkey go round and round. Before she had gone to Paris she would not have dared to walk barefaced through a Syrian village. Through Damascus, yes, but never in this hinterland where life went on as it had for centuries. She walked up the dusty street, past the mud houses whose doors were full of women in their black *abayahs*, veils drawn, staring at her in astonishment.

Dressed in her Paris wool suit, she looked as appropriate as a cowboy in a harem. At the edge of the village she had been assaulted with that smell that took her back to her childhood, dried excrement, as pungent as if the sun had been beating down on it for 5,000 years, the smell of the Middle East. You can smell it flying over Egypt at 20,000 feet, so pervasive is it and not at all unpleasant. It fixes the Middle East in your nostrils as incense fixes a church. Part of my heritage, she thought.

She was just outside the tiny village now, the children following her like twittering birds after a trail of crumbs, and here was the house she was looking for—a mud brick house, set in a stand of date palms, surrounded by a mud wall, camel thorns like barbed wire set on its top to keep out intruders. A tribesman with a long kaffir rifle stood outside the door, and he stepped into her path.

"*Shlonak*, Hamid," said Chantal coolly. "Have I changed so much?"

Hamid's rugged face split into a toothless grin. "Chantal! *Ahlan wasahlan!*" He beamed and salaamed and beamed again. "You're alive! *Al Hamdu Lil Lah!*"

"Oh yes, thanks be to God," said Chantal cynically. But more thanks to my fleet feet. God takes care of those who take care of themselves. Where had she heard that? Surely it was not a Muslim sentiment.

She strolled past Hamid (What a bodyguard! He'd have been killed in a second by Israeli gunmen, who would already have been inside, slaughtering them all!) and into the cool courtyard rimmed and shaded by date palms. It was a big square mud-brick house, more elegant than those in the village. Chantal walked straight up to the heavy wooden door, studded with ornamental nails, nodding curtly at the guard, who was too taken by her appearance to try to stop her. She let herself into Sheikh Ahman's private *diwan*, as if she owned it, although she had never set eyes on it or him before.

The three Arabs were seated around a table, smoking and talking, and she marched up. "I am Chantal," she said briskly, wondering at her daring, even as she did it. She would never have done such a thing before the Paris assignment. But now she was a celebrity. She had read all the papers in Rome, and those in Beirut, and those in Damascus. It was a heady experience, being a celebrity.

Ahman rose from the table and extended his hand, something he would never have done before she had been caressed by fame. He was a tall man with sad eyes, very stately in his white robes. "These are my sons, Ibrahim and Abdul. Pray be seated. We have been expecting you."

Chantal sat down with the three men, the first time in her life she had ever been asked to join a group of Arab men, taking it all in, as she had taken in all the other new experiences, as if it were happening to someone else. I must keep my wits, she was thinking. I am a very important person now, and I must not for a minute forget it, and I must not for a minute let *them* forget it.

"You have done well," said Ahman.

"I survived," said Chantal bleakly. She had thought over this speech many times. Not much of a speech but in its brevity earth-shaking. She was contradicting her Sheikh, leader of Selima, earth-shaking heresy. "Survival is hardly doing well," she said icily.

She let them chew on that for a moment. "The operation was a catastrophe. We accomplished nothing. We lost three of our best men. Months of training out the window." Then for the clincher, "The operation was badly planned." This was a direct affront. Sheikh Ahman had planned much of it himself and approved all of it. She, a seventeen-year-old girl, telling off a sheikh. She could get both hands chopped off for such impudence. And be left out on a hillside to be eaten by jackals. It had happened in her village before. Knowing all this, she gazed somberly straight into his fierce eyes. They'd never beat the Israelis if they wallowed forever in self-delusion. It had been a damned bad operation, and it had to be said.

In the oppressive silence, the two sons, Abdul and Ibrahim, waited for their father to do something delicious, like chopping her head off right there and then. They were true medieval children with all the proper instincts. Ahman was wearing his long curved scimitar around his waist, every inch a medieval king in that most medieval of Arab nations. But Ahman was a far more sophisticated person than his two sons. He'd been not only to Damascus but to Mecca and even to Geneva. For an Arab sheikh he'd been around.

Besides, he was deeply curious to hear her story. He needed her, her experience, her information, and her ideas. After that, there would be plenty of time to chop off her hands, her feet, and her head.

"Strong words," he said mildly, dumbfounding his children. "Pray go on."

It took the breath out of Chantal, this mild tone. A very wily fellow, she guessed quickly. She had a strong suspicion that he was outraged underneath all that suavity, but she respected him for throttling his instincts long enough to hear her out. After that, he might easily revert to the Middle Ages. She'd have to tread carefully.

"We must get rid of some of our most comfortable illusions," said Chantal, moderating her tone to his. Suddenly she was very respectful, hands clasped in her lap, head bowed.

38 ·

"We must rid ourselves of the most comforting illusion of all—that we have not been penetrated," said Chantal submissively, to make the truth a little more palatable. "The Israeli pigs knew everything, where we waited for the stolen car to pick us up, our mission, our destination. The Israeli Ambassador had been warned and was taken to safety." She'd got that from Hassim Hakkim, who'd got it from a customer. "They knew our numbers, all except one. They didn't expect me, or I would be dead."

That was enough for the moment. Chantal had enough cunning to let it alone for a while, to let the Sheikh take the initiative. He showed no eagerness to do so. He simply sat there, his anger drained by the very enormity of what she had told him. It had been their one shining triumph among a string of failures, the idea that the Israelis had never penetrated Selima. They had accomplished exactly nothing in three years, but always there was the hope that next time they would do something spectacular. Always there had been the comfort that their operation, and even their existence, was the best-kept secret in the Arab world. Now even that had been dashed. Sheikh Ahman felt the closeness of despair.

Silence for five full minutes, then the Sheikh said: "Why do you think they missed you? Why did they not know you were part of the mission—if they knew everything else so fully?"

Chantal dropped her submissive pose. "Because I'm a girl," she said simply. She let that sink in a moment. Then she added: "I think whoever has penetrated Selima doesn't take girls seriously enough to include them in his intelligence. That would indicate—to me, at least—that whoever has penetrated us is an Arab." She dared a smile directly at Sheikh Ahman. "The West takes girls more seriously than Arabs. They would never have left me out of their calculations."

Sheikh Ahman stroked his beard thoughtfully. "An Arab?" he said. "Turning his information over to the Israelis? Are you suggesting a traitor?"

"No," said Chantal, who'd thought that one out long and hard. "I don't think it's that kind of treachery. I think it's a different kind altogether. Somebody in Selima is spying on us for the benefit of another group of guerrillas—and that group of Palestinians has been penetrated by the Israelis—and is passing along what he hears about us."

There were two dozen Palestinian groups, some of them being

formed and dropped within a matter of weeks. They were all furiously competitive for cash, for prestige, for glory. They all spied in various ways on each other.

"It's the only explanation I have," said the girl sadly.

A very plausible explanation, the Sheikh was thinking.

He clapped his hands, and a servant came in. "We'll eat," he commanded. Then he turned to Chantal and pronounced the unthinkable. "You'll join us, of course."

Chantal sat between the Sheikh and his two sons at the filigreed table. It was the first time she'd had a meal at the same table with Arab men in an Arab country. It was certainly the first time an Arab girl had ever sat down with a sheikh in that area. The servants—to say nothing of Abdul and Ibrahim—were totally unstrung.

It was a silent meal. Chantal thought she'd given the Sheikh enough to think about for the time being; she wolfed the kebab, the two kinds of rice, the chicken in tomato sauce, the chicken livers, with intense pleasure. French food was for the French; Italian food was for Italians. She was an Arab girl at heart when it came to food.

The Sheikh offered her a cigarette. She shook her head. Like all Arab girls, she had smoked like a chimney—the harems stank of tobacco smoke—but she'd kicked the habit when she was hustling. The men didn't like it. She had no intention of lumbering herself with that addiction again.

The Sheikh smiled for the first time. A thin smile. "Where did you get that name? Chantal is a very French name."

"My mother was Lebanese," said Chantal bleakly. "The Lebanese are very French and pass for French very easily. That's why I can speak French so well. I must go back to Paris because that is where the leak is. It's not an Israeli leak. It's an Arab leak. I shall find it—and plug it. This time, I want money. I want the names of our friends and fellow fighters."

"I suppose," said the Sheikh coolly, "you want to be the leader of the operation."

"More than that," said Chantal, equally cool, "I want to *be* the operation. All of it! I think one of the reasons we were spotted is because we were a group of four, leaving our footprints all over the sand. That Israeli who gunned down Abou, Ali, and Muhammad came and went alone, very fast, very efficient."

The Sheikh stroked his wedge of a beard and thought about it.

Then he barked a series of hard questions. Where would she stay? How would she travel? What would she do when she got to Paris? What would be her methods of covering her tracks? How would she report back?

She had all the answers to hand because she had anticipated—had, in fact, asked herself the same questions.

"But I shall need money. A lot of money," concluded Chantal.

"You shall have money," said the Sheikh.

"I shall need a name. Not just any name. The better the name, the easier it will be for me to get where I want to go."

"You shall have the best. You shall have my name," said the Sheikh.

He was a Hassimi.

"There are quite a few Hassimis in Paris," said the Sheikh. "Though few of them use the name anymore, they are still Hassimis. You will find them very helpful."

# CHAPTER 6

Ferenc was caressing the naked Frenchwoman, putting his full mind to it, as was the only way, when the telephone trilled. Trill is the only word for a French telephone, a feminine sound, beckoning and infinitely trivial, as if it were impossible to hold serious discourse on such an implement.

Ferenc strangled an obscenity and rolled onto his back, eyes on the ceiling. He considered letting it ring, but then he could not engage in sex halfway. It demanded everything. Philippa lay there, eyes closed. She'd been caressed almost into insensibility, or, as Ferenc liked to think, into a higher sensibility.

The phone rang again like a purring, slightly hysterical cat. Ferenc answered it, the mission swimming back into his consciousness. It might be Jepthah.

It was.

"He's landed at Orly," said Jepthah.

"Who?" said Ferenc, not quite with it.

"Robert," said Jepthah and hung up.

Ferenc sighed and dropped the phone back into its French cradle. It was a very female phone even by French standards, white and gold, very old-fashioned in design, with the old cup for a transmitter. He contemplated the woman, who was swimming slowly back into awareness from the depths of sexuality where she had so comfortably rested. She opened her eyes.

"Ferenc," she whispered.

He smiled at her ironically, lazily. Oh, what a tangled web, he was thinking.

"What was it?"

"Your husband has just landed at Orly," he said, amused.

Philippa didn't stir; she smiled lazily. "Orly is a very long way," she whispered invitingly and pulled his head down to hers.

"You are supposed to be home when he gets there, remember?"

"I will be," murmured the woman.

He succumbed to emotional pressures. After all . . .

Later, he watched the slender, very French body slipping into her clothes. It was one of his favorite aesthetic pursuits, watching naked women get dressed. Especially Frenchwomen. They dressed so beautifully. She was stepping into a slip as daintily as if it were a cobweb, which indeed it was, one leg uplifted, eyes on her work, preoccupied. "I don't like to hurry you, Philippa, but we don't want Robert making any trouble."

"Why should Robert make trouble? It's not at all difficult, getting an invitation to one of Armand's parties. My God, everybody is there. You could have just called yourself, Ferenc."

But that was the last thing in the world he wanted to do.

"Did you just lure me into your bed to get an invitation to Armand's party?" Philippa laughed at the very ridiculousness of her own suggestion. She was a very confident adulteress.

"Perhaps," said Ferenc, playing her game.

"Marianne would have been easier. She lives much nearer your apartment," said Philippa. She played adultery hard and clean, enjoying the dialogue almost as much as the act.

"Marianne talks too much," said Ferenc. "The nice thing about you, Philippa, is you're not given to boasting."

"Well, I can't afford to," said Philippa, laughing. She was slipping into her tweed skirt now, very fetching. Ferenc watched appreciatively. It was marvelous to watch a woman's personality change from the unclothed to the clothed. Very different animals altogether, with their clothes on.

"You are incredible, Ferenc," said Philippa lightly. "Do you have men stationed at Orly to warn you of the approach of husbands?"

"At all the airports," said Ferenc. "It's a service you can buy now—like an answering service. French socialism is a wonderful thing."

"Marxism, I hate it. They've abolished adultery in Russia, did you know? By government decree."

She was fully dressed now, a very chic Frenchwoman, scarved, gloved, toqued, brushed. "How will I get this ridiculously irrelevant invitation to you, Ferenc?"

"Give it to your doorman in an envelope marked *Ferenc*. It will be picked up."

"My God, you are mysterious," said Philippa, loving it.

*Merde!* The last thing in the world he wanted to do was to arouse her suspicions. But it couldn't be helped. This plan was far too complex. Plans should be simple.

"What are you playing at?" asked Philippa, a true conspirator.

He took her gloved hand and pressed it to his lips. He was very fond of Philippa. Anyway, she was the safest of collaborators. She had to be very careful. She had, in consequence, become one of the best and most experienced liars in all France.

"I'll see you tonight. We can exchange distant glances."

"Keep them distant," said Philippa sternly. "We barely know each other." She brushed his lips with hers, not disturbing her lipstick. "Robert can smell intrigue a mile and a half away. That is why he is such a good banker."

Robert was a Hassimi, one of the richest of that very rich family. Rich and intensely political. The rich had got very much more political in France in the last twenty-five years, Ferenc was thinking. It had arrested their decadence momentarily or, rather, had provided a new outlet for it, as if the older forms of decadence—women, food, luxury, even aestheticism—had proved too thin and uncomplicated for their complicated French tastes. Politics made the decadent Frenchman a more dangerous animal; he was playing with more dangerous fire, for one thing, and for another he was paying attention to social undercurrents that had hitherto escaped his attention. But in another way it made Ferenc's task easier. They were too politicized to worry about the activities of their wives. Ferenc smiled.

"When will we two meet again?" she asked.

"I'll have to let you know." Not ever, thought Ferenc. Alas. He'd have liked a bit more of Philippa.

She left with the briefest of smiles.

An hour later Jepthah was in the flat and Ferenc was explaining the idiosyncrasies of high French society. "Oh, he's a Hassimi all right, even if his name is Pinay. Hardly any of the Hassimis are called Hassimi anymore, even in Arabia, where they've become Husseins mostly but also a lot of other things."

Ferenc had done homework on the Hassimi family since he was about to join it.

"He's very, very French, this Pinay, because actually he isn't, really. His great-grandfather was Moroccan, his mother is Algerian. Those are the ones that get impossibly French, the ones that aren't French at all. Just as the most British Britons are Greeks—like Prince Philip—or Germans like the Queen. You will always find—if you scratch an ancient French name hard enough—that they came from Poland when not, in fact, Russia."

He was in high good humor, elevated out of his normal black pessimism by Philippa's delicious body, with, of course, the added irony that he was at the same time getting his work done. Philippa was very much a part of the plan, and to enjoy the girl and at the same time move one's mission that much closer was the very apex of high performance for a member of the Institute of Special Tasks. Ferenc congratulated himself. He was, he reflected, a very moral seducer as he was also a very moral killer. One must have one's reasons, and then everything was all right. But wasn't that the story of civilization?

The two men bent over the plans for the house, a very grand house on the Avenue d'Iéna. "I know it from attic to cellar," said Ferenc. "I played in it as a child with André, who is also a Hassimi and also not called a Hassimi. His name is de Quielle, Robert's cousin about three times removed. Like Robert, the Hassimi got dropped somewhere when his grandfather or somebody married someone with a more French name, which they promptly took. You'll only find Hassimi on his baptismal records—along with about twenty-five other names which they never quite lose because someday they might come in handy if there is a change in regime or occupation. If the Russians moved in, for example, these ancient French families would suddenly remember a Russian forebear—you understand?"

"No," said Jepthah.

"Well, you don't have to," said Ferenc in high good humor. "Only I have to. Now attend."

He pointed to the cellar, which was of Byzantine complexity.

"You can get lost very easily down there. You had better memorize it absolutely. This is the room where the transformations—both of them—will be done. It has two advantages. You can get in and out there"—he pointed—"through that iron grating, which looks very solid but isn't. Do you understand how to get to that grating all right?"

Jepthah nodded. "It's not easy. I have to go through another cellar to get at it. I had a practice run last night."

"How did it go?"

"Very well. There's a doorman here, but he's no problem. But then I didn't have a body on my hands. That will be a very large difficulty." Jepthah had never liked this operation from the outset, which is why he had been brought into it. Not liking the risks involved, he had been hypercautious about every element, testing and retesting both theory and practice a dozen times in his mind. "You said there was a second advantage to that room. What is it?"

"It's never used," said Ferenc. "It's too far from the stairs for one thing—which is a bit of a problem since I'll have to carry the body that much farther. André and I used to hide there as children because no one ever thought of looking there."

"Are you quite sure that situation still exists?"

"Yes, I checked it last night."

Ferenc looked at his watch.

"Go pick up the ticket," he said to Jepthah. "It should be in the doorman's hands by now."

It was—marked simply *Ferenc* on the envelope, not on the ticket itself. It was just an odd ticket to Nobody in Particular for one of those big shapeless *tout Paris* parties attended by "everyone who was no one," Ferenc used to say. The trouble was there were lists kept, and it would never do to have his name on one. Arab counterintelligence had got very good, disturbingly good, lately. It was best not to leave any names around at all. Especially on lists that might get printed in the papers, as *tout Paris* party lists frequently were.

Ferenc lay out the dinner jacket carefully, making a little face. It was not that the thing was in bad taste, but that it was in no particular taste at all. Nondescript. This was one of the handicaps of his work. One had occasionally to be totally nondescript, and it ill suited his temperament. He picked up the scissors and carefully cut out the labels of the dinner jacket, which had been bought in Switzerland and was intended for a business type, not his type at all. Next came the shirt, of a terrible acrylic, truly a nonentity of a shirt. The police and their forensic department were not going to get much out of these clothes. The socks were of black fiber, purchased in Pris Unic. There must be a million such socks sold a month in France. Let the police try to trace it. And they would. They would.

He put on the clothes slowly, feeling anonymity grip his limbs, subduing his youth and his flamboyance in the grayness of the dinner jacket that had nothing to say. Last came the dark coat. He had to be careful with the scissors here. The coat must be without a label but must not be seen to have been too carefully put into that condition. He tore out the label, leaving the threads still hanging, as if it had been torn out from too much hanging on a hook. Let the flics chew on that! They loved little messy details like that. It occupied their empty lives.

Finally, the hat. My God, what a hat! Black, featureless, a nothing of a hat. Again he left the label alone. Ferenc had quietly lifted it from a hatrack in a café while its owner had his face deep into his ratatouille. Let the cops trace it back to him, then. It would serve him right for not watching his hat more carefully.

Ferenc looked at himself in the mirror. A triumph of nothingness. He made a face at himself in the mirror, as if to divorce himself from that costume, but the costume now became the man, extinguishing Ferenc. The last of Ferenc, he thought, for a good long time.

He examined his wallet carefully to see he had everything—money, forged identity cards, the works. Then he put the wallet into the breast pocket of his nonentity of a dinner jacket. He left the key on the table for Jepthah to dispose of. Jepthah was coming back to clean up and close up.

He let himself out of the flat at exactly 10:00 P.M. The party would be well along by then. Out on the street, he walked briskly for eight blocks before hailing a taxi and asking to be taken to the Avenue d'Iéna, in one of the most fashionable quarters of Paris—and one of the richest.

## CHAPTER 7

The most ancient city in the world, Chantal was thinking. The city which in truth belongs to Zeus and is the eye of the whole East, sacred and mighty Damascus, as the Emperor Julian had written.

Chantal was dressed in her chic Paris wool suit, and it was far too hot, but it was important to her new identity. No longer Chantal; she must not think of herself as Chantal. She was Nicole Bernier now, and in the soft Italian handbag she'd bought in the most fashionable store in Damascus lay wads of identity—passport, *carte d'identité*, credit cards, driver's license—the whole paraphernalia of modern personality without which you were hardly anyone at all. She felt a flame of proletarian anger at the selectivity of credit cards—and quickly throttled it. No time for wallowing in revolutionary emotion. She was a proper member of the bourgeoisie now. In her expensive black leather handbag lay her credentials, not only the credit cards but a fat roll of French francs, almost the hardest currency in the world now (next to the Swiss), and it was astounding how possession of so much naked cash changed a girl's point of view. She caught a glimpse of herself in a shop window and almost burst out laughing. She looked like a film star—serene, confident, and bottomlessly young—the clean and beautifully cut short hair, like a boy's, framing an artful minx of a face. Those fresh eyes! Where was the hot-eyed little savage born in the hovels of Syrian dispossession? Where even the Paris call girl and her flat, cynical gaze? The gaze had been washed into innocence by sheer money. What an idea! She laughed aloud, ignoring the passersby, something she'd never before have dared do. Nicole. Lovely French name. She felt very Nicole, now she'd caught a glimpse of herself.

She strolled now, head high, down the covered market of Hamidieh, past the women in their black *abayahs,* ignoring their resentful stares, past the tarbooshed sheikhs and the endless priests in their effeminate gear. It was a hubbub of a street, and she reveled in the color and noise, eyes alight, mouth open. The smell ignited her—nectarines, figs, dates, almonds, all nestling together in joint aroma. Muslims liked to think of Damascus as the original Garden of Eden, and it was still the greatest orchard in the Middle East. She would have liked to sink her teeth into a nectarine, but she was afraid the thin veneer of Frenchness would melt away and she'd become an Arab urchin again.

She walked on now, the streets dissolving into an anarchy of little lanes, shops pressing in on her on both sides, beckoning. One could spend a week in this market, caressing each shop with her covetous eyes, if one only had time. What an irony! Time was the only thing the Arabs had had for centuries, lots and lots of time—and very little else. And now she had no time. Or was it the clothes that hurried her steps? When one assumes the mask of the West, one takes on their bad habits, their hurry, their materialism. Ugh! I must be careful. I'll dissolve into one of *them.*

The street threw her directly at the high Roman wall which sheltered in it the immensity of the Great Ommiad Mosque, and she felt rise in her the pure springs of that most Arab emotion—hatred. We have nothing but our hatred, but, *Allahu Akbar,* we have that in quantities unsuspected in the West. For this mosque was the greatest relic of the Ommiad Dynasty, the Damascus rulers who had murdered the family of the Prophet, extinguishing the line of Muhammad. It had happened twelve hundred years ago, and she hated the Ommiads as if it had happened yesterday. It was the dumbfounded glance of a passerby that reminded her she couldn't afford these Arab extravagances of emotion, dressed as she was. She hurried on, composing her face back into Frenchness, arranging her mind in a pattern of Frenchness. How very quaint, she thought in her Frenchness, to be so aroused over a murder which had happened twelve hundred years ago. Truly it was said that an Arab has no gift for forgiveness.

She hurried on now down The Street Called Straight, which was mentioned in the Bible as the street where Judas lived—no, not that Judas, a different one. She slowed now to look into the wondrous Middle Eastern shops. Brass. Leather. Jewelry. Linen. Damascus had always been famous for linen. Damask from Damascus, back to the days when it was truly the hub of commerce of the whole world. O Syria, she thought ironically, the most Have nation of the whole world to have become the most Have-not of all the world. What tricks the centuries played!

From the minarets came the silvery song of the muezzins.

*"Allahu Akbar. Ash-hadu An La Ilaha Illallah."*

God is great. There is no God but God. Oh, but there is! There is me, thought the girl. There is all of us. She was a revolutionary first and a Muslim afterward, a long way afterward. She could lose herself in only one dogma at a time. On the path of God they shall slay and be slain, said the Koran. I am on the path, all right, and I shall slay and be slain (she yawned in a splendor of indifference at the boredom of death), but it is not for God I am doing it. No, it was a more sacred flame than God that burned inside her, fires of patriotism for a country that she had never set foot in. That was the greatest irony of all. Most of the Arab urchins she had been brought up with, many of them fighters for the liberation of Palestine, had been born in refugee camps, and yet they would tell you "I am from Galilee" or "I am from Rehovot" though they'd never been in those places. The hottest patriots of all had never laid eyes on Palestine.

The Street Called Straight ended in the last of the old Roman gates, the Gate of the Sun, still impressive and massive. The girl Nicole who had been Chantal walked through it, causing a little stir among the Bedouin boys loitering there. *"Baksheesh,"* they whined.

Out of the Inner City now, she swung north. The house she

sought was set in a garden fragrant with eucalyptus, orange trees, and jasmine. It was a very Arab house with thick walls and small slits for windows with ornamental iron grillwork over them.

"We have been expecting you," said Selim Seleucid. He was squatting on his haunches on a thick Omid carpet beside a low mother-of-pearl-inlaid table, this most publicized of all Palestinian leaders. He was disappointingly unimpressive, thought the girl, with that absurdity of a little goat beard. The eyes, though, were more promising—hot and flat, in which she could read nothing.

"Sit down, please," said Selim, indicating the carpet.

She smiled, "I am afraid," she said submissively, "that my clothes are too Western."

Selim acknowledged the blue wool suit with a flicker of impatience. "Bring her a stool," he commanded. The stool was brought, and Nicole (as she now thought of herself) sat, higher than the Great One by a foot and a half. Well, she thought. This is fame indeed. Selim was the custodian of secrets hardly guessed at in the village she had left. His name had been that of the Organization—though that was changed now.

From Sheikh Ahman she had got money and the loan of his ancestry. But only Selim knew where the contacts were in Paris—and who they were. From Selim would come the mission itself. Selim flicked his flat eye at his young bearded secretary and at the guard, who departed instantly, leaving Selim and the girl alone.

"Not even my secretary knows what I am about to tell you. There are only three who know—you will be the fourth."

He sucked on his cigarette and sent out a cloud of scented smoke, taking his time. Finally he said, "The Paris operation, which has banked all our European missions, has always been kept very small—for security. But now, as we both know, there is a leak—probably an Arab leak. The man I want you to report to is a Hassimi—like yourself—but that is not his name as it is not yours. His name is Robert Pinay. You are to live with him as his niece. You have been in a convent, which is why no one has seen or heard of you—but of course you have been told all about your convent background. I want you to be a very loving niece, but I don't want you to trust Robert Pinay, or anyone else, at all. You must not tell him what you are there for. He is accustomed to secrecy from us so he will not ask, but if he does, you must report it to me immediately."

He turned his flat gaze on her fully now, and she felt for the first time—and powerfully—that this was not an unimpressive man at all. There was tremendous strength in this man. He kept it out of sight until needed. He was unimpressive only when he wanted to be, that was all. A fine trick, especially for a business such as ours, she thought. I would like to learn it.

"Now, here is your mission," he said.

# CHAPTER 8

It was a babble of a party, a *tout Paris* frenzy, full of people who did not really know each other at all. Ferenc wandered, impassive, from room to room. That was the way to stay alone—impassivity, the gaze not quite meeting anyone's eye. And keep moving. A slow pace, never resting.

In the great salon with its ridiculous and priceless Louis Quinze chairs that one was discouraged from sitting on (and were not very comfortable anyway), and immense Louis Seize gilt mirror that reflected and distorted the immense room, with the great chandeliers that had been electrified in the nineteenth century and gone back to their original candles—the very hallmark of elegance—in the mid-twentieth century, he saw, at the very end of the room, Philippa Pinay. She was standing next to her husband—her devotion to Robert at parties was legendary—and she was, in her long multicolored patchwork dress, both very chic and very innocent. Clever Philippa. She had everything both ways. His gaze took her in and turned away in an instant. Did she see him? Of course she did. Philippa would never miss anything, not that one! Ferenc, under his eyelashes, gave her husband a quick, thorough scrutiny. He'd encountered him at parties, knew him not at all well. He wondered about him now. Robert Pinay was one of those rotund Frenchmen like Pompidou (who was himself a not at all rare French type) who radiated bonhomie that didn't even begin to conceal the agility and toughness of mind underneath. He was reputed to be a very good banker—and also rather a dab hand with the ladies. Not an ordinary cuckold at all. He was chatting now with a pop singer—a girl who, with her short hair and cap, looked like a boy and was, in fact, rather resplendently bisexual—as they all were in that set.

There were the usual rumors that the Pinays, *femme et mari,* liked to enjoy the same girl from time to time. But Ferenc was not interested in that kind of rumor. What interested him much more was the fact that Pinay could talk with such camaraderie to a guttersnipe like that singer and few seconds later with the more august members of the French banking community and a minute after that with Quai d'Orsay characters. He was the new French aristocrat, all right, versatile. Tough. And very cold.

Ferenc moved deeper into the room, past one of those splendid French *grandes dames,* reputed to be eighty, and still breaking up other people's marriages, with her gay white mop of hair and twinkling blue eyes, who was chatting with a tall straight Frenchman who must be, Ferenc guessed, an Army man, past or present. He pushed through the mob collected around Yves Montand, then eddied around Foufou Nimes, who had written that god-awful collection of lies about her life in the brothel, not one word of which was true, but which had sold in the multithousands, past a collage of dazzling and lithe young Frenchmen who all looked like Belmondo but weren't. That brought him within inches of Philippa, whose eyes remained adoringly on her husband. What a girl! thought Ferenc with admiration. As he sidled past he couldn't resist—for the sheer French hell of the thing—running his hand appreciatively over Philippa's shapely and passionate ass—because, after all, there was absolutely nothing she could do about it, could she? And a man must enjoy his work, he thought gravely, passing into the great hall beside the main stairs which was choked with *tout Paris,* coming up and going down, chattering and smiling and laughing very noisily.

Ferenc pushed up the great curving staircase to the third floor, partly to see who was there, and partly because the food was up there. The food would be marvelous, and Ferenc knew it would be the last he'd get for a while. A man needed a square meal before he killed, he thought wryly. Very hard on the *nerfs*, killing. François Duvillard would not be there for a while—he always came late and left early—so Ferenc had a little time. But he was by no means on holiday in this interval. He was quite deliberately casing the entire party, filing away the names and faces of all who were there and not forgetting to make a mental note of who was *not* there. One couldn't afford later to make any mistakes about who was out at the moment. This was a very useful exercise.

The food was laid out on an enormous table and was, as he had suspected, truly heroic—lobsters in their shells, brushed with brandy and sautéed; Mediterranean prawns of epic size with a sauce diable; a venison stew of exquisite aroma; four different kinds of salad. Ferenc helped himself to every last thing, not neglecting to file away the visages of the men who served him. He knew at least three of those faces. Armand Pinay, whose party this was, was Robert Pinay's cousin; he had borrowed servants from some of his relatives. One of them looked a moment at Ferenc as if he recognized him but then said nothing. That was a blessing. It was too much to hope that he would get through the party without anyone noticing him (besides Philippa, who could be counted on to keep her mouth shut), but Ferenc hoped to keep recognition down to the barest minimum. Already he'd passed some old school chums whose eyes had dismissed him utterly. After all, he'd been away for years, and then there was that totally anonymous dinner jacket he was wearing. It made him all but invisible. Ferenc wanted to see everything and everyone—and not be seen himself.

It was not to be. He was wolfing his third Mediterranean prawn when a hand spun him around.

"Ferenc!"

"André!"

Much embracing.

"Careful of the lobster. Very messy."

"You didn't call me. Beast!"

"I just got here." A big lie. But what could one do?

Ferenc smiled fondly at André de Quielle, his old school chum.

Oh, what a charm was André's! Good looks. Marvelous manners. Decency. Kindness. Brains. And rich to boot. The gods were unfair. They ladled out the largesse to some with absurd profligacy while giving nothing at all to others. André de Quielle had much too much of the good things. But then he would go through life never knowing the agonies and aspirations of failure, the stimulation of deprivation. Poor fellow! Ferenc smiled lazily at the exuberance of André's affection for him. He was one of those entirely natural fellows who let their love spill right out on the carpet. It took great confidence these days when love for one's fellow was out of style.

"But what are you doing here?" André was saying. "You are in Israel being Zionist. At least that's what everyone thought. Being the noble Jew, rescuing those benighted heathens from the wilderness with your French civilization. Isn't that so, eh? So what are you doing in the middle of all these ghastly people!" André made a very French face to show his opinion of *tout Paris*, which was very low.

"Eating," said Ferenc easily. "One can endure the food in Israel only so long. Then one needs a square meal. Have a prawn. They are superb."

"And you didn't call me, Ferenc? I am heartbroken."

"I just got off the plane. I came straight here—knowing full well you would be here. Much as you despise all these people." Ferenc laughed, not quite all the way. He hated telling lies to André. To anyone else, yes. But not André. Still, that's the way it was. Oh, hell!

"But how marvelous! We shall have lunch together tomorrow. You shall tell me all. And right now, we shall. . . ."

Ferenc had to cut that off. He put down the plate of food reluctantly—there were still some very good things on it—and, putting his arm through André's, drew him to the edge of the room, away from the crowd of eaters.

"André," he murmured, improvising. But on familiar territory. He knew André inside out—what he would accept absolutely, what he would not accept. "I must tell you something." He looked around conspiratorially, then let his voice drop. "I am in love."

"Aaah!"

"But she belongs to someone else."

"All the best ones do." André's eyes were alight. This was his territory all right.

"I have been very foolish."

"It is the only way to be."

"I should not be here because if her husband saw me. . . ." Ferenc rolled his eyes, a French gesture he hadn't made in years.

"Aah!"

"I've got to slip out of here before he notices. And for God's sake, no mention that you saw me. Promise now!"

"But . . . but . . . which one is she? Show me! My God, they all have husbands. You shouldn't worry about husbands."

"This husband is trouble. Big trouble. Look, André, I can't tell you the whole thing. It's . . . oowoo . . . so . . . so . . . wow!" That would give some idea. "I'll call you tomorrow at noon sharp. Okay?"

Ferenc took his old friend in his arms and crushed him in a great bear hug. Then before André could quite get his breath back, Ferenc skipped through the crowd on the stairs to the floor below, leaving André bewildered but very happy for his friend. An illicit, foolish, secret affair! It was right down his alley.

On the first floor now, Ferenc looked for his quarry. He was in a real pickle now. If André came down and found him still in the house after he'd fabricated an emergency requiring that he leave, what then? Questions, that's what. He could not afford any talk about his role in Paris. The nice thing about a woman, somebody else's wife, was that it would not cause talk because that sort of thing went on all the time.

The vast salon seemed peopled by the same cast as when he had left. With a few differences. One of them François Duvillard. Ah! Ferenc took a deep, deep breath, taking it in very slowly, yogi-style, then out very slowly, yogi-style. It helped calm him but also it slowed the racing brain. Quieted it. He needed it for this work. Especially this particular job, which was technically complicated.

Duvillard had a girl on his arm. Damn. That was unexpected. Ferenc looked at his watch. The man was early, too. Usually he arrived half an hour later. That is, if you could say anything was ever usual about François. He specialized in the unusual. That girl. Good bones, dark hair. Did he know her? Heaven help him if he did.

Ferenc started to push through the crowd a little more quickly than he would like. There was still André upstairs. François's cousin. He could cause no end of damage if he appeared and took it into his head to join them. This damned plan depended not only on too many things happening but also on too many things not happening.

One of the things that were not supposed to happen was that girl. Duvillard had been appearing at these big *sorties* alone. But now . . .

"*Pardon,*" murmured Ferenc, slithering past the girl singer in the boy's cap. He held out his hand and smiled his lazy smile.

"François Duvillard?" said Ferenc. "I am Gerard."

This was the moment of truth. Ferenc smiled into the cold blue eyes of the man whose life he was about to take over. His mind racing, in spite of the yoga exercise. If, he was thinking, his old school chum André was the best of the French, of a charm irreplaceable, this man was the worst of the French. Cold. Contemptuous. With a destructive intelligence, playing venomous games with his wit and his wealth for his own private amusement.

The intelligent, contemptuous eyes looked him over before the hand was extended.

"Oh, you're the man," said Duvillard.

The moment had been carefully prepared by letters. Only the place was unexpected. To Duvillard. Not to Ferenc. There were excellent reasons for catching Duvillard by surprise.

"I didn't expect you here."

"I saw you come in," said Ferenc. "I thought I'd introduce myself."

"Hélène Labuisse," said Duvillard, indicating the dark-haired girl.

Ferenc smiled a grimace of a smile in her direction. Then back to François: "If I could just have a minute, monsieur. We might settle this now—to our mutual advantage."

Duvillard had taken to collecting opals. It was a very recent game with him. The sort of extraordinarily bizarre game that would appeal to him. Opals had got very expensive, and each one was different, not like diamonds, which could be cut. It was like collecting people, really. Opals came complete—and the game was to outwit the other collectors by trading back and forth, at 100,000 francs a throw, tempting a man with a gem of a jewel into parting with, perhaps, an even bigger gem, by throwing in a few lesser morsels. It was the kind of meaningless, enormously expensive diversion the French aristocracy had played for centuries. Ferenc despised it and the whole aristocratic stance that went with it. Here he was playing it—for he was, as Gerard, a collector of opals. The letters had described a little dandy calculated to attract such a one as Duvillard. It was a registered opal he was offering—a beauty—in place of a couple of Duvillard's beauties. The advantage lay marginally with Duvillard. That was the fun of the game, not possession (in itself pretty ridiculous) but the measureless satisfaction of doing another out of an expensive possession. Lovely game.

"Of course." Duvillard turned the barest sliver of attention to the dark-haired Mlle. Labuisse. "You'll excuse us, Hélène." He was coming along much too easily, and Ferenc wondered if he was doing it simply to administer this disdainful apology. You'll excuse us. Not will you, but you will. The girl was hurt and just a trifle alarmed at being left alone in the midst of this savagely self-centered crowd. It showed in her dark eyes. Oh, good, thought Ferenc. That'll keep her emotionally occupied just enough to stop her wondering about me. He took Duvillard's arm with an excess of obsequiousness. Duvillard would despise the obsequiousness, and this would put him, to a very slight degree, off guard. Because, of course, he enjoyed despising people. Duvillard was one of those who passed a large part of each day despising this one and that one. It afforded him immense pleasure and was, in fact, one of the great pleasures of aristocracies of all nations. But in surrendering to the delicious pleasure of despising a fellow human, Duvillard failed to notice that he was being steered very rapidly toward the small door in the staircase that one tended hardly to see. Unless you knew it was there.

"In here," said Ferenc, smiling his obsequious smile.

"In *here?*" questioned Duvillard, stopping dead in his tracks. He had become aware that he was being steered. He was not liking it a damned bit. He threw off Ferenc's guiding hand angrily. "What do you mean 'in here'? This leads to the cellar. I don't do business in cellars."

He was taking alarm. Ferenc played his trump.

"It's a very nice cellar," cooed Ferenc, gazing straight into his quarry's eyes, holding the man's eyes to keep them from wandering around. "I spent many hours playing in it as a child."

"You . . ." Duvillard was flabbergasted. This fellow! Spent many hours playing in his cousin's cellar! As a child! It opened a whole concatenation of dazzlingly new possibilities, changing the social level he had assigned Ferenc (or Gerard, as he thought him), changing the nature and the enjoyment of the swindle he was about to perpetrate (swindling friends of the family was a wholly different pleasure from swindling total strangers), and otherwise occupying his mind and emotions just enough to put him off guard yet again. Only for a moment—but that was enough. Ferenc turned the tiny, gilt, almost invisible knob in the baroque door and opened it.

"I used to come here often as a child," said Ferenc, still holding the man's eyes, while deflecting his attention with a bit of truth. There is nothing so disconcerting as truth in high French society. It is so rarely heard that it blots out thought for a moment or two, which is all the diversion that Ferenc needed. His hand grasped the elbow which had so recently shook it off and steered Duvillard into the little opening under the stairs. With the other hand Ferenc closed the door behind him. It was as black as the inside of a bear.

"What the devil!" spluttered Duvillard. His last words.

Ferenc put the silken cord around his neck expertly and quickly, listening the while to the demented cocktail roar of voices outside. That had been one of the great virtues of this otherwise far too complicated plan—that penetrating roar of hundreds of well-liquored guests. It drowned out a simple throttling, which, in fact, turned out to be not all that simple. Duvillard, for all his eating and drinking, was a muscular French aristocrat who hunted and played golf and did all the other social exercises. In extremis his arms and legs thrashed wildly, rocketing into the little baroque door like hammer blows. The Israeli pulled the flailing figure across his back by means of the silken cord and carried it down the pitch-black steps, feeling Duvillard's heels kicking wildly at him. In the pitch blackness, holding the flailing body well away, Ferenc went down four steps and then, with the familiarity learned in childhood, turned a sharp right and descended four more steps. The flailings weakened and then, as Ferenc concentrated his grip into a mighty spasm, ceased altogether. Ferenc held the body in the vicious vise for a full twenty seconds. Even in that blackness, death was dankly present. Ferenc could taste it. So many bodies. Stretching back to his time in Algeria with the French Army, which seemed a hundred years ago. He listened to his own beating heart for a moment in the clarity of afterkill, when, as in all the previous ones, he experienced a thrill of triumph. Oh, it was all very well to disapprove in the abstract of murder. But the fact was that at the very moment of a kill, one felt this flash of total triumph, a throwback to the primordial. He would like to throw open his mouth and scream like Tarzan. Afterward would come the guilt, the nightmares, all the rest of the human subconscious process, but at the very moment after killing always there was this marvelous and unutterably deplorable feeling of triumph. He couldn't help it.

Ferenc luxuriated in triumph for only three seconds. Then, in the inky blackness, he threw the body over his shoulder and felt his way to the bottom of the steps, counting. Five. Six. Seven. Quick right turn. One. Two. Three. Four. Counting to the beat of his heart, which was returning to normal. Five. Six. He felt the concrete on the soles of his shoes. Straight ahead now—twelve paces. He felt for the door that should be there, found it, and passed through. Once on the other side, he felt for the light. It was safe now. The lights showed a gloomy vista of brick, piled high with the very neat detritus of the French bourgeoisie, chairs that were not quite right for the expensive salon but were too good to throw away; packing cases full of Tante Marie's old china that could be pillaged for wedding presents to one's less desirable relatives but never, never (mon Dieu!) used by oneself; brocaded sofas that had passed over the precipice of fashion but might (one never knows, does one, about these things?) be right back at the apex of good taste next year. (Who would have thought Louis Quinze would ever come back? thought Ferenc in one icy corner of his mind.) He walked rapidly through the piles which had changed quite a lot in quality but not at all in quantity since he was a boy. The French never threw anything away that had only recently been counted as a virtue. Even the identity of the corpse over his shoulder was going to be reused just like a milk bottle.

At the end of the long passageway of cellar that ran completely under the house, a very long way indeed, was the little room whose great advantage was its distance from the stairs. Ferenc slipped the passkey into the lock with his free hand and opened the door. Jepthah was there ahead of him, laying out the two heavy sacks on a thick cover of newspapers. In his hand was the long butcher knife with its razor-sharp edge. He put it next to the sacks.

Ferenc lay the body next to him silently and returned to the main body of the cellar to turn off the lights. No one would come down there at that hour, but there was no point in taking chances. When he got back, Jepthah was already undressing the dead man very carefully, slipping the dead arm out of the velvet Yves Saint Laurent jacket as if he were undressing a little girl.

"Any problems?" asked Jepthah.

"Yes." Ferenc started to undress, too, divesting himself of the awful dinner jacket. "He brought a girl."

"Complications," murmured Jepthah. He was pulling off the dead man's trousers. "What are you going to do with her?"

"I haven't decided." Ferenc was on his knees now, half naked, his eyes fixed on the dead, staring eyes of François Duvillard. He took the dead man's chin in his hand and smiled, appreciating the irony to the very depth of his Gallic soul. "How far had you got with her, *mon vieux*, hmm? Must I carry on? And at what point did you leave off, eh? And did she like your brutal style? You weren't very nice to her, leaving her in the middle of all those terrible people as if you were parking a car. But maybe she likes that kind of treatment. Some women do. I shall try to be every bit as nasty as you, old fellow, but it's not going to be easy."

"Ferenc," protested Jepthah. "For God's sake, get on. You're not Hamlet."

"Oh, but I am! We all are!" Ferenc was in the full tide of postmurder exhilaration.

"We haven't time for monologues."

Ferenc chuckled and resumed his undressing. "You needn't worry, my friend. We are safe as tombs here." He slipped out of his trousers, and then out of the Pris Unic socks, and handed them to Jepthah. The dead man was naked now, and so was Ferenc. He was still talking directly to the corpse, now a close friend. "Killing a man forms a very close bond, did you know that, Jepthah? Oh yes, I feel I know him much better now that I have killed the poor bastard! *Regardez*, Jepthah, I am feeling sorry for so big a bastard as he was! But I do! I do! I know him much better, you see, now that I've killed him! There is a moment of understanding—oh, what an exhilarating experience—at the precise moment when the soul departs the body when you feel most intimate with the man whose life you are taking!"

Ferenc was in full flood now, his eyes glittering with a special postmurder madness. Jepthah didn't look at him; he had gone through this before. He was opening the little briefcase now, looking through the rubber bits in search of a particular scar.

Ferenc ran on like a car with the brakes off, talking again directly to the dead man: "I forgive you your viciousness, which I am about to embrace—will I also assume your sins? Will you go to heaven now? Shorn of all your misdeeds by my intervention? What a fortunate fellow to be murdered! It may easily be the nicest thing that ever happened to you. Maybe the only nice thing in your useless life."

There was a small scar under the nipple, and Jepthah measured it and then measured the same spot on Ferenc's chest, Ferenc talking away the while: "After a life of unremitting activity, much of it damned hard work, how will I be at uselessness, eh? It will be a very new trick misspending my time."

Jepthah fixed the bogus scar expertly on Ferenc's chest. "This will take hot water, soap—or caresses," said Jepthah wryly. "They make this stuff pretty good these days. Now you'd better put on your face, Ferenc. That girl is waiting."

Ferenc throttled the euphoria and got down to the serious business of transforming himself into someone else. First the acetolin base, half the thickness of tissue paper, tougher than rubber, twice as resilient, and soft as a baby's bottom. Too soft, really, for a man's face, but it couldn't be helped. The acetolin was covered with a surface of tiny ridges and was grayer than Ferenc's skin, adding ten years to his face. Next the lips, thin, contemptuous, tight. All done with a rubber substitute called cyrotel, developed in the Israeli laboratories only six months before, more versatile than skin and longer-lasting. "Oh, they have made vast strides in the impersonation business since Benedict Hermann," said Ferenc exultantly. "We've computerized identity. Very sophisticated stuff." He was putting on his nose now, a mathematical perfection of a nose, which gave to Ferenc's face that precise degree of exhausted fastidiousness of Duvillard's.

Ferenc smiled into the mirror, feeling his identity slip away as Duvillard's took hold. He was doing the magic of acting, transforming himself into someone else from the inside out. Meanwhile, graying the hair a bit, putting a touch of vein in the temple where the veins showed ever so little through Duvillard's skin. It all took a total of ten minutes, the real work having been done long ago in the laboratories.

Jepthah had piled a fresh, very thick wad of newspapers on the floor well away from the two piles of clothing and was engaged, grunting with the strain of it, in cutting the dead man's head off. The body would be found floating in its nondescript dinner jacket in the

Seine. With any luck the head would never be found. It would lie securely weighted on the bottom of the Seine, where its pleasant roundness, smoothed with cement, would resist grappling hooks. It was one of the most useful and thoughtful contributions of the terror laboratory. It took one-fifteenth the amount of concrete to sink a head as it did a whole body and speeded up the time needed for the operation sevenfold. Ah, science!

Fifteen minutes later, Ferenc was François, a miracle of tired contemptuousness in a well-fitting velvet jacket.

"God bless," said Jepthah, holding Ferenc's right hand in both his. He felt more friendly to the hand than to that face.

"Jepthah," said Ferenc, looking sadly at his old friend, "after you report in, ask Tilsit if you can come back. I am too tied down by this damned disguise—and the girl may be trouble. Explain, will you, that I can't operate as freely as before, that I need help?"

Jepthah nodded. "You'd better get back to the party. The girl may be a little annoyed. You've been gone twenty minutes."

Ferenc sighed heavily: "With any luck she will have got furious and left."

# CHAPTER 9

Nicole was appalled. She tried to conceal it, but it was too great a shock, too divisive. She felt Selim's flat gaze on her and knew he knew.

"You don't like what I'm asking?" he said. It was a statement really, not a question.

Nicole, her eyes the size of saucers, didn't answer. She rose abruptly and took a turn around the room, taking quick, short strides, fighting her bewilderment. Selim waited patiently. He'd asked a great deal.

Nicole stopped the pacing directly in front of the man who was the top Palestinian terrorist. "I have given my life, such as it is, to this movement. It is the fire of my existence," she said. "I didn't do this to kill Arabs, my brethren."

"I appreciate your loyalty to your comrades. Do you also appreciate treachery?" said Selim. He was in a difficult position. The fires of patriotism instilled in this girl since birth made her unswerving in her devotion to the cause. But this very devotion was a difficulty. She asked questions. What one needed for this kind of work was someone bright enough to accomplish the complexities one demanded and at the very same time stupid enough not to ask questions like "why?" Unfortunately, no such division of intelligence existed in human society.

"Why?" asked Nicole.

"You are not to ask why."

Nicole faced her leader, almost fainting with defiance. "I cannot kill my brethren unless I know why."

Selim was in a quandary. The girl already knew too much. If she refused to carry out the mission, she would have to be disposed of. She couldn't be allowed to run around loose with all she knew. That would simply cost him a valuable operative—and where else would he find a seventeen-year-old as dedicated, as bright, and as personable as this one? Especially one who spoke French like a French girl?

Selim sighed a Levantine sigh. "Sit down," he said peaceably. One could not, of course, tell her everything, just enough to still her love of her fellows, her brethren, her comrades.

"There are loyalties and loyalties," began Selim in tones of greater warmth than he had used all that long evening. "We must make a choice if we are to achieve our great objective. There are Arabs—quite as sincere and dedicated as yourself—who are misguided. Or who are—even worse—fainthearted. They are willing to accept a permanent division of Palestine."

"Ah," said Nicole, her despair lifting like mist in the sunlight. She was an all-or-nothing girl to the marrow. She would never settle for less than all. She would never have become a guerrilla warrior in the first place if she had been prone to compromise.

"Let me tell you something about Arab politics," Selim spoke in warm, caressing tones, his brown eyes melting sadly into hers now, turning on all his charm to soften the cynicism of the message. "And when I have finished telling you, you will be, alas, older. You will leave a little of your youth behind you when you comprehend the infinite uncertainties of human nature—especially among Arabs. You will be much wiser but a much sadder girl."

For an hour he spoke of the factionalism of the Palestinian movement, the growing bitterness and hatred among the splinter groups, the necessity for solidity of purpose at the center; the passionate partisanship of the warring groups that was threatening to split the Palestinian movement from top to bottom.

"Somebody must perish, or we will all perish together," said Selim softly. "And the ones we have selected are no less dedicated or devoted to the same high purpose than yourself. This is a tragedy—but the lesser one."

It was 11:00 P.M. before he finished.

# CHAPTER *10*

Ferenc popped out of the concealed cellar door like a jack-in-the-box, pulling the door shut behind him. I am François now, François, François, he was saying. *Attention!* he was saying to himself. His very bones felt different.

He stood a moment, back to the door, holding himself very straight, ready to stare down anyone who dared question his popping out of that unlikely door. No one noticed at all. The party had shifted to the upper registers of sound. There is a period in every party where alcohol is served where the number of talkers suddenly doubles and the number of listeners is halved. Everyone tries to express himself at once, and the decibel count doubles along with it. The partygoers' perceptions are at their lowest ebb at moments like these.

He stood a moment, settling into his part, letting his face assume the arrogance it must carry naturally, settling his mind into the patterns he had studied so thoroughly, especially the voice. Where had he left the girl? Already he was thinking as François, not as Ferenc. Ah, yes. Upstairs.

He pushed through the crowd and up the grand curving staircase to the salon. He walked through the uproar slowly, confident that people would get out of his way—and they did—his eyes searching. The young woman was not where he had left her. He had a moment of optimism. Perhaps she had gone home in a fury. That would simplify things, but of course it was too much to hope. Everything had gone according to plan—except that woman—and he knew from experience that one thing always went wrong. No plan ever went 100 percent right.

Aaah, well, there she was. She had moved the length of the great room, probably searching for companionship, and was now at the far corner under the great baroque mirror over the fireplace, talking to a small dapper man with a rosette in his buttonhole. One of those innumerable people who not only had the Légion d'Honneur but actually wore the rosette to parties, which told a lot about him. Did François Duvillard know this dapper boutonniered character? Ah, that was the question. It would be the first of many such encounters in which he would have to feel his way with infinite delicacy. His great weapon was arrogance. He elbowed his way through the partygoers, feeling immensely exhilarated. He had never been in such danger in his whole danger-filled life, and he was loving it. Already he was François to the very core.

"François!" said the woman icily. "How good of you to come back."

Marvelous, he thought. She's in a temper. We can have a splendid quarrel; one learns a lot in a quarrel. People let fly with their inmost secrets.

He nodded at the dapper man absently. A good nod. For a man like François it could be the nod he'd give a total stranger. Or one he'd give his oldest friend. He was that kind of man. Rude. It made things very much easier.

"Sorry, *chérie*," murmured Ferenc—no, not Ferenc—François, silkily. "I have made a most enjoyable acquisition. It took a little time."

The woman was meeting his eyes now in a sort of icy rage. Oh, good. He preferred that to tears. She didn't look the tearful type. What were they to each other? There was no Hélène Labuisse on the intelligence estimate.

"We were discussing the Exhibition, François," said the man with the rosette of the Legion of Honor in his buttonhole.

He knows my name. We're on a first-name basis. He wears the Legion of Honor rosette. And he discusses the Exhibition at affairs like this rather than who is going to bed with whom. That tells me much but not nearly enough.

"And what did you think of the Exhibition?" asked Ferenc.

"Worse than last year. And that was very bad," said the boutonniered one.

"I think we should do away with the Exhibition altogether," said Ferenc. François Duvillard was renowned for his outrageous utterances at parties.

"Do away with the Exhibition!" The boutonniered one was scandalized.

"Oh, François doesn't mean that. He just says things like that to make people angry, Colonel Frère," said Hélène.

Colonel Frère, thought Ferenc. Well! Well! Head of Special Branch Police Intelligence. What on earth was he doing at a gathering like this? Why not ask? It's what François would do.

"What are you doing at so frivolous an affair as this, Colonel? Protecting us from Selima?"

It was a shot in the dark—and a very unfortunate one. Colonel Frère became very icy indeed. He surveyed Ferenc now like an objective.

"And what made you say *that*, Monsieur Duvillard?"

Now we're not on a first-name basis, thought Ferenc. Well! Well! Ferenc smiled his most malignant François Duvillard smile. "One hears things, Colonel. One gets around and one hears things."

"About Selima?" said the Colonel, thin-lipped. "Not many people in France have ever heard of it."

Oh, Lord! Ferenc felt a distinct jar. He'd forgotten how well informed he was about Middle Eastern guerrilla operations.

"Oh, he makes jokes," said Hélène Labuisse irritably. "About everything under the sun, our François."

"I would be very grateful if Monsieur Duvillard would rack his mind and tell me where he heard of that particular organization," said the Colonel.

Ferenc became almost excessively François Duvillard at this point, laying one finger against the side of his nose in one of François Duvillard's more infuriating mannerisms, thinking aloud in a mocking way. "Well, you know, Colonel, one remembers the gossip. One doesn't always remember who told you it." He laughed wickedly.

"If you recall, will you let me know?" The Colonel bowed in the direction of Hélène Labuisse—and strolled away.

"Why in the name of God did you have to say such a thing to Colonel Frère? Of all people! Do you want him to suspect?" She was furious.

Suspect? Suspect what?

"Sometimes it's the best way to throw off suspicion," said Ferenc, watching her very carefully now. This was fascinating territory indeed. Were they in something together—François Duvillard and Hélène Labuisse? What fun!

"You should not have said it! It was a ridiculous bit of attention-getting, François. Anything else but that! And to anyone else but him!" Ferenc was learning things about her every second. She was no fool, this one. What's more she was almost acting as if she were in charge—not François. Well! Well!

"We had better go—before you put your foot in your mouth again," said Hélène coldly.

"We have not yet eaten," protested Ferenc, "and my cousin's food is famous."

"Oh, we'll feed you," she said irritably.

We?

"Come on. You've been seen with me. That should start some hares."

Curiouser and curiouser, thought Ferenc, every fiber of him alive with the possibilities. "Well, you're the boss," said Ferenc lightly.

Another shot in the dark.

"I am not the boss," said Hélène coldly. "Robert Pinay is the boss, and you had better not forget it. He's a very dangerous man, François, even if he is your cousin. Sometimes I think you don't know your cousin at all well."

"Sometimes I think I don't know my cousin at all well either," said Ferenc, laughing. He couldn't resist it. He certainly didn't know Robert Pinay at all. He knew his wife, every last dimple. It now almost seemed as if Robert might be the more interesting of the two.

There was a very awkward moment over the girl's coat. It seemed that François Duvillard had arrived in nothing but his dinner jacket. But the girl had had a coat and in forgetting it Ferenc stumbled again. Still, François Duvillard was such a self-centered son of a bitch that it could very well be something he would forget. He retrieved the coat from the cloakroom as Hélène waited in the entranceway, and stole a quick look at the label—a Lanvin original, which meant money—and then the two stood outside.

The doorman went in search of the Duvillard car and chauffeur, and now would come a very tricky moment indeed. The Duvillard chauffeur, old Jacques, had been with the Duvillard family since before François was born. If he could stand François's rheumy scrutiny, he could bear up under any other. That consideration was the very hub of this otherwise too risky plan. François Duvillard would arrive at the party in his own car with his lifelong chauffeur—and if he returned with the same car and the same lifelong servitor, who on earth would suspect that this was not truly the real François Duvillard?

The ancient Isotta Fraschini—it had been in the family since 1915 and was a symbol of inestimable prestige, since it was the only 1915 Isotta in all Paris—drew up. Jacques stepped out and held open the door. He was a French ancient of truly terrifying mien, the face of such antiquity as to have lost all mobility, the eyes tiny, ferocious, intelligent, thoroughly nasty, very French.

"*Merci*, Jacques," murmured Ferenc, as the man held open the door. He was just trying out his voice on the man. The face was perfect. But the voice?

Jacques said nothing at all, but the eyes glittered disdainfully. Ferenc felt suddenly cold to his very toes. This man hated François Duvillard.

Inside the ancient tonneau, the woman took charge.

"One Sixteen Rue Valenciennes, Jacques," she said confidently.

Now what would they be doing there?—116 Rue Valenciennes would be Robert Pinay's house.

Ferenc knew the value of silence. He settled back comfortably into the extraordinary comfort of the ancient car and, as it were, settled also into his skin as François Duvillard. He felt an immense surge of confidence at having got through the first enormously important steps in this charade. He was on stage now, the curtain was up—and no one had thrown any ripe fruit yet. That in itself was a great stride forward. He recalled an interview with Laurence Olivier he'd read once in which that great English actor had said that makeup was a very important part of acting. It was! It was! Every moment he spent in François Duvillard's skin he felt more like him, more—what was the precise word he wanted?—imperturbable. Here he sat with a girl he didn't know, involved in some caper about which he hadn't the foggiest notion, headed for a conference with the boss of the caper, where the perils of his ignorance were unimaginably great. Yet here he was—making the girl do the running. And—yes —enjoying her discomfort. Enjoyment of others' distress, particularly that of lovely ladies, was not normally his scene; yet here he was, enjoying very much the discomfort of this pretty woman. He was slipping—had slipped—into his role almost too completely.

"I don't think I shall ever understand you, François," said the woman finally.

"Praise God," murmured Ferenc cynically. "You wouldn't like it if you did."

François had obviously bewildered her before. It was a remark that had quite clearly been made on many occasions.

"It was very foolish of you to go ruffling the waters right now," said the girl. "Robert thinks Colonel Frère has tumbled on the Chinese connection."

*Chinese* connection! Ferenc, steeped in months of close study of the Byzantine complexities of Arab politics, and particularly Palestinian politics, felt a moment of giddiness. Enough was enough! *Chinese* connection indeed!

"Oh, I don't think he has," said Ferenc, wrapped in his cloak of imperturbability behind his superb Duvillard mask, talking with confidence about he knew not what. "Frère is just suspicious by profession. It's what he's paid for—to smell smells that aren't there."

"He wasn't at Armand's party for the wine," said Hélène.

"What was he there for?" asked Ferenc languidly. "I was trying to smoke him out."

"You succeeded only in thoroughly arousing him," said Hélène angrily. "For heaven's sake, don't tell Robert what you've done. Promise me that!"

She put her hand on his arm pleadingly, her eyes huge. Ferenc found himself laughing right into her face, an act so foreign to his true nature that it startled him. It was done without thought, without premeditation. Truly he was wallowing in the depths of Duvillard's nature! He said nothing, waiting for her to play her hand.

"The Chinese are not such ideological infants as you think, François. They are obsessed with ideology only because that is a phase in their development. They are good revolutionaries. They see Palestinian nationalism as just a phase which must be gone through before the Palestinians become true Socialists. But this doesn't mean they are not very clever conspirators indeed—in fact, cleverer than your beloved Russians in many ways."

Ferenc smiled a loathsome smile and rubbed his hands together. "I'm frightfully hungry. I wonder what Robert has for us to eat."

CHAPTER *11*

Supper in the simple breakfast room just off the main salon of Robert Pinay's lovely house was very good indeed. A lobster casserole with spiced wine over toast, very rich, very filling, with buttered extra toast on the side and a slightly sweet white wine from Pinay's own vineyard. It had been prepared by the servants and was waiting for them. The Pinays—Philippa and Robert—arrived within minutes of Ferenc and Hélène. Philippa sent the servants to bed, took over the supper altogether, serving them with downcast eyes.

Ferenc watched her with a slight smile. She'd dropped her adoring wife pose altogether and was now efficient waitress, maitre d'—all in one. What a woman! He'd seen her in three roles now—passionate adultress, adoring wife, gracious hostess. Marvelous in all of them. Never did she meet his eyes, and he got the clear impression she did not like François Duvillard at all. That would make things a lot easier.

The party they'd just left, Robert Pinay told them, was just stripping itself down to the hard drinkers and merrymakers and would go on certainly until the small hours. So and so was making eyes at the wife of such and such, and her husband was furious. And so forth. All party gossip. Interesting stuff—and Ferenc paid close attention—but hardly what he'd been summoned to listen to. Ferenc played his role, dropping acidic remarks from time to time, wary and watchful in his François Duvillard skin. Philippa added a bit of chatter that was almost too frivolous—what the women were wearing, and so forth. Hélène said nothing at all. All very innocuous. So innocuous as to be very dangerous indeed. He mustn't be tempted into the indulgence of relaxation.

In fact, though, they paid him little heed. Hélène Labuisse had already accepted him, and since she had, they did. People, Ferenc thought, sunk deep into his François Duvillard skin, were so full of themselves, they had no time for you. Even his voice—his greatest worry, since physically he was almost too perfect—attracted no attention. They were so sunk in their own stratagems they took no notice. Their very intelligence was a great shield. The idea that he was *not* François Duvillard was too inherently improbable for such intelligent people to entertain. He had stumbled upon a great truth, he thought. It's not going to be the sophisticates who are hard to hoodwink but the simple people who use their eyes and ears and noses rather than their brains. Such as that antique chauffeur.

At midnight Philippa served them coffee, cleared away the lobster, kissed her husband absently, and, quite abruptly, said goodnight. She was gone in an instant. The atmosphere changed.

Robert's beaming party manner dropped off him like a raindrop. He fixed Ferenc with a straightforward gaze, neither friendly nor hostile, and rubbed his hands together briskly: "The situation has taken a turn for the worse. The pressure is very great now for the Arabs to use the money weapon on top of the oil weapon. The Russians are pouring on the persuasion to get the oil money out of Western banks and put it in their hands. As you know very well, we are bankers first and Hassimis second. What they are saying is to take the cash out of Western banks, which is to say out of *our* banks. This is not even very sensible ideology. Economically it would be a catastrophe—not only for our bank but for them as well. Money that disappears into Russia has a way of never reappearing—at least not as money. The Russians will provide anything from their excellent tanks to their rotten machine tools. The one thing they never give back is money."

"Tell that to Faisal," said Ferenc negligently, "as if he does not know."

"Oh, Faisal knows all right, but he's dazzled by the Russian airplanes. He wants some of their two-thousand-mile-an-hour ones which he can't fly and which the Russians would under no circumstances give him anyway. However, it's not Faisal who is the problem, it's Qaddafi. As you know, Qaddafi doesn't give a damn about capitalist investment; he has huge quantities of cash whose sole purpose is ideological. The main reason all of it hasn't vanished out of our banks into Russia is that he thinks the Russians are far too conservative and non-Marxist and nonrevolutionary. The other reason is that we are the only even remotely Arab Western bank. But he's getting very restless. We have to show him something to keep him quiet."

Ferenc's mind was racing along three levels now. So Duvillard, the ne'er-do-well Hassimi, was already in on Hassimi planning? He'd been sent to Paris to push the fellow into the inner councils; he was already there. Aloud he said: "What do you want exactly, Robert?"

"Blow up something," said Hélène Labuisse. It was the first time she'd spoken.

"Preferably with a Russian rocket with the markings all over it. The nice thing about Russian rockets is that even after they blow up they are so identifiably Russian."

"Hmm," said Ferenc thoughtfully. Double cross, he was thinking. Triple cross. Quadruple cross.

As if reading his mind, Robert said: "Preferably with some Arab casualties—moderate Arabs, of course."

"Oh, of course," murmured Ferenc.

Whose side was Robert on anyhow? It was inconceivable that this rich French banker was on the far left revolutionary Marxist wing of Fatah. Or was he just making trouble to keep Qaddafi quiet to keep the money in his bank, an entirely capitalist aim? His head ached with the strain of sorting out these subtleties.

"You see, the great weakness of the Russian position in the Middle East"—Robert was yielding to the French passion for logical, coherent explanation, which was very helpful—"is that they hate the sheikhs, they loathe Faisal, and they despise Qaddafi. They have great difficulty concealing their dislike, and this has undermined their position with the very people they're trying to woo. Every time a Russian rocket is found in the wrong hands, suspicion grows."

"Has your Russian friend any more of those nice rockets he can lay his hands on?" asked Hélène Labuisse.

My Russian friend, thought Ferenc grimly. What Russian friend? Aloud he said: "Oh, I think so. Have you anyone to handle it?"

A calculated risk. It might show his ignorance, but he had to know.

"We have a very good operative coming in. Very well trained. Very personable. Very fanatic. We can count on her for anything, including blowing herself up if necessary—and it may be necessary."

*Mon Dieu*, thought Ferenc. This is Paris, is it? The most civilized city in the world? Aloud, he said: "She?"

"The girls are better than the boys," said Hélène Labuisse almost triumphantly. "They're prettier than the boys, they look less like Arabs, you can get them in and out of countries easier—and some of them are much brighter than the boys. This girl is the only one to escape that Israeli massacre at the Café des Pyramides when three Arab men were gunned down. She got away clean—and clear out of the country."

Ferenc didn't turn a hair. "Did she now?" he murmured. "And have you picked out what she is to blow up when I get her a few Russian rockets?"

"No," said Robert. "We must think about that. It will take a lot of thought. The girl, of course, has no idea what we are about, and you must tell her nothing. The idea is to pick a target that will infuriate all moderate Arab opinion, implicate the Russians, placate the Chinese, and point the finger of suspicion at the wild-eyed militants in Palestine Liberation."

"A very large order," said Ferenc.

"And kill a few right-wing Arabs, too," said Hélène Labuisse mildly. "Don't forget that. The chief idea is to torpedo the peace conference. We must prevent peace breaking out in the Middle East."

"Well, there's little likelihood of that," said Ferenc ironically.

He was swept by exhaustion. It came on in waves, suddenly and overwhelmingly. Immense reserves of adrenaline had pumped into his blood, carrying him through a killing, through a masquerade that involved tremendous mental agility. Now he felt as if he'd been on his feet for twenty-four hours uninterruptedly. He was sagging, physically and mentally, and that was very dangerous indeed. He couldn't let down in front of this man and this woman. He stood up abruptly.

"*Bonne nuit.*" François Duvillard was renowned for abrupt departures. He suddenly got bored and left people, sometimes without even saying goodnight.

Robert Pinay opened his mouth as if to protest, then shut it again. Obviously he'd been through this before.

"*Bonne nuit,* François," he said courteously, resignedly.

Ferenc looked at Hélène Labuisse enigmatically. He had no idea what to expect here. Was he supposed to take the lady to his bed? Or to some other bed? Or what? Let her make her move.

"*Bonne nuit,* François," she said dismissively, holding out a hand. He shook it with a quizzical smile. My goodness, her *hand!* Not even her cheek! Well. Well. Neither Pinay nor Hélène Labuisse showed the slightest inclination toward getting up. Clearly he was supposed to see himself out, which meant he was a very familiar visitor indeed.

And Hélène was obviously an even more familiar one. Spending the night, was she? So. She was Pinay's girl, not Duvillard's. And a much tougher cookie than he had imagined. "And kill a few right-wing Arabs." She'd been very casual about killing—even more significantly, about killing Arabs.

Oh, God, he was tired. Outside, old Jacques bundled him into the tonneau (no other word for that ancient interior, he thought) with practiced contempt. The vehicle purred through the Paris night like an ancient dragon. Inside, Ferenc hung on to wakefulness like a drowning man to a life belt. He pinched himself. He tried to alarm himself by dangers yet ahead. Among other things he had to find his bed. The Duvillard ménage had been well scouted by Israeli intelligence. He knew where the house was—on the edge of the Bois de Boulogne, very expensive, very chic—and even where the bedroom was. What he didn't know was where the lights were, whether any servants would be up, what steps on the stairs creaked, all those tiny details of long familiarity that he should know. And didn't.

Another thing he didn't know, he soon found out, was the lock-up system.

Jacques stopped the ancient car outside the great iron grilled gate that led to the garden. The chauffeur held open the car door to the aged Isotta. Ferenc clambered out, taking a great gulp of night air to wake himself. Then he stood on the pavement with an uncertainty he'd never have permitted to show if he'd been more awake. Would old Jacques open the iron gate? No, he wouldn't. Or anyway, didn't. Ferenc let too long a moment slip by while he waited for Jacques to do something, but the old man was an even better waiter than he was. Old Jacques just stood there, the car door handle in his hand, staring at Ferenc with his hooded eyes.

Too late, Ferenc nodded and crossed the pavement. He tried the door. It was locked. Damn! He should have known that, shouldn't he? Jacques's gaze, hostile as ever, was still on him. Now what do I do? thought Ferenc, wishing he were more awake. Keys. Keys. He felt in the dinner jacket—François's own dinner jacket—right jacket pocket, left jacket pocket, right trouser pocket, left trouser pocket. No keys in any of them. Jacques gazed his hooded, implacable gaze at him throughout.

*Merde,* Ferenc was thinking wildly now. Am I to founder on a simple matter of keys to the gate after I have stood up under the scrutiny of Robert Pinay and Hélène Labuisse? He was feeling his breast pocket now, an unlikely place for a key, but what was left? It was not there either.

If only my mind were working a little faster . . . "I've lost my key, Jacques," he said.

Jacques slammed shut the car door. Very slowly he crossed the pavement to Ferenc, unbuttoned the single button holding the dinner jacket closed, sent a gnarled finger groping into the pocket of the frilled, ornate waistcoat, and came up with a pair of keys.

"Where you always keep them, Monsieur François," he said.

The old servitor opened the iron gate with a great show of servitude, waved Ferenc up the path, and again with a display of Uriah Heep obsequiousness—surely an exercise in mockery?—opened the front door to the house and handed Ferenc his keys. Inside was cavernous blackness. Ferenc had no idea where the light switches were—unless they were just inside and to the left as you entered, as most switches are. Ferenc was not going to take any chances. He stepped into the inky blackness. *"Bonne nuit,* Jacques," he sang out—and slammed the door.

*Mon Dieu,* it was black. It took a good five minutes of groping and stumbling about before he found a switch that turned on not only one light but a half dozen bulbs that lit the entrance hall, foyer, and stairs.

At the head of the stairs was a whole bank of light switches. He turned them on—every last one—to find out what lights they lit. His bedroom was right opposite the head of the stairs, overlooking the Bois. He found the lights in their usual place inside the door and turned them on before dousing the hall and stair lights.

I should explore the whole house while everyone's asleep, he was thinking, but the hell with it. He tore off the dinner jacket, his borrowed clothes, dove into his borrowed bed, and fell instantly to sleep.

Then came the nightmares, the worst he'd ever had, worse even than the ones after the torture detail in Algeria. François Duvillard's bony sneer of a face loomed big as a balloon under the strangling hands, laughing. And why not? For Ferenc was suddenly aware that those were *his* hands and *his* sneering face. Strangling himself! What a futility!

Ferenc was swept with the ultimate horror of all—the knowledge that it *was* a nightmare. He tried to wake himself up, and so profound was his slumber he could not. He just lay there sunk 10,000 meters deep in fathomless sleep, strangling himself with his own hands again and again.

# CHAPTER 12

"You've been to Paris before?" said Philippa. She was sizing up Nicole from head to foot. That blue wool suit—*Mon Dieu!* Robert had told her little except that the girl was a distant cousin. She didn't believe him. Robert's explanations about the roles of pretty girls in his life were rarely to be trusted. But if *that* were what she was all about, then what would happen to Hélène Labuisse? It would get very crowded in Robert's bedroom.

"Once," said Nicole primly. *"Avec ma tante!"*

*Ma tante*, my ass, thought Philippa. This is not a girl who travels about much with her aunt. And while she looked delectable enough, Philippa doubted, too, that sex was what she was there for. Something to do with the bank. Robert never told her about the bank, and until recently she had had no curiosity. Moneymaking bored her. Philippa was by nature a spender. Where the money came from was not only boring but vaguely indecent—like where babies came from to Victorian ladies. But lately affairs at the bank had pricked her interest, if only because she had begun to suspect that money was the least of what was going on there. Too many late-night evenings with the likes of that bottomless shit François Duvillard, to say nothing of a whole assortment of improbable characters who came and went at improbable hours and whom one didn't meet at anyone else's house or at Deauville or—anywhere. So what were they doing in her house at 2:00 A.M.? Plots and stratagems—and Philippa loved plots and stratagems almost more than love itself.

They were driving in from Orly in the Pinay Facel-Vega.

"It's very nice to be in Paris again," said Nicole, thinking of the last time. Would she run into any of her old customers? All those rich Greeks? But she didn't look like that girl at all anymore. Meanwhile, there was this chic lady with the clever eyes. She would have to be careful. This was in many ways a more dangerous game than shooting Israelis. Instinctively she drew into total naïvete—and her looks would support this. She looked totally innocent—so marvelous were the beauty salons of Beirut.

It had quite the wrong effect on Philippa. Such innocence was not to be believed in the modern world. Certainly not from anyone thrust on her household by her husband, who was totally devoid of innocence in the bedroom, the counting room, and the drawing room—and she had no idea which of these rooms the girl was destined for. "Where do you live?" asked Philippa.

"Zurich," said Nicole sweetly.

"Nobody lives in Zurich," said Philippa.

"Oh, some do," said Nicole. "I do." She instantly regretted it. I should just have acted dumb and confused, she thought. I mustn't trade ripostes with this clever lady.

Innocent as a fox, thought Philippa. "We must do some shopping," said Philippa, trying it out.

"Oh yes, please," said Nicole eagerly. "You must show me how to dress. I know nothing at all."

*That* I believe, thought Philippa, looking at the blue wool suit.

"We'll go this afternoon and spend a lot of Robert's money. Nothing is too good for a niece of my husband." She watched closely to see if that sally had hit any particularly tender area. If it had, it didn't show. She doesn't care about money at all, this one, thought Philippa, but I think she loves clothes.

"This is your room," she said later, showing the girl into a second-floor room overlooking the garden at the back of the house. "It's two flights up, but a young girl like you shouldn't mind."

The little staircase from the first to the second floor was right next to her room—and no one could get up or down that staircase without Philippa knowing. It creaked like a ship in a gale. Philippa was immensely curious as to who would go up those stairs and why.

"It's lovely!" cried Nicole rapturously. Inside she was cursing Arab curses. How could one do what one had been sent to do up a staircase that creaked like that? She'd have to do something about that.

Ten minutes later Philippa, watching narrowly, introduced the young girl to her husband.

*"Enchanté,"* murmured Robert Pinay, kissing the girl's hands one after the other, looking at her with his most eager smile. "You are even prettier than I'd been led to expect."

*Merde,* thought Philippa; he has never laid eyes on her before. Robert had told her he had never seen the girl before. I've caught him telling the truth, thought Philippa; this is even more sinister than I believed possible. What is she doing here?

"She needs clothes, Robert," said Philippa.

"Hélène can take her shopping this afternoon."

So! Hélène is in this, too, thought Philippa. That rules out sex altogether. "I said I would take her shopping," said Philippa, eyes on her husband.

"Perhaps you both can take her shopping."

"That will be most interesting," said Philippa blandly. Most interesting indeed. Wife, mistress, and mysterious cousin from Zurich? What a ménage à trois!

Ferenc awoke with a growl and sat up staring. All one movement, hands raised as if to ward off ... whatever needed warding off. His head seemed like cotton. Who in God's name was he? And why? Especially why?

He examined the room minutely, the great French windows, the proliferation of mirrors everywhere (intelligence had said nothing about this mirror fetish), the Corot over the Louis Quinze white marble fireplace. Oh, he was going to live well—if he could manage to stay alive.

He got out of bed and took a good look at himself in the gilt mirror over the fireplace. François Duvillard stared back at him, horror-struck, the nightmares still etched on his false self. Ferenc ran his fingers over his cheeks, rubbing out the horror, reassembling himself psychologically. He felt ghastly, as if he'd had no sleep at all. He looked at his watch. Eleven A.M. Half the morning gone. And to what purpose?

A discreet knock. Oh, good. That would save a half-hour hunt for the bell. The damned bells and switches were more trouble than the infinite complexity of Arab politics and Palestinian terror.

*"Entrez."*

She was a little old lady in black bombazine with hair as white as a cloud—and as insubstantial. She was about four and a half feet tall, bent almost double, with eyes as piercing as searchlights, and Ferenc guessed she must be eighty. Another antique, bloody hell, thought Ferenc. He felt as naked in front of that searchlight gaze as before that of ancient Jacques. He did much better with the bankers than with the peasants in this masquerade.

*"Bonjour, m'sieu,"* said the old lady merrily (was there a touch of malice in that silvery laughter?) and placed the tray she carried on the table next to one of the French windows, as if she did this every morning. "You slept late."

Ferenc said nothing. His silence gambit had worked wonders so far.

"M'sieu Vassily called three times," said the antique lady merrily. (What was so funny? Or was she always like this?) "He wishes you to call back the moment you awake."

Vassily? Russian? My Russian friend perhaps?

"Oh, he'll call back," said Ferenc, trying out his voice on the ancient merry lady. What was her name anyhow? Damn intelligence! An old white-haired lady in his bedroom at first waking, and he hadn't a clue! It made him angry—and instantly he felt better, more awake. He strode over to the breakfast tray and gulped down his orange juice.

"What else?" he asked. Why not? He couldn't wait all day for the information to come to him. If I can just get through this first day, past these damnable servants, I have a chance to survive this idiotic masquerade, he was thinking. If I were a betting man, I would give me about fifty-to-one odds against managing to get through today unscathed.

The crone was handing him his mail. Three letters. Each one, dynamite.

"Madame Pinay phoned. She'll call back."

Philippa? Now what did that magnificently gifted lady want? Especially since she seemed to hate his guts. Or rather François Duvillard's guts. *His* guts she rather liked, he remembered. He opened a letter. An engraved invitation. No, not an invitation, a reminder that he was expected at dinner that night at the home of—oh, my God!—André de Quielle, his old childhood chum. A slim icicle of dismay pierced him. That would be some fun, running the gauntlet of André's blue eyes. Why was André having François Duvillard to dinner anyway? He didn't like him. What an infinitely incestuous mare's-nest Paris society was! One rubbed elbows with far too many people—including many elbows whose owners one loathed—at this level. Life was much simpler down at the proletariat levels of terror where he had operated before. Much simpler and much less dangerous. Anyway, he knew his way around André's house, so that was all right.

He opened another letter. Another social affair—what a popular fellow, considering how unlovable he was—this time an invitation to dinner at the American Ambassador's. My goodness, François certainly got around. Three weeks away, this one. He wouldn't have to worry about that for a while—if ever.

The telephone rang.

"Answer it," said Ferenc to the old lady.

"*Chez* Duvillard," said the lady into the phone. She handed the instrument to Ferenc. "M'sieu Vassily."

Ferenc sighed. This was the toughest hurdle of all—telephones —and he summoned all his superb gifts of mimicry. His voice was exquisitely noncommittal: "*Oui.*"

"François!" The voice was urgent; it was very Russian; it was also very cultivated—not the Gromyko-type voice—more White than Red Russian. But then, of course, they were all one now since World War II, all Russians together. "I must see you this minute!" Tremendous urgency. Very friendly.

Ferenc took the plunge. "Of course," he said. "Why don't you come here right now?" That would save him the trouble of finding him. If this were indeed the Russian friend who supplied those lovely Russian rockets.

"Well, I'll get there as fast as I can. It may take an hour. The Embassy cars are all out." The Russian rang off.

Embassy? Well, well. He didn't sound like an official Soviet type—but then Paris civilized even the Russians. Ferenc sat down to his croissant and brioche and took a tiny sip of coffee, savoring the chicory. He missed French coffee in Israel.

Israel.

Had everything gone all right? Had Jepthah got rid of the body and got out of the country? *Figaro* lay on the breakfast tray. He opened it and turned directly to the crime page where the bodies were always laid out for French popular consumption. No bodies. At least none that he knew. The old lady lingered, her piercing gaze never leaving him. She seemed quite fond of him—the first person he'd found at all fond of François Duvillard. If she was indeed fond. The trouble with ancients is that their surface is not always a reliable mirror of their depths. That fixed grin could conceal purest malevolence. He had no way of knowing. He couldn't very well order her out because this might very well be the morning routine. Perhaps he was expected to chat with her.

"*Ça va?*" That French question that meant nothing—and everything.

"Jacques said you couldn't find your keys last night?" The old one was cackling with glee, the old bones rattling with merriment.

"Oh, it's not that funny," protested Ferenc.

"Oho! You do tease the poor simpleton!" She was off again in a gale of squeaks and catarrhs and rumblings. Ancient laughter. A terrifying sight. Hatred below stairs between these two ancients? He filed it away with all the other things.

"*Eh bien,*" Ferenc shrugged a French shrug. He would accept credit for that bit of sadistic teasing without absolutely committing himself to it. It was something to be kept in mind. François liked tormenting ancient Jacques, did he? Sounded like him. And that was perhaps why. . . .

The telephone bleated its female bleat. This time the ancient picked up the instrument without being asked. "*Chez Duvillard. Ah, oui, madame.*" She handed the phone to Ferenc. "Madame Pinay." Sniffing a little as she did so, as if they shared an opinion of *that* one.

Ferenc essayed a wink to see how it would go down. The old one doubled up with mirth, the old wrinkles heaving and splitting. Well,

well, thought Ferenc. She and François were conspirators together. Against old Jacques? And who else?

"Philippa," he murmured into the phone.

"François," the voice was cold with dislike. Very crisp, very businesslike. "Can you come to lunch?"

"Today?"

"I realize it's very short notice. I tried to ring through twice before, but Madame Blanche flatly refused to wake you." Here the voice was venomous. Clearly Philippa and Madame Blanche—so that was her name, thank God—were not enamored of one another.

"We have a . . . cousin staying with us." There was an almost imperceptible pause before "cousin." Philippa's editorial comment. "Robert is dying to introduce you to her. He says you already know about her."

Ferenc's mind went blank for a moment. Cousin? Oh, *that* one. The young lady who was so easy to get on airplanes.

"Oh, yes. The cousin," said Ferenc. "And what do you think of her, Philippa?" He already knew pretty well from the tone of voice that Philippa entertained enormous doubts. He wanted very much to hear what Philippa would *say* about her.

"Very pretty," said the cool voice. "But much too young for *you,* François. Luncheon will be at one thirty sharp. *Au 'voir.'*" She hung up abruptly.

Ferenc looked at his watch (or rather at François's watch). Eleven fifteen. Oh, it had been a busy fifteen minutes since he had first opened his eyes. He had perhaps forty-five minutes before that mysterious Russian arrived. He wanted very badly to do some exploration. He threw down the tiny cup of coffee and rose. *"Au 'voir,* madame," he said roughly—using Duvillard's celebrated rudeness to get rid of her. Perhaps François had not treated his ancient servitor like this, but it was a good bet that he had, the uncertainty of his temper being almost the only certainty about the man. The old one instantly gathered up the tray and fled—cackling—as if she not only expected this kind of treatment but reveled in it.

The moment she was out of the room Ferenc went through the desk. There was plenty there—letters, appointment calendars, bills. All very interesting when he got around to it, but now he was looking for François Duvillard's diary. Intelligence had found he kept one but had not managed to get their hands on it. One of the things that

Ferenc had found in François Duvillard's pocket was a long, thin, decidedly odd key, and he had more than a hunch that the key was to a wall safe and that the diaries were there. He began to look for the safe—behind pictures, books, even under the carpet. If there was one thing he prided himself on, it was finding hidden objects in a room in the shortest time, using an intense concentration on the most unlikely areas. And it was in the most unlikely spot that he found it—in the baseboard behind a wall plug. The long, slim key fitted into one of the screw holes of the wall plug, which then opened a whole foot of baseboard. Behind that was the safe, which opened to the same key. Inside were the diaries.

He had only forty minutes to dip into them. It was a dumbfounding forty minutes. Intelligence hadn't begun to assess François Duvillard at his true worth. But then neither had anyone else. Except perhaps Robert Pinay. François Duvillard was truly an astounding fellow.

He was still in his dressing gown forty minutes later when Madame Blanche's knock came.

"M'sieu Vassily," she trilled.

# CHAPTER *13*

Vassily was very charming, very amusing, and altogether he gave Ferenc one of the worst half hours in his life.

"What is Pompidou really up to?" Fine brown eyes, Ferenc was thinking all the while. Very sympathetic, which Soviet eyes rarely were, but oh, so intelligent. Vassily was white-haired, urbane, and actually well dressed—almost unheard of among Russians. His discourse, in any' other circumstances, would have been fabulously entertaining.

"He has Qaddafi to lunch two days running. How can anyone endure two successive lunches with Qaddafi? The man's mad. He takes your excellent Mirage airplanes, which his people can't fly, and gives them to African countries, which not only can't fly them but don't want them. And what for? To demonstrate that he is more revolutionary than we are." The Russian permitted himself a silvery laugh. "My dear François, all Arabs are insane, but some are more insane than others, and none more insane than Qaddafi. So what kind of game is Pompidou playing with Qaddafi, eh?"

Am I supposed to know? thought Ferenc. Or is he just being amusing? He gave a Gallic shrug, marvelously noncommittal. The Russians wanted to get Qaddafi's oil money out of the French banks and into their own hands, Robert Pinay had said. But did *this* Russian want that? Or was he playing a separate game? Ferenc arranged his face into inscrutability and prayed for guidance.

"We must get Pompidou out of bed with Qaddafi," said the Russian.

Why? To get him into bed with the Russians, who could then take his money?

"Pompidou, my dear François, is giving that madman a dangerous and entirely unwarranted respectability."

Ah, there it was. To the Soviet Union, there was only one revolutionary respectability—their own.

"The Quai d'Orsay in this matter is, as usual, being fearfully clever—but not very smart," said the Russian. "Because you and I know Qaddafi is playing the Chinese game. Right now he is furious with most of the Arab world because he was cold-shouldered by Egypt. It was he who sent the Young Palestine League to the Chinese, who supplied everything they wanted to blow up airplanes and murder diplomats in Khartoum."

Oho, this was an Establishment revolutionary all right! Russia had got too respectable for its own good. These were all the sort of terrorist activities the Bolsheviks once did—but no longer did. Ferenc, a committed Israeli . . . what, fanatic?—felt a surge of kinship with Qaddafi and against this urbane Russian.

"So, my dear François, we must do something to discredit. . . ."

"Qaddafi?" ventured Ferenc.

"No, the Chinese connection."

There it was again. The Chinese connection. My God, everyone was in this—twelve different kinds of Arab, at least a dozen warring groups of Palestinians, French, Russians, and insane Libyans. Did they need the Chinese as well? Of course, that was what the Russians were terrified of. The Chinese had backed Fatah in almost all its operations against Israel, particularly the more bloody ones. The Russians were totally opposed to this kind of adventurism—external operations, as they called them—all the plane hijackings, the kidnappings, random murders. They considered all this terror irrelevant. Yet, by adopting this maiden aunt posture, they were losing glamour to the young revolutionaries, and they knew it. Suddenly Ferenc knew it all. The Russians were playing three games at once—one for the benefit of the young, one for the stuffed shirts like Pompidou, and a quite separate one for Qaddafi. O serpent, thy name is Russia!

Ferenc smiled a venomous Duvillard smile and leaped to his feet. "You'll pardon me, my dear Serge." He'd got that first name from the diary. "I must get dressed. I'm expected at Robert's for luncheon. Go right ahead. I'm listening avidly. You are being even more amusing than usual."

Indeed he was.

"Robert never has you to lunch without some purpose, usually wicked," said Vassily. But lightly, very lightly. "What is it this time?"

"I won't know until I get there."

The soft brown Russian eyes gazed at him thoughtfully at this, as if it weren't quite the right thing to say. Had he put a foot wrong? Ferenc slipped into one of François Duvillard's soft Egyptian cotton shirts. Ferenc hated the Egyptians with his whole soul, but, my God, they made marvelous cotton. Meanwhile, he listened.

"We must get Qaddafi's mind on something else. He's doing much too much traveling. In the wrong places. Now perhaps if there were trouble at home, eh?"

Ferenc's mind raced now. He knew precisely what Vassily wanted now. He was trying to fit it into what Robert Pinay wanted —not forgetting, of course, what Israeli intelligence wanted. (He *had* almost forgotten that.)

"I think I can arrange exactly the thing you're looking for," said Ferenc. "If you could manage to get me some more of those . . . rockets."

The Russian was all attention now. Sitting up very straight in François Duvillard's Louis Quinze chair. There was a long silence. Ferenc spent a long time selecting a necktie, tying it with exquisite care, conscious of the soft Russian eyes on him all the while.

"No one must be caught this time—by anyone, Arabs, Palestinians, French, or anyone at all. No one must be questioned by anyone—not even by our friends."

"No one will be caught." Ferenc's eyes gleamed with Duvillard mirth. "There will be no survivors. You may rest assured." Actually, he hadn't worked it all out in his mind. But that much he already knew—no survivors.

"Everyone will know they are Russian rockets, and we cannot afford. . . ."

"Oh, but we will take care of that, Serge. They will be Russian rockets that Qaddafi procured from Egypt—against your express wishes, mind you, and therefore Russia can in no way be blamed for the loss of all these lives—and put into Palestinian hands via the Chinese connection—thus effectively. . . ."

"Say no more," said Vassily. "I don't want to hear anymore. In fact, I know nothing. I shall be properly horrified when it comes about. The Soviet Union, you know, thoroughly disapproves of terrorism as practical politics."

Ferenc smiled a malevolent Duvillard smile. "Well, you didn't always feel that way, dear Serge."

"Neither did you French," said Vassily, smiling a silvery smile. "We have all had our revolutionary ardors, haven't we? And outgrown them. Have a splendid luncheon with your despicable cousin, François. And I'll call tomorrow to find out just what Robert had in mind. He never gives anyone luncheon without a motive, invariably a deplorable one. Good-bye."

He left smiling, erect, crisp, exuding good looks and bonhomie. A thoroughly un-Russian Russian, thought Ferenc. Or perhaps not. The Russians were getting more civilized every year. It would be their undoing someday, all that urbanity. It came from getting rich. Very bad for you. Ferenc hummed a capitalist tune and thought smugly that it would be a long time yet before Israelis faced corruption from too much of anything.

Oh, the Russians. Playing their triple games. And I, thought Ferenc. How many balls have I in the air? I've lost count.

"Nicole Bernier—François Duvillard." Philippa did the introductions, eyes on her husband's noncousin, looking for clues. She got few.

"Comment allez-vous?" said Nicole, looking extraordinarily seventeen, fresh as spring wine, her clear eyes drinking in François Duvillard like a debutante meeting her first dance partner.

"Ça va," muttered Ferenc, playing François Duvillard lightly now. He didn't want to scare her away. It took a bit of composure to reconcile this fresh young geranium with what he knew. The last time he'd seen this girl was down the barrel of a gun. It seemed wildly improbable that this freshly laundered young mademoiselle—she looked about fifteen—was an Arab terrorist of impeccable credentials.

"I didn't realize you had such a pretty cousin, Robert," said Ferenc.

"She's barely out of pinafores, François."

Nicole said nothing, eyes following the conversation by flitting from speaker to speaker.

They were five at luncheon—Hélène Labuisse, the Pinays, the girl, and Ferenc—in the formal upstairs dining room, far too grand a room for so informal a meal. Lunch was a tissue of lies from beginning to end. Philippa was fishing for information, knowing she'd get nothing but lies, nevertheless hoping that the very quality of prevarication might bring a few clues.

"Where did you go to school, Nicole?" she asked.

"Madame Fouchard's," said Nicole sweetly. "It's a convent. Near Lausanne." Lausanne teemed with convent schools, some of them so tiny as to be almost invisible.

"What did you learn, mam'selle?" inquired Ferenc with a profound show of disinterest.

"The catechism," said Nicole radiantly. She hoped they wouldn't ask her about it, although she could have managed all right if they had. For a young Muslim girl, she was well briefed on the higher idiocies of Christianity. "French literature"—God help her if they asked too many questions about that—"and needlework!"

"What a waste of time!" said Ferenc, a properly François remark.

"Which subject? The catechism? French literature? Or the needlework?" asked Philippa.

"All of them," said Ferenc. "Any cousin of Robert's ought to learn karate and banking. The catechism is a set of rules our family has never used."

"Surely French literature can't do her any harm," said Pinay with his rotund shark smile. Playing uncle, thought Ferenc.

"French literature has debauched more young French girls than Satan," said Ferenc. "And the catechism has ruined all the others."

Nicole had let the conversation play around her. She was trying to adjust herself to the idea that these jaded, negligent French were actually cousins—distant ones, of course—to the Hassimis, the most powerful Arab family of all. Nobody had prepared her for François Duvillard—although he was supposed to be part of the family. An Arab? That supercilious elegant? Hardly.

"Do you know the catechism, m'sieu?" said Nicole, trying it out.

This brought a bleat of laughter from Robert and smiles to Hélène and Philippa. "The catechism? François? What an idea!" said Robert Pinay merrily.

"I'll teach it to you, m'sieu," said Nicole. "They say it's more virulent the later it's learned. You might become a pillar of the Church."

"That would be the worst thing that could happen to the Church," said Philippa.

"Are you trying to interfere with my religious education, Philippa? Shame on you!" said Ferenc. He'd love to be taught the catechism by this little Arab terrorist.

"It's not your education I fear for. It's hers," said Philippa. To Nicole she added, "You must observe our cousin carefully—everything he says or does—then never, *never* do any of those things. François is a superb example of how *not* to conduct yourself in French society. He gets away with it only because he's so rich and highborn."

Ferenc smiled his François smile. "You are very wrong, Philippa," he said. "I get away with it *not* because I'm rich and highborn but because that is the temper of the times—mockery and disdain are, in fact, the rules of social behavior, not the exceptions. Disbelief is the absolute pinnacle of good manners in our times. The very best people don't leave cards at the Ambassador's house. They blow up the Embassy." He was being outrageous—but wasn't he supposed to be? He was observing little Nicole closely, and she gazed back, innocent as spring water. He gave her high marks.

On her side, she felt a frisson of reluctant admiration. He was not, after all, so supercilious as he looked.

"You, my dear cousin," continued Ferenc, knowing full well it would infuriate Philippa, "are out of touch with the modern realities. You are a nineteenth-century *grande dame* at heart." Nothing, he thought, would enrage this very tough modern woman more than being called nineteenth-century—except that phrase *grande dame*.

"We'll have coffee in the salon," said Philippa coldly.

CHAPTER *14*

It was the longest day of his life. Ferenc was gazing into his François Duvillard face, tying his necktie, trying to reawaken in himself a sense of peril. He was in danger, he thought—amused at the thought—of relaxing into his role to the point of forgetting what he was there for. What a quaint trap his sheer excellence at this masquerade had dropped him into! He was in danger of *enjoying* himself, which was almost the most terrible thing that could happen to a terrorist of distinction. The phrase made him wince. Terrorist of distinction. That's what he was, all right. A dedicated disciple in a holy war of extermination. He mustn't be sidetracked into enjoyment, betrayed by his own sense of humor.

He gazed into his Duvillard face. Short life indeed! It stretched interminably, devoted almost exclusively to torture, mayhem, and killing, back through an infinity of horrors to his childhood. André de Quielle. Childhood chum. He was going to dinner there at the end of this very long day, his first as François Duvillard. Why André's? He hoped from the very bottom of his soul that André was not involved in this charade. Was André a Hassimi? No, he was a distant cousin on his mother's side (he thought) in this bewildering family galaxy. André. His closest and oldest friend. If he could stand up to *that* scrutiny. . . . But why was André having François to dinner? André had no use for François Duvillard. Maybe it was a very big party and Duvillard was just another name.

It wasn't a big party. They were eight at dinner—all men. Not a social occasion at all. Quai d'Orsay types, every last one. He'd forgotten André was a Foreign Office specialist. Specialist in what? He'd been gone for years and he didn't remember. In fact, he doubted that he'd ever known.

It was an unsmiling André, different altogether from his radiant chum, who greeted him at the door. André's manners always got extraordinarily precise when he didn't like you. When he did like you, he rumpled your hair.

Ferenc was the last to arrive, and when André ushered him into the little first-floor drawing room, the other six were already there. André (praise God for small mercies!) introduced him to each and every one. So—he didn't know anyone except André. That made things much easier. Now all he had to do was figure out what he was there for. It didn't take long.

A desiccated pince-nez type, real Quai d'Orsay mummy, thought Ferenc, was droning on about money, obviously resuming a discussion that had been going on before he got there. All seven men were bending their total attention to this discourse, even André, that fun-loving Frenchman, immensely solemn.

". . . fourteen *milliards* in ten different kinds of currency— American dollars, Belgian francs, French francs, a great deal of German money," the man was saying. "We traced it through various accounts in Beirut banks. Iraqi oil money mostly—as you know, we get fifteen percent of their annual production. It arrived here—our people kept an eye on it all the way—in cash, packed in a wooden crate under heavy guard marked Oriental art, 'handle with care.' Now, we all know the only reason for such an immense quantity of currency. But why *here*? We are already selling French arms—quite legitimately open to anyone's inspection—to Iraq. To say nothing of the Saudis, the Egyptians, and the Libyans. Why fourteen *milliards* in *cash?* To buy illegitimate arms? From whom? And for what? And why here in Paris? Mostly these transactions take place at the other end of the Mediterranean."

Now seven sets of eyes, asking all these questions, turned on Ferenc. I'm supposed to know, am I? thought Ferenc. As a matter of fact, he had some very good suspicions. But how much was he supposed to tell these Foreign Office types? Whose side was François Duvillard on? His cousins, the Hassimis? Palestinian terror? The Russians? Or the French Foreign Office? Or was that remarkable man playing all against each other and laughing his Duvillard laugh? He was a very complex character, this man he'd murdered. Ferenc had found some astonishing things in the diaries.

Meanwhile, fourteen eyes were boring into him, demanding explanations he didn't intend to give.

"Where is the fourteen *milliards* in currency now?" asked Ferenc casually in his François Duvillard manner.

"In Robert Pinay's bank," said a square-cut man. Security type, thought Ferenc. "We think," added the square-cut man.

"You *think!*" said Ferenc mockingly. That let him off the hook.

"Oh, come on, François," said André. "Most Arab oil cash lands in Robert's bank. You know that. The fact is, we lost it. They pulled the old double shuffle on us. The cash has disappeared—but we suspect Robert knows where it is. The big question is, what's it for?"

"Robert doesn't tell me everything," said Ferenc, playing it cool. "He is mainly interested these days in keeping the Arab money in his banks and out of Russian hands."

"We *know* that," said another Foreign Office type impatiently, as if he were stating the obvious. "We know, too, that he is acting as payoff man for some very questionable Palestinian outfits, and we realize the pressures they are exerting and the threats they are using. We don't care how much Arab terror he is financing so long as it's not *here.* The police are very nervous about Palestinian terrorists being shot in our cafés. Now we have this shipment of money that has disappeared. What is it doing here?"

"If anyone knows, Robert Pinay knows," said André. He was looking directly at Ferenc, right into his soul, thought Ferenc. Oh, God, he wished André weren't in this. It took his eye off the ball.

"Well, I'll find out," said Ferenc coolly. Was François Duvillard working then for the Quai d'Orsay intelligence? Had the French government decided to plant him on Robert Pinay before even Israeli intelligence had? What a situation.

"Please do." This came like a pistol shot from a very young ramrod-straight type with eyes like holes. "You upset Colonel Frère very seriously, you know. He has not stopped talking about Arab terrorists ever since you dropped that bombshell at Armand's party. What on earth did you do that for?"

Oh, God, I wish I hadn't, thought Ferenc. Everyone has been on my neck about that ever since. "I was just putting him on," said Ferenc in his François Duvillard manner. "He is such a stick, that one."

"It was a very foolish thing to do," said the young man, whose name, Ferenc recalled, was Fourchet. "Frère has not stopped wondering what you meant. Now he is inspecting your background, your antecedents, everything. The last thing we want is Frère hanging around *you*. You won't be worth anything to us if he finds out."

Dinner was announced. In the nick of time, thought Ferenc. I was getting into a corner I couldn't get out of.

It was a working dinner party. Eight men discussing business. Not a joke, not a *mot*, no light banter at all. All business, and the business was terror.

"In America they've not had a skyjacking in a year," said that ramrod-straight character named Fourchet. "There have been none of the airport killings we have had in Europe. Why? Very tough security both on and off airplanes. Yet America is the number one enemy next to Israel."

Airport security, Ferenc was thinking. Is this a concern of the Foreign Office? But of course it was. Terror was a Foreign Office concern now—almost *the* Foreign Office concern of highest priority.

The pince-nez one was speaking now: "We know very well the Libyans are running terrorists through our airports using diplomatic immunity. It is our policy at the moment not to anger Qaddafi by picking them up. If we had a massacre like that at Leonardo da Vinci Airport in Rome, well, policy would change overnight. Are we to wait for that? Because, believe me, gentlemen, it *will* come—if we wait and do nothing."

Ferenc was remembering the words of Tilsit: French foreign

policy is immensely pro-Arab while French popular opinion is immensely pro-Israeli. Why? He was beginning to get a clue: money. But money was by no means the all of it. There were other high-level considerations. But what? And whose?

André turned now to the square-set man, a Foreign Office security specialist. "Would you tell the others what you have told me this afternoon? Monsieur Henri, as you know, is our liaison with both British and French intelligence. British intelligence has had a tip from the CIA that something very big is brewing. A terror coup—bigger than Munich, bigger than the Lod or da Vinci airport massacres. And it is headed our way—that is to say, Paris."

Everyone munched away, busy with his own thoughts but not so busy as to interfere with his eating. Neither terror nor badinage ever interrupted a Frenchman's enjoyment of food, thought Ferenc.

The manservant holding the platter of duck stood at that very moment at the side of the square-cut Frenchman, who helped himself generously. "I don't mean to say, gentlemen," he was saying, lifting a sliver of orange, "that the massacre"—he paused to consider whether or not to take another potato—and decided in favor—"or whatever terror is planned"—he cut up a piece of duck and inserted it into his square-cut mouth and masticated vigorously—"is going to take place in Paris." He took a piece of bread, ran it around the plate sopping up gravy, and bit into this with immense enjoyment. "We don't know actually"—a sip of wine to wash it all down—"where the outrage is to happen." Now he took a sliver of potato on his knife and transferred it carefully to his fork, then with the knife glued it down with bits of duck and gravy. "We know only that it's being planned here"—he bit into the tasty conglomerate with immense pleasure and chewed awhile—"financed here"—another sip of wine—"and, gentlemen"—here, for the first time, his eyes left the food and swept around the table, because this was important—"the weapons are being assembled here."

Marvelous performance, thought Ferenc. His mind was veritably exploding with an unasked question: How on earth do we know all that? He didn't dare ask it for fear he was supposed to know the answer. André asked it for him.

"Where did the CIA learn all this?"

The square-cut man was helping himself to another roll. "The CIA doesn't give out that kind of information. But we think we know. Our intelligence in Damascus has told us that the Young Palestine League has sent a terrorist here. Very recently. A girl."

A girl, thought Ferenc.

"The Young Palestine League is the most extremist of all the Palestinian guerrilla outfits. It still clings to the hope that the Israelis can be driven out of Palestine into the sea. . . ."

The square-cut one was now eyeing the cheese board with immense deliberation. Everything stopped while he made up his mind. Finally he took the Brie.

"The Young Palestine League wishes to throw a wrench into the Geneva peace conference before any settlement is reached short of total victory for the Palestinians." The square-cut one now chewed a huge bit of cheese and was silent.

"Why should the two things be connected?" asked André.

Good man, thought Ferenc. Just what he wanted to know.

Monsieur Henri, as usual, took his time. "We don't. But she is the only known terrorist headed here, and we *know* she was sent with a specific mission. *Eh bien . . .*" He helped himself to an orange.

This time Ferenc couldn't resist: "Where is the young lady terrorist now?"

The square-cut man had the orange on a fork now and was peeling it with a knife in one long continuous spiral—a true masterpiece of orange peeling. "We don't know. She slipped through the net at Orly. The girls are very hard to catch. They don't look like Arabs. They look like girls. Some of them are very pretty."

André was very thoughtful. Ferenc had never seen this side of André. The serious career Foreign Office specialist. But what was his specialty? Right now, he thought, everyone was deferring to him, waiting for him to make up his mind.

"Financed here," said André finally. "A lot of Arab terror operations have been financed here. That is what too many people are saying. The Germans have been giving us hell about that all along. And, lately, the Chinese."

The Chinese connection had yet to show its head—except in conversation.

"As we all know, gentlemen," said André, "it has suited our purpose—up until now—to let this go on. Because we have permitted the Hassimi banks here to finance these guerrilla operations, we've been left alone. Nobody has been massacred at Orly—yet." The voice took on tones of exquisite irony. "And, of course, also we have assured ourselves that all this lovely Arab oil money remains in our banks and does not get transferred to some other national banks. But this policy is beginning to be—as the English are so fond of saying—counterproductive. The Germans are threatening to take the matter up in the United Nations. We cannot afford that. The Chinese are being very difficult about a Franco-Chinese hydroelectric plant that we had thought was all sewed up."

Now why, Ferenc was thinking, were the Chinese acting like that about Arab terror? The Chinese were financing Arab terror themselves. The Chinese had banked and given arms to Fatah, the intelligence wing of Palestine Liberation; Chinese encouragement had been almost entirely responsible for the Palestinian commando raids on Israel. Israeli intelligence knew that. But then, of course, Fatah was a moderate organization. *Moderate* terrorists—what an idea! But anyway, to the very proper Chinese revolutionaries, Fatah were very proper ideological *nationalist* revolutionaries. The Chinese distrusted the wild-eyed Palestinians—and there were no wilder-eyed Palestinian outfits than the Young Palestine League.

Again he felt that wave of exhaustion sweep over him. Playing a role his every waking hour (with nightmares in his every sleeping hour) was draining his reserves to the very bottom. My God, the intellectual agility needed to keep straight in his mind the double-dealing Chinese and the triple-dealing Russians alone, to say nothing of the lies he had to tell *this* group as opposed to the lies he had to tell Robert Pinay....

He was conscious of André looking at him piercingly. In fact, all of them. "Are you with us, m'sieu?" said André in light, dry tones. "Your mind seems to be wandering."

"*Pardon*, m'sieu," said Ferenc. "I was simply wondering why the Chinese, of all people, were getting so high and mighty about Arab terror."

"I think you had best leave the Chinese position to the Chinese specialists in the Quai d'Orsay, François," said André, masking the command in that statement in tones of courtesy. Still, it was unmistakably an order. So André was François's boss, eh? "You have other duties at the moment," said André. "You must pay attention."

Ferenc concentrated. A very great effort. André told him in his light, musical tones what he wanted François Duvillard to do, and above all, what information he was expected to wring—by any means he saw fit—from Robert Pinay. And from the bank. The others chimed in from time to time with advice, instructions, or information. Ferenc was suddenly the very center of attention, and he got the idea that he was the very reason for this dinner. He also found out what position he occupied at the Foreign Office, and for how long. He perceived at least a fragment of what François had already accomplished for the Foreign Office.

If I were not so fatigued, he thought, I'd be outraged. It was not so much the duplicity of François Duvillard's role—although that was bad enough—but the duplicity, the sheer moral decadence of the French in this affair that horrified him. Or would have horrified him if he were not so very tired. I'll file it all away for later horror, he told himself. Meanwhile, he listened and tried to keep his wits from nodding off. It went on for hours.

It was 2:00 A.M. before Ferenc found himself back in the tonneau of the ancient Isotta, and then, in spite of himself, he did a terrible thing. He fell asleep.

He awoke the next morning in François Duvillard's bed wearing François Duvillard's pajamas. Who had put him there? Old Jacques? Had he noticed the fake wrinkles on his face and fake scars on his body? The very thought of old Jacques peering at his naked body with those hate-filled, rheumy eyes made his blood run cold.

# CHAPTER 15

Nicole Bernier looked out of place on the Rue Chanson. It's a mildewed street, charming, but decayed, far up the Seine, above the fashionable Ile St. Louis. She was in the white Courrèges suit Philippa had picked out for her, and it made her look young, which she was, and fragile, which she wasn't. Anyway, it was all wrong for this street, which was best suited to old crones in black and fierce-eyed Algerians. It was a tiny street, and she felt conspicuously wrong in it, but she was told to go here so go here she must. Actually, she would have liked to go there first thing off the plane—but she couldn't get away from the Pinays quite that easily the first day. It had been bad enough that morning of her second day in Paris. Philippa showed signs of wanting to adopt her as a sort of house pet, and Nicole rejected *that* role. Pet indeed! She could eat Philippa for breakfast—but she had to simper. If sometimes it was fun, today it made her sick. She was behind schedule.

She strode down the very center of the tiny back alley of a street, eyeing the upper stories of the mildewed houses with their forbidding, drawn shutters. Very much an Algerian hideaway. She walked fast, remembering Ali's teaching: Move fast, because if they're following, it makes a pursuer conspicuous by making him hurry. It also makes him make mistakes. This one, so far, had made no mistakes. She had wheeled, whirled into shops, ducked behind buses for a quick look—and seen nothing. So why then did she know he was there? She'd not been a fugitive all her life for nothing. She could smell pursuit.

She stopped now to look into a shop whose window could contain nothing of interest for so chic a lady as herself. It contained, in fact, Disque Bleus, those French cigarettes that were so strong they made her cough even when someone else was smoking them, villainous-looking Algerian hard candies that looked as if they had been in their glass containers for generations, and vicious French comic books featuring torture and murder. The window had been recently washed, and Nicole got a lightning reflection down the street. Ah! She caught him this time, as he vanished into a storefront. Big man in blue. Looked like a flic.

In a flash Nicole was inside the grubby shop, just as she'd been taught. Pursuers, Ali said, when driven to cover, took their eyes off their quarry for just an instant. That was the moment to get lost. There was no one in the shop but the woman, an Algerian ancient, black as coal, leaning against the dusty glass counter, reading a newspaper.

Nicole took a chance. *"Allah wayaki,"* she said.

The ancient's eyes gleamed.

Nicole dipped two gloved fingers into her purse and drew out a 100-franc note, showed it to her fellow Arab, and then crouched, still holding the 100-franc note, under the counter. With her other hand she wagged a finger knowingly. The ancient showed a wicked tooth in a smile. Then she bent again over her newspaper. Minutes passed.

After a while, the crone said, *"Il est disparu, madame."*

Cautiously, Nicole straightened. *"Quelle direction?"* she asked.

The ancient pointed down the street. Almost with the same motion, she helped herself to the 100-franc note. *Merde!* Nicole was thinking. If the flic (if it *was* a flic and not an Israeli gunman) went that way, how was she to get where she was going, eh? She took another chance.

*"Ma soeur,"* she cooed. For weren't they sisters after all? She explained her predicament in Arabic, to make it seem even more a shared predicament. The Algerian ancient smiled knowingly and told her how to get to the house from the opposite direction. It was not very far, and there were houses through which one could walk straight into alleys. Two minutes away, said the ancient, if she walked fast.

Nicole shook hands with her in the French style, smiling. *"Al-salam alaikom,"* she said, and gave her another 100-franc note.

The ancient eyes gleamed with irony: *"Tiji dayman,"* the old one said, and Nicole burst out laughing. "Come often," in Arabic! What a delicious idea!

*"Peut-être,"* said Nicole, and took to her heels on a dead run. In twenty seconds she was inside the house down the street that led to an alley, and that in turn led to the Rue Dragoman, where she was headed. She gave the Rue Dragoman a close inspection from her vantage point in the alley. Not a soul on it. A murderous-looking street, too narrow even for cars, the buildings beetling down on it from both sides. The house she sought was only three doors away. She ran to it. Get it over with, Ali had said. Once inside a house, you are tenfold safer from pursuit than in a street. Much good all that wisdom had done him.

The dark hallway smelled of neglect and poverty, that unmistakable odor that reminded Nicole—not altogether unpleasantly—of her childhood. She'd bet anything there were fleas here. She could smell flea just as she could smell pursuit. There was not a sound in the house, and she'd have been disturbed if there were. The Young Palestine League, Selim Seleucid had said, owned the house from top to bottom. The action was all on the top floor. If anything stirred on the lower floors, look out! Nothing did. Nicole made her way to the top of the verminous stairs, which grew more dilapidated at every landing. At the very top, she listened. Not a sound. She felt in her handbag and drew the key Selim Seleucid had given her—very sophisticated for so fleabitten a building. She slipped it into the lock and let herself in.

It was a bare room, wallpaper hanging in tatters from the walls. Next to the window, which was shuttered, stood a plain pine table illuminated by a lamp. At one of three chairs around the table was Hélène Labuisse, bending over a map.

*"Bonjour,"* said Hélène Labuisse. "You're very late." She looked directly at Nicole, who was standing in shadow.

"I was followed," Nicole said. "Every step of the way." She looked at Hélène Labuisse as if it were her fault.

Hélène Labuisse looked thoroughly alarmed. "You were followed *here?*"

"No, I got rid of him. But just! Why should I be followed? What kind of security is that? All the way from Robert's house."

"One of Colonel Frère's men. Police terror squad. They are following everyone who leaves Robert's house lately." She was very calm about it. "It's a nuisance. But not much more. At least not yet. The French police have been told to lay off us—for the time being, anyhow. French policy at the moment is not to tread on any Arab heels."

I am not an Arab heel, thought Nicole. I am a Palestinian toe.

"But, of course, they are very nervous. And with good reason," Hélène Labuisse laughed. "Sit down. This arrived only this morning—from Beirut."

The two huddled over the map. Hélène pointed to the center of the paper. "That is where you must stand—for hours. I don't envy you." She looked at Nicole with open curiosity. She was so young. "You've had experience with these rockets?"

"Oh, yes," Nicole said flippantly. She didn't like Hélène Labuisse. She would have wished to work with a man. If she had to work with her, she didn't have to like her. "Actually, I've never fired one. I've had dry runs. I can take one apart in the dark. When do we get it?"

Hélène Labuisse shrugged. "That's up to François Duvillard."

"Him," said Nicole bitterly.

"Yes, him," said Hélène sharply. "Oh, he has his faults, but he has been invaluable at getting things out of the Russians. And he is the last person in Paris anyone suspects of being in this business."

Nicole remembered that mocking voice—talking about the truly modern aesthete.

"And Robert Pinay?" asked Nicole.

"You must not tell Robert anything," said the other woman.

"That's what Selim said. But it's hard not to tell him *anything*. He knows I'm in the movement."

"Yes, but he doesn't expect information from you. That's not your job. Tell him nothing."

"He was very curious at breakfast."

"He's a very inquisitive man. A proper French banker."

"Proper?" Nicole laughed.

"He is very proper, no matter how devious he may seem in this business. Robert's sole concern is keeping the Arab money in his hands. You must never forget *that* is his interest. *Our* interest is very different. Now look here. . . ."

The two women bent over the map again and concentrated on the business at hand. "You are at liberty to change things if you like," said Hélène Labuisse.

"I know," said Nicole. It was her operation. Her life she was throwing away.

Quite casually she asked Hélène Labuisse, "Do you trust François Duvillard?"

"No," said Hélène, "but in this business you have to make do with what you have. He can get things out of the Russians none of the rest of us can."

"And how does he do that?"

"Genius," said Hélène Labuisse. "For recognizing Russian self-interest before they even recognize it themselves. He plays on their self-interest like a cello." Then, with unexpected bitterness, she added, "He plays on everyone's self-interest, does our François."

Nicole smiled her Arab gamine smile. "Yours?"

"Perhaps once," said Hélène Labuisse. "No longer. You'd better be careful."

What counsel to give a terrorist, thought Nicole. Being careful was not in her line.

"And Robert's self-interest? Does he play on that, too?"

"Incessantly. Torments him with the possibility of all that Libyan cash vanishing into a Chinese hole."

Nicole sighed. "I don't understand the Chinese position in this business."

"Understanding the Chinese is not your job," said Hélène Labuisse sharply.

Nicole said nothing. She bent over the map again. It was a detailed drawing in pencil of the airport at Geneva. Her position was marked with a small red cross. In parking lot 6 on the fence near the runway.

Nicole shook her head. "A very bad position," she said. "The Swiss police will be all over that parking lot. You don't know Swiss airport security."

"Do you?"

"Very well," said Nicole. "I've been through this airport four times. Security is fantastic. And for the conference it will be even more formidable. It will be very difficult to get into this parking lot at all, much less with a rocket launcher six feet long."

"Much easier to get into the parking lot than into the airport."

"I'm not against the car park. I'm just against *this* plan, and especially this position."

"Where instead?"

Nicole folded her hands carefully. "I don't think I shall tell you. Or anyone."

"You can't handle this alone!"

"I don't intend to. I just don't think it necessary to get too specific about plans three days ahead of time."

"You distrust me?"

"I distrust everyone," said Nicole calmly. "I have been shot at once in Paris. Somebody knew precisely where we all were and at what time. To the minute. I just don't want anyone knowing where I am to be—that precisely—on this operation." She laughed her gamine laugh. It went well with the Courrèges suit. "I'll be somewhere in that parking lot. It's a big area." And it was, she admitted to herself, admirable for concealment, for flight, for self-defense, for gun battles. Lovely spot, that parking lot with its row after row of cars.

Hélène Labuisse didn't at all like being talked to like this by a seventeen-year-old Arab girl. But there was nothing she could do about it. The girl was an operative, apparently a good one, and operatives had privileges not given to ordinary members of the group like herself. If it was any comfort—and she admitted it was a very great comfort—the girl was going to die. There was no way she could manage this without getting killed. Hélène Labuisse couldn't resist saying it.

"You are going to die, you know." Watching very closely to see what effect it had.

Nicole stared back unwaveringly. "My life is unimportant."

That's what they all said, these Arab girls. They seemed to mean it. Hélène Labuisse was a dedicated Marxist who had heard that statement many times before and even said it herself, though not recently. She had never meant it. Not really. I'm getting old, she thought. I'm getting old. Young fire. She'd had it. Once. Seventeen, my God!

Hélène Labuisse dropped her eyes and began folding up the map. "You are certain no one saw you come into this house?"

"Certain," said the Arab girl. "*You're* certain it's a flic, not an Israeli?"

"Certain," said Hélène Labuisse.

"Well then, he knows the area—but not the street or the house. In fact, he can't even be sure this is the area. I led him a chase all over Paris before I came here. He could assume I was still leading him a chase when I lost him."

Grudgingly Hélène Labuisse felt a flicker of admiration for the Arab girl.

"Come on," she said. "I'll show you the rest of the house. We may need it when the day comes."

# CHAPTER *16*

Ferenc took the package from Madame Blanche at the door of the bedroom. For a change, she wasn't cackling; she looked *farouche*. What the hell! "It arrived—special," she snapped. Whatever that meant. She was furious about something.

"Something is the matter, madame?" asked Ferenc pleasantly. He was in a tearing rush to get at the package but he couldn't afford domestic discord. Not after he'd been undressed and put to bed by alien hands the night before.

"Old Jacques," spat the white-haired one, "makes my life a misery."

She disappeared down the hall. Ferenc closed the door and locked it. Old Jacques making her life a misery, eh? Usually it was the other way around. The postmark on the package was Zurich, which was not where it came from. Everyone in his business, thought Ferenc, wanted a Zurich postmark. It was supposed to guarantee anonymity. Actually, he thought, it did nothing of the kind. If he had been a police inspector, he would open all packages and letters from Zurich. Zurich was the letter drop of all the world's terrorists.

Ferenc lifted out the microscope carefully. François Duvillard had enjoyed a passion for butterflies, one of his many brief enthusiasms that Ferenc planned to revive. But this was a very special microscope.

Ferenc unscrewed the top of the eyepiece and drew out the tiny miniaturization camera. He flipped open the lid, found it was loaded with its tiny roll of film, and flipped it shut again. He put it back into the microscope body and screwed the eyepiece back again, and looked through the lens.

Out of his dressing-gown he drew the communiqué he'd just typed to Tilsit.

> The overriding reason for pro-Arab tilt in French policy is cash. French cash reserves are one-third less than public estimate. Last public estimate French reserves was 39,105 million francs. Actual figure closer to 25,585 million francs. French Finance Minister cooking the books to conceal French foreign loans of 9,570 million francs and future additional loans of 7,183 million francs. If these figures were publicly known, bourse would panic and franc would go through the floor.

Ferenc had got the figures from the diaries of that enigmatic figure whose scars he wore. Where had François Duvillard got them? Certainly Robert Pinay wouldn't tell him things like that. Ferenc didn't know, but he believed them absolutely, based on what he'd got out of the meeting with the Foreign Office types the night before. Without the diaries, he'd never have put it together.

> French Finance Ministry is paying for Arab oil with borrowed Arab cash, which it hopes to keep in French bank, a swindle not permitted ordinary mortals like you and me.

Tilsit wouldn't appreciate jokes told on microdots, but what the hell!

Arabs wouldn't like it if knew they're paying for their own oil with their own cash. Over to you.

Just what mischief Tilsit could make with that information, Ferenc knew not nor cared. His job was to get the information. As blackmail material on the highest foreign policy level—if, for instance, it were slipped to the CIA—it had great uses, he had no doubt.

Ferenc slipped the communiqué on the floor piece of the microscope, adjusted the lens, and snapped the picture. He drew out the miniaturization camera and rolled out the little square of film. He punched out a dot of film, already processed. On that microdot was the entire message in an area the size of a punctuation mark. From his dressing room, he picked out a postcard he'd bought the. day before. The Eiffel Tower. On its message area Ferenc wrote in a spindly hand:

Chère Tante Louisa. Il fait mauvais temps. Mais ça va. Je t'embrasse. Marie.

At the third full stop, next to va, he stuck the microdot film. It made a full stop, a period. He addressed the postcard to Madame Louisa Fusil, Box 26, Zurich, a letter drop which, Ferenc thought wryly, was probably cheek by jowl to an Arab terrorist letter drop. They all used Zurich, the Young Palestine League, the Japanese Red Army, the Turkish People's Army, all the world's undercover guerrilla outfits, all crisscrossing the world with plots to blow each other up. Well, no, not each other. Most of them were loosely allied against the Israelis. But not all. The Palestinian terror groups were fragmented and at each other's throats. That was a blessing.

Ferenc put the camera back into the microscope and photographed his other communiqué. This one was about the operation at Geneva. Ferenc had to explain the Russian position, Robert Pinay's position, and what he thought was the Chinese position. And, of course, the severe modifications he was going to have to make to make the operation fit Israeli plans. It covered, when finished, six separate microdots, and Ferenc put them on six separate postcards.

He dressed slowly and carefully, inspecting his mask, his scars, for damage and slippage. Then he walked out of the house and swung down the street fronting the Bois. Out of the corner of his eye he saw the flic step out from behind a car and stroll after him. He sighed. His own damned fault for that crack to Colonel Frère. He had paid through the nose for his sole mistake—if it was his sole mistake. For all he knew, he might have made a half dozen others. There was that slightly alarming frigidity of Madame Blanche. He didn't like that. Old Jacques had let slip something, had he? But what?

Ferenc whistled a Paris tune and cut across the road into the Bois. His pursuer followed. Oh, well. He needed a little exercise. He walked briskly through the woods with their yellowing fall leaves, shook his head, smiling, at a whore who wanted his business in the bushes. He dropped into a riding school to watch the practice show jumping. The poor flic tried to look interested in riding, which is very hard work if you're not. After that he strolled leisurely around the park lake and approached the little Café Verdurin, which had always been his favorite of the Bois restaurants. He sat at an outside table under the towering elms and ordered a *fine*. His tail was at a table behind him. Ferenc summoned Albert, the headwaiter, and instructed him. For the next ten minutes he fell into a profound reverie—and let the tail make of that what he would—reflecting mostly on the details of the Geneva operation, which, with his modifications, would take the most hair-raising timing. Ferenc didn't like timing to be too demanding. One should have alternative arrangements because of what he called the Rule of One, which was quite simply that, no matter how meticulous the plan, *one* thing always went wrong. He pulled out a piece of paper from his notebook and drew a map outlining exactly the walk through the Bois he had just taken.

Ferenc saw the taxi he had ordered Albert to get him as it approached the winding Bois road. With long strides he was down the graveled walk and into it. He told the cabbie where to go, and they moved off—the flic standing helplessly by the road. He'd stand there a good long time. The hardest thing in the world was to get a cab in the Bois that had not been specifically ordered for you.

In the St.-Germain-des-Prés area, safe from police eyes, Ferenc mailed all his postcards. Theoretically the French post was sacred, but Ferenc knew better. If that flic had caught him dropping those postcards in a box, every letter in the box would have undergone the most minute police scrutiny—and microdots were hardly a secret anymore.

After dropping the postcards, he climbed back into the waiting taxi and had it drop him off at the Café des Truffes, on the Boulevard St.-Germain, much beloved of students. It sits up on a slight embankment so that the drinkers may gaze down at the passersby without being much disturbed by the passersby gazing back. He ordered a *fine* from the waiter, bought *Figaro* from a street urchin, and settled down for a read.

Twenty minutes later Serge Vassily sat down opposite him. Ferenc favored him with his thin François Duvillard smile and returned to his paper. "The Congressman from Hawaii," he read aloud, "says his constituents are split fifty-fifty on Nixon. Fifty percent want to impeach him, fifty percent want to hang him." He folded up the newspaper and summoned a waiter. "Monsieur wishes ice water," he commanded. "He thinks it's good for his gizzard." He'd got that eccentricity from the diaries. If it annoyed the Russian to have it ordered for him, his urbanity seemed totally unmoved on the surface. He looked around at the noisy students.

"I've never approved of this place," he said smoothly. "I don't like being reminded so blatantly of my age." Then, without a change in tone, he added, "You're being followed, you know."

"Colonel Frère's men," said Ferenc, "being overzealous."

"Still, it's a nuisance. Where is your appendage now?"

"I left him in the Bois—looking for a cab. What have you learned?"

"The answer is—No." The Russian said it smiling, as if he were making a *mot*. "No matériel. Unless one of our people is in charge."

Ferenc picked up his *fine* and looked at it and through it, as if he were a wine taster observing the color. "Impossible," he said. The thing was difficult enough without Russians underfoot. To say nothing of being in charge.

The Russian said nothing. His ice water arrived, and he sipped it like champagne.

Ferenc observed him. "Paralyzes the digestive process," he said. It was a French superstition that Ferenc didn't believe—but François Duvillard would believe. Then without a change in inflection, he threw in, "We'll have to get it from the Chinese."

The Russian took another sip of ice water. "Inferior workmanship, the Chinese."

Ferenc smiled. "Undoubtedly. But it's not Chinese. They have quite a few of yours, my dear Serge."

The Russian hated to be called "my dear Serge"—especially by François Duvillard.

Serge Vassily chuckled—a friendly chuckle. "I don't believe they'd give them to you, François, to sabotage themselves, now would they?"

"But aren't you doing the same thing? Sabotaging your own operation?" Ferenc smiled at him with the best nature in the world. "I thought we were getting Qaddafi out of bed with Pompidou, weren't we?"

Vassily showed elaborate unconcern. "Merely a suggestion. In the best interests of the French. I assure you."

"Oh, assuredly," said Ferenc mockingly. Catch the Russians ever doing anything in the interests of anyone but themselves.

"Anyway, there are other ways of deflecting Qaddafi."

"I'm sure there are," said Ferenc. "In that case, I bow out entirely and leave the field to you—and to your people."

This was a gamble but not much of a gamble. Vassily would not have come to him in the first place if there were not compelling reasons for them to need a front man. This request to have a Russian put in charge sounded to Ferenc as if someone was masterminding this thing over Vassily's shoulder—and perhaps even against his will. The mastermind, whoever he was, wanted a Russian in there to keep an eye on François Duvillard, but he didn't want a Russian to take over the operation. The Russians were getting much too conservative in their revolutionary old age for terror.

Vassily sipped his ice water. And thought it over. "Perhaps we might . . . modify our concern. If we had details of the plan so as to be sure. . . ."

"No," said Ferenc. "The fewer who know anything at all, the better the chance of pulling it off. You know that, Serge."

"Oh, I know that," said Vassily with a rueful smile. "But does *he*. . . ." He jabbed a finger straight up at his superior.

"Well, you'll just have to educate him then, won't you?" said Ferenc politely. "Otherwise we might have to scrub the thing entirely, and that would be a pity, my dear Vassily, because"—he leaned forward now and whispered it—"Pompidou is very close to a ten-year pact with Libya assuring them a hundred more Mirages and"—he smiled a poisonous Duvillard smile and just breathed the wicked words—"one nuclear submarine."

That penetrated even Vassily's composure. Its great virtue as a threat was that this terrible rumor about the submarine had rumbled around the intelligence underground and been picked up by Israeli intelligence. The Russians must have heard it, too.

Vassily sipped a sip of ice water.

"Not the missiles, of course," said Ferenc with a smile. "Only the submarine."

The Russian gave a thin smile. Even the thought of the Libyans having one nuclear submarine gave them the shudders. That was the stick. Then the carrot. "Speed is of the essence. There are very strong voices against this deal in the Foreign Office. A nice massacre . . ."

The Russian winced visibly. "Please, François. What a terrible word!"

". . . at this time would blow the negotiations sky-high."

The Russian rubbed his nose and surveyed the passing throng of students and Left Bank habitués, girls walking proudly one step behind their lovers, their hands on their shoulders, the lovers themselves striding heads up, eyes alert for fresh conquests, the bearded men with little white dogs, the bedizened and bedazzled of many nationalities and many skin colors, forever one of the most colorful throngs in the world. "It's as if the nineteen twenties had never ended, my dear François," he said, changing the subject—and surrendering all in one graceful sentence. "Outcasts all of them, but you know, François, I feel like an outcast among outcasts. They belong to each other, these outcasts, and we don't fit in, do we? You and I could never fit into that passing crowd. Now, could we?"

Ferenc sipped his champagne, savoring his victory.

The Russian leaned forward urgently. "We can't deliver the matériel to your house. Not with Colonel Frère's men crawling all over it. You have a hideaway. . . ."

But Ferenc was not about to give away that address. They'd have the Russians looking over their shoulder in a different way.

"The Bois de Boulogne is very nice in the fall, Serge. Lovely colors and lots of leaves on the ground. I have just taken a walk there, and I drew you a little map because it was such a delightful promenade I'm sure you would be enchanted to make the same promenade."

He drew out the map he'd drawn in the café and showed it to him. "You enter the Bois there, follow this path—now right here—a half mile off this path there's a ravine, deep with leaves at this time of the year. I just looked at it. Right there"—he drew an X—"is a towering chestnut whose foot is drowned in leaves. A little hole under the leaves . . ." He gave the Russian the map. "It had better be tonight. We have only a few days and much to do."

The Russian slipped the map into his pocket almost absently, his eyes playing on the crowd. "You know, François, I almost settled down here—right here in St.-Germain-des-Prés—in nineteen twenty-two. I didn't have to go back to Russia. I could have stayed here. I'd have been one of them, like that fellow there." He pointed to a grizzled, bearded fellow parading his girl as if she were a mastiff.

"Never," said Ferenc, rising to his feet. "You'd have died of boredom, Serge. You're much too complicated to be a bohemian. They are very simpleminded, these folk, and you and I haven't the gift of simplicity, have we? Pay the man, will you?" Ferenc smiled and slipped away. One of François Duvillard's little games, he had discovered from the diaries, was always to stick poor Serge with the check.

Vassily made a grimace, summoned the waiter, and pulled out his wallet. He watched Ferenc as he threaded his way through the passersby to the cab rank opposite the massive square church, one of the oldest in France. The taxi disappeared straight up the boulevard, which didn't mean a thing because that was the only way traffic ran on the Boulevard St.-Germain.

CHAPTER *17*

Ferenc climbed the verminous steps at the Rue Dragoman hideaway swiftly, pausing at each floor to listen. Nothing. He waited a long time at the first landing to be quite sure no one had followed him in. He wasn't altogether enchanted with this hideaway. The two sides of the street were a little too close together. If someone had staked out the house opposite? François Duvillard seemed sure that they hadn't. But was Ferenc?

On the top floor, he drew out a key, fitted it into the lock, and stepped inside. Nicole was alone, seated at the plain pine table, her head bent over the map of the Geneva airport. She didn't look up. *"Bonjour, m'sieu,"* she said.

Ferenc eyed her silently. Seated, with her dark, curly mop of hair bent over the map, she looked, even more than at their first meeting, as innocent as spring water. In her way she was. They were the new nuns, these young ladies of terror. Totally dedicated to their work, which was to kill—among others, him. Theirs was a purity of motive akin to the virginal ladies who became the brides of Christ. Precisely.

They were offering their bodies, their minds, their souls up to their faith. Was terror any more lunatic a way of life than a nunnery? After all, it was his . . . vocation, too. He was in the priesthood, wasn't he? But innocence was not his lay, as it was hers. Seventeen years old! She was not destined to be eighteen, this young lady. He felt a tremor of pity for this young nun of terror and shook it off savagely. He could not afford the self-indulgence of pity. Her dedication was to destroy not only him but his country. Still, the sight of that delicious envelope of flesh tore—if only momentarily—his heart. It always did. No matter how experienced he was at this game. The human personality often caught him by the throat just before he squeezed the trigger. Each victim, no matter how impersonal, had his own truth, his own gift of separateness. It was as if he were extinguishing a species. It shook him to the marrow every time. Especially when it was so young, so delicious a morsel, as this girl. An Arab, was she? She didn't look it with her golden skin tone, her dark short hair, her Courrèges suit. He felt his Frenchness bubble up in him, drowning his Israeliness.

The silence was as lead. Nicole looked up finally, her eyes questioning. "Have you come for your first catechism lesson, m'sieu?"

Ferenc found himself looking into the mocking black eyes and sharply revised his opinion. Innocence, my ass. "You look like one of those nubile medieval ladies in one of the paintings of Hieronymus Bosch. As if you had got to Hell without losing your virginity."

"Do I indeed?" She laughed merrily. She had no idea who Hieronymus Bosch was, but it was a delightful thought. A virgin? Me?

Ferenc leaned against the door, his arms folded. "You're much too beautiful for this work. People will remember that face."

She gazed back at him, still feeling a delicious merriment. "They haven't so far."

"How do you know?"

"I know. People don't remember beautiful girls. It's the ugly ones who attract attention."

"So—you are quite aware you're a beauty?"

"Quite, m'sieu."

"And have you been in so many operations you can afford to be so sure of these things?" She couldn't possibly have been in all that many at her age. On that score, he had to be her superior by several miles.

"Enough," said Nicole, smiling faintly. Actually, only one. And it had been a flop. But she had got away and back to her people alone and unscathed. After that she would never again be a beginner.

He glanced around at the damp walls of the shuttered room. This was his area all right, his turf, these peeling walls. Very restful. It was the luxury of François Duvillard's house that was foreign territory. That was masquerade area, not at all restful. This was home. He sighed and walked across the room to the plain pine table. He circled the table, keeping his eyes on her, catching her, as it were, from all angles. It was a device, pure and simple, to unsettle her a little. He had his work cut out with this young girl. He wanted to unsettle her a little, to ruffle her composure.

Then he saw the map of the Geneva airport. He circled that, too, studying it from all angles. So that's where it was to be. Up to then, he had had no idea. He had his modifications all planned without knowing exactly what he was modifying. But then one didn't need to know all that much. A massacre was a massacre. They were all pretty much alike. The geography was unimportant.

He bent over it.

Silence. They were both expert at it.

He drank in the map, absorbing it into his pores, a sort of osmosis, so it became part of his bloodstream. He always did this because —according to his inflexible Rule of One—one thing would go wrong and then a man needed to be able to flash into the mind a map, brightly lit, possessing a dozen alternatives, to get out of the mess.

He drank it in, and while he did, she drank him in, studying the line of the disdainful lips, the curve of the jaw, outwaiting him. He was going to be trouble, this one. She'd known it the moment she laid eyes on him.

Silence hung in the moldering room like a rain cloud.

"Mam'selle?" said Ferenc finally.

"M'sieu?"

Clearly she wasn't going to volunteer anything at all.

"Do you like it—this plan?"

"No."

"Well, then?"

"I've decided to change it."

"How?"

She smiled and shook her head. "There's no need for you to trouble yourself over these little details, m'sieu. They'll just give you nightmares."

122 •

Nightmares!

She'd stabbed his most vulnerable point. He stared at her, hating her. She stared back coolly, still smiling, not knowing what she'd done, but knowing she'd done something. He'd frozen on her. Well! She froze her own smile. It was still a smile but cold as winter.

"*My* operation, Monsieur Duvillard," she snapped. "It's best that as few as possible know anything at all about it. Then if the police ask you, you may say truthfully you don't know."

Nightmares! Ferenc was thinking. Why had she hit on that word? Or had she hit on it? Did she . . . ? No, she couldn't know. How could she? A lifetime of suspicion welled in him. He struggled for control because this would never do, this giving way to emotion, very unlike him. He rose now and stared out the one window at the narrow, malodorous street, at the house across the way, almost touching it, so close was it.

"Security," he muttered. "That house is so close, a person might almost see the map."

"That's why the venetian blinds, m'sieu," she said sweetly. The thought struck remotely that it was odd for him to worry about that room now. François Duvillard had been in that room many times. Why was he worrying about security so late in the day? Aloud, she said, "We have not much time. Have you the rocket?"

"I will have it tonight," said Ferenc absently. Nightmares! The panic was receding, but it left him feeling sad. And worse, ominous. As if someone had walked on his grave. And me not yet in it, he thought.

"And when will I have it?"

Ferenc rubbed his nose, playing François Duvillard again. For a moment he had forgotten to be infuriating. It was a weakness. He made up for it now by making her wait.

"That depends," he said finally. "There are complications, Mademoiselle Bernier." (What is her real name? he wondered. Samira Hamid, more likely.)

"Complications are your problems, m'sieu," she said crisply. "Solve them. My problems are operation. Yours are supply. May I have my rocket?"

Ferenc smiled his most irritating François Duvillard smile. "Not quite that easily. We need guarantees."

"My life is guarantee enough."

"No. There have been too many failures." This was a dart aimed at her most vulnerable point. The Arab terrorists had not yet pulled off an operation that went entirely to plan. Their record was fairly terrible, in fact. "We need to know something of the plan."

"Who is *we?*" spat Nicole. There were too many people in this thing, too many altogether. My God, she knew nothing of this supercilious elegant. She'd been told to distrust Robert Pinay. She hadn't been told to distrust François Duvillard, but then she hadn't been told to trust him either. She didn't trust him.

"I don't think you need to know that," said Ferenc. "*We*"—he hit it hard—"are the ones providing the rocket. We are very nervous about rockets. We are absolutely opposed to turning it over to one seventeen-year-old girl." This was a damned lie, but she would never know. "There has to be accountability, mam'selle—or no rocket."

"No rocket—no operation!" she blazed at him.

She was using the same threat on him as he'd used on Serge. But he was not so vulnerable to it as Serge. He could afford to be indifferent—and she couldn't. She had her orders, and the Palestinian guerrillas brooked no delays. It was one of the great weaknesses of extremism in politics; it was impatient by its very nature.

He folded his arms. "Well, then, we'll just have to scrub the operation," he said as unpleasantly as he knew how. "A great break for you, mam'selle—your life."

"I have not asked for my life back," she stormed.

He stared, incredulous. The awful thing was that she meant that, every word. This beautiful young girl. Everything to live for—as the expression so inaccurately went. But she wanted to fling away her life. Positively ached for it. In the cause of—what? Hatred was what. These girls lifted up eyes shining with hatred and asked to be sacrificed on the noble altar of hatred. There was nothing on his side of the fence to match this splendid hatred. He could only observe and wonder and beware such dedication. These young people were not playing games. They were, in the highest sense, serious. Thank God he had the rocket. He changed his tactics swiftly and became conciliatory.

"The rocket launcher is six feet long, Nicole," he said, using her name for the first time.

"I know *that,*" snapped Nicole. "I know how long it is, how much it weighs, how to assemble it, disassemble it, and fire it, m'sieu. Far better than *you.*" She spit out the *you,* despising him for every-

124 ·

thing—his color, his nationality, his elegance, his wealth, his education, his clothes, his life-style.

It was a mistake, Ferenc saw, to attempt to mollify her. She considered that demeaning. She had to be fought with naked argument, not gentleness.

"I have the rocket, mademoiselle," he hurled at her, using the entire word, rumbling over its syllables like a truck. "You have no choice. Either accept the weapon on my terms—or no weapon and no massacre." If that was the way she wanted it, that was the way she should have it.

It cleared the air like magic. Nicole smiled and relaxed—now that she wasn't being treated as a kitten.

"And what are your terms?" she asked very casually, coolly.

"I'm going with you to Geneva. To the airport. And to the final destination."

"You!" Nicole burst out laughing. "You would faint dead away at the first sight of blood. You'd vomit with terror at the first bullet shot at you. You would be an albatross around my neck. Have you ever *seen* bloodshed, m'sieu?"

Ferenc calculated the odds in a microsecond, decided he had to take the chance and work out the consequences later. "More than you have ever seen!" he said.

"Where?"

"Algeria," he said coldly. "I've seen men scream. I've seen them bleed. In fact, I have *made* them scream—and *made* them bleed. I was on torture details that would have made your guerrilla training seem like nursery school."

François Duvillard had never been in Algeria and certainly never been on a torture detail, but she could not know that, and he just had to take the chance she wouldn't find out—or that if she did, that he could square it, as a device for winning her confidence.

Because he *was* winning her confidence. Ferenc thought that he would never live to be admired for having served on one of France's official torture squads in Algeria—yet that was exactly what she was doing. Her lips were parted with astonishment; she gazed with admiration. It was not that she admired torture or torturers; it was simply that she had not thought François Duvillard, this supercilious elegant, capable of such a thing—and if he was, she would have to recast her whole idea about him.

She rose now and, as it were, took the offensive. It was she now who circled him, looking him over mockingly, as if he were a prize steer. She reached out and felt his biceps, which he obligingly tensed for her exploratory fingers. Her mouth formed into a little O of admiration. Muscles he had, thought Ferenc. So had François Duvillard, who did all the fashionable things like riding to hounds and tennis and some no longer fashionable things like fencing.

He remained silent under this scrutiny, letting her enjoy herself, allowing her the rope to ensnare herself in his preposterously tortuous toils. She tired of the game first and sat down again, frowning now and looking twice her years. The question when it came caught him by surprise.

"Why did you get mixed up in this business?"

Now he had to examine not his own motives, which, God knows, were tangled enough, but François Duvillard's. There was no point in even attempting to pretend to her sort of dedication. François Duvillard would scream with laughter at such an idea. But just why *had* he got mixed up in this business? Even the most careful scrutiny of the diaries had not yet given Ferenc the slightest clue. Perhaps that was as good a pose as any.

"I don't know," said Ferenc, smiling his most provoking smile. "I frequently ask myself that question. Why should I who have . . . well, most things—money, social position, a fine house, possessions—why should I risk all this in a cause which—I hope this doesn't offend your passionate sensibilities, mam'selle—bores me utterly. Why, I ask myself? And so far I have not found an answer."

"Cheap thrills?" She was angry again, as if he'd desecrated her purpose.

He moved swiftly to put out the fire. "I don't think so," he said politely. "Cheap thrills are not my line. I'm much more . . . complicated than that. You must not underestimate me, mam'selle."

"I don't," blazed Nicole. Underestimate him! My God! She was fascinated by him, repelled by him, infuriated by him, perhaps even a little scared of him.

"I have considered whether I am perhaps looking for a higher . . . shall we say, plane of endeavor for my life, and that doesn't satisfy me either. I think I am drawn to this . . . business by its Byzantine complexity. I am a very complicated person, and I am drawn to complexity as a moth to light."

She was contemptuous. "There is nothing complicated about terror. You kill—and get killed. Bang! Bang! It's finished. What attracts you to that?"

She was a simpleton about some things, Ferenc was thinking. Harshly he asked, "Do you know how many governments, how many Arab guerrilla organizations, how many French ministries—each with its own interest, most of them sordid, all of them conflicting —are involved in this enterprise? No, you don't—and I'm not going to tell you because it would just confuse you, baffle you, and anger you. But believe me, this . . . bang bang is a maze of complexity so twisted, so various, so black, so devious that it almost defies mortal comprehension."

She was silent then, remembering her horror at Selim Seleucid's explanations. She felt a baby again, helpless in the face of these monstrous adulterations of her own lofty purpose. She was a terrorist, pure in heart, wandering among wolves, forlorn.

"Even if you wanted to tell me, I wouldn't want to listen," said Nicole sadly. She stared at the ground silently. Ferenc let her work it out for herself. There was a time to keep silent in these affairs. Finally, she made a little shrug, as if making up her mind. "I don't —it's true—understand those things you spoke of. I don't wish to. But do *you* understand what you're getting into? Do you understand that the theory of terror and the cold reality of terror are very different things? You will probably not survive this, Monsieur Duvillard. Do you know that?"

He nodded. It was best not to speak at this juncture. Let her work out her own self-destruction.

She shook her head, as if banishing her momentary despair, and rose to her feet. "Okay," she said briskly. "But in the operation I am the boss. You are an amateur."

Ferenc bowed sardonically.

CHAPTER **18**

Ferenc had been avoiding old Jacques deliberately. All morning he
had been on foot or in taxis, staying away from the ancient Isotta,
which already loomed large in his plans. It couldn't continue forever.
When he returned from the Rue Dragoman hideaway, letting himself in with his key like an old hand, he ran into the antique chauffeur
in the front hall, polishing the great gilt mirror that hung over the
little Louis Seize marble-topped table. He was in his houseman's
apron, eyes on his work. Ferenc threw his gloves on the marble,
throwing a wrench into his concentration.

Reluctantly, the old eyes turned from their work to him. Old age
hated violent distraction. Ferenc wanted to unsettle the old man,
force him into betraying . . . whatever there was to betray. The old
eyes gazed into his, guileless, far too guileless.

"M'sieu?" said old Jacques.

"You put me to bed last night, Jacques." A statement, not a
question.

128 ·

"M'sieu was asleep," said the old man far too gently. Where was the old man's bottomless hatred now? "Deeply asleep. I considered it the better part of wisdom not to awaken m'sieu but to carry m'sieu to his room and put him to bed." There was not so much as a particle of mockery in the tone. There was instead a deep and thoroughly alarming courtesy. Then he did something even more alarming. He winked a very large, almost buffoon of a wink—and quietly went back to his polishing.

Ferenc didn't even bother to conceal his dismay. What was the point? He backed away to the stairs, his eyes never leaving the old one polishing the mirror. What in hell did he do now?

"Jacques!" A bark.

"M'sieu?"

"I wish to talk to you."

Ferenc shot up the stairs, the old man following slowly, impassively. Inside his bedroom, Ferenc tore off his coat and waited what seemed hours for the old man to make his appearance. Old Jacques shuffled in, the old eyes inscrutable, closing the door behind him. Ferenc took him by the throat and slammed him up against the door. It had no effect whatsoever. The ancient, rheumy eyes looked back at him unclouded, uncaring. He was too old to terrify. Too old! What then? Kill him? *Merde!* A body. Explanations. But to leave the old bastard alive in the very middle of these agonizingly complicated betrayals involved a degree of trust he felt in no one.

He stared at the old man with a ferocity almost bestial in intensity. The old man stared back totally unmoved. When he spoke up, it was with the simple finality of the aged. "I hated him, m'sieu."

"I know that."

It solved nothing.

"He humiliated me every day, every hour of my life."

"I know that, too!" Much difference it made!

"You have won my undying fealty, m'sieu."

*Fealty!* Lovely antique word! Ferenc had never heard it spoken aloud. The old man was a throwback to the Middle Ages.

"You have already alerted Madame Blanche," snarled Ferenc. "She's quivering with suspicion."

"I'm deeply sorry, m'sieu, that I was unable to conceal my joy at the demise of that terrible man. Madame Blanche does not like to see me joyful. She has no idea why. No idea at all."

Ferenc stood stock-still in the center of the room. His whole professional being was revolted at the thought of admitting this stranger, this ancient, this amateur, into his deepest secret. But what in Goddamned hell could he do about it? To kill him would just arouse questions, point fingers, when Ferenc needed his energies elsewhere. The man was too old and had too little to lose; you couldn't terrorize him.

*Fealty!* Ferenc examined the ancient word. Oh, he'd be faithful, probably. But how many blunders would the old man commit? Had he already committed? What choice have I? thought Ferenc. It's the best of a bad situation. He made up his mind.

"Return to your work, Jacques. And don't, if you love me, be so *joyful* in front of Madame Blanche. You are to say nothing at all to Madame Blanche beyond a growl—not even *bonjour.*"

"I never say *bonjour* to Madame Blanche," said Jacques with dignity, and left.

Three hours later Ferenc was bent over the Duvillard diaries, admiring, among other things, their style:

We are in the neo-Freudian age where guilt has changed imperceptibly from a symptom, a malaise, to an enjoyment, indeed a status symbol. In the most advanced—by which I mean depraved—civilizations, like New York—a quite separate civilization from the rest of the United States as Rome's was quite distinct from the rest of the empire—guilt is now *the* status symbol of status symbols. Originally, in the primitive era of guilt, one shared one's guilt with only one's psychoanalyst and kept the fact that one had such a thing a deep secret. Today guilt—possession of—has overflowed its banks. One parades one's guilt in one's books, one's conversation, one's paintings, one's life-style. The richer a man is, the guiltier he is to be richer than his neighbors; the more celebrated he is, the more guilty that his small talents are so unfairly celebrated over others just as talented or even more so; therefore the very display of guilt is inversely a way of showing off one's wealth, one's fame.

Mocking, sardonic was the tone; yet Duvillard was a true philosopher. He dug incessantly deeper into his own being, searching for clues and coming up with observations of sometimes staggering brilliance about his fellow humans, but never quite pinning down the one butterfly he most wished to inspect—himself. Did Duvillard enjoy this game, as the mocking style made it seem? Was he not instead a soul in torment—and this mockery a cover-up? Or am I making all this up, thought Ferenc, am I finding some justification for him because I—more and more—am *becoming* this son of a bitch?

He threw himself on the fourposter, that medieval monstrosity, as out-of-date as the whole life-style of François Duvillard, and tried to clarify his position. Who am I? Well, of course, I'm Ferenc. All I have to do is pull off these rubber scars, this rubber face, and I'm Ferenc again. Just as Laurence Olivier is Laurence Olivier, not Shylock at all. But is not the actor—the good actor—indeed the human he's playing for a few hours? Is it not a form of demonic possession so complete as to change a man's mind and heart and liver as well as his appearance and personality? Have not wives of actors complained that their husbands, playing drunks and wife-beaters in long-running plays, actually *become* drunks and wife-beaters?

Then: Why am I asking myself all these questions? It's not my style, questions. It's *his* style. It's because I'm trying to stop myself going crazy, that's why I'm asking questions. I am playing a role of a man playing five different roles—one to Robert Pinay, one to André de Quielle, one to the world at large, one to Serge Vassily, and—the most important one of all—one to himself. All immensely ingenious, all conflicting. Meanwhile there is me, a quite separate person altogether. I am suffering from that greatest of modern clichés—an identity crisis.

It was too much. Ferenc let out a bellow of laughter, an explosion of self-mockery so violent it threw him clean off the bed. Groping on the floor, on hands and knees, still convulsed with laughter at the insanity of his position, he caught himself unexpectedly in the full-length mirror on his open bathroom door—and confronted the maniacal appearance of François Duvillard. Not Ferenc at all. It froze the laughter from his lips in an instant.

My God, I'm acting like the bastard in private! This is what François Duvillard would do—these maniacal fits of laughter at the human race and especially at himself. Who am I playing this role to now—God? François Duvillard doesn't believe in God. It says so in the diaries.

The diaries! Ferenc had turned to them for clues, for help in playing his role, but they'd become a drug. He was eating the sacred mushroom. He was taking a trip, not seeking information. For how much information had the diaries actually provided? Some, it's true. But for every clue he'd found a half dozen riddles that led him on. Like all diaries Duvillard wasn't writing for him—Ferenc—he was writing for himself, François Duvillard searching for his own clues. François Duvillard *knew* all the things Ferenc wanted to find out—so he didn't bother to write them down. Ferenc had had to guess them by indirection, from hints in Duvillard's lucid self-questionings. Ferenc was looking for clues to the identity of François Duvillard, and so was François Duvillard looking for clues to the real meaning of François Duvillard. *Merde et diable* (one of François Duvillard's favorite oaths), what am I doing on my knees to myself in front of a mirror? I am Ferenc, an Israeli operative on a most delicate and murderous mission, and must try to cling to. . . .

Ferenc became aware that he was looking at a pair of ancient legs like sticks supporting, as his gaze shifted upward, the ancient cacophony of Madame Blanche. She was staring at him openmouthed.

"What are you doing, m'sieu?"

"I am making faces at myself in my mirror, you ancient bag of bones!" snarled Ferenc, playing François Duvillard with savage enjoyment.

In reply the old servant cackled with dry, bony laughter, a terrifying sound, her old face split into little rivulets, dry as creek beds in Arizona. Ferenc watched her with a sour François Duvillard look.

"Why are you walking in on me, bag of bones?" inquired Ferenc ferociously.

"I knocked. M'sieu did not answer."

Hell! Was he so carried away by this masquerade he didn't hear knocks? Or, as was more probable, was the old bitch lying in her bloody teeth? "What do you want?" he snarled.

"A man to see m'sieu." Not a gentleman. A man. "He says he is the gardener m'sieu has sent for. I told him we already had four gardeners."

Gardener? "What is his name?" asked Ferenc.

"Schutzanzug," said the old one contemptuously. "Hans Schutzanzug. A *boche!*"

Oh! Schutzanzug! German for "overall"—an old code word.

"Send him in, Madame Blanche. I did indeed send for him to teach old Raoul a few German tricks—and also to help out old Jacques with the Isotta. He is getting a little old, old Jacques."

Madame Blanche's mouth tightened. "Old Jacques won't like that," she snapped. Anything old Jacques didn't like usually filled Madame Blanche with joy. But not this. If m'sieu was to start bringing in young people to help out—and usurp the jobs of the old ones—where would it end?

She shuffled out, glowering.

A minute later, Jepthah walked in, expressionless as always. He was the perfect operative, thought Ferenc. Nothing deflected him or worried him or ruffled him.

"Shut the door, Schutzanzug," said Ferenc coolly.

The two men faced each other across the room with slow smiles. "How goes it?" said Jepthah.

Ferenc threw up his hands. "Oh . . . it goes not badly. If I can stay on top of it—but it is much, much more devious than we ever suspected, Jep. And you? You can't have been to Tel Aviv and back."

"Zurich is as far as I got," said Jepthah. "Tilsit sent me back to warn you there's trouble. Do you know a Colonel Frère?"

Ferenc threw back his head and laughed a Ferenc laugh. He felt light as a feather, like Ferenc again. He felt—what?—free, if only for a bloody moment. "Oh, I know Colonel Frère all right," he said gaily. He pummeled Jepthah now, roughed up his hair in the French manner, and gave him a great big bear hug.

"*Mon Dieu*, I'm glad to see you, Jepthah," he whispered. "I was beginning to drown in my own lies. Sit down and let me tell you about life in somebody else's skin!"

Jepthah stood well back from the French windows and looked out at the Bois. "There's one of them there." He pointed. "Another one behind that viaduct. There may be others I haven't spotted. You're well staked out."

Ferenc was at the mirror, touching up his scars. "How did Tilsit find out what Frère was up to?"

"We have a man inside. The French think they've turned him around. They haven't."

Ferenc felt his nerves tighten like violin strings. "I blew it in the first two minutes after I left you. I didn't know who Frère was. I made some flippant reference to Arab terrorists. He turned those blue eyes on me—and he hasn't stopped. It's my one error, at least the only one I know about."

Jepthah was, as usual, practical. It had happened. One accepted it and thought around it. "You can't keep it here. Not with Frère's men crawling around the shrubbery."

Ferenc told him about the hideaway on the Rue Dragoman.

"How do we get it there? The Isotta is the most conspicuous car in Paris."

"Precisely," said Ferenc. He sketched out his plan, using a map of the Bois and two sets of diagrams.

Jepthah smiled faintly. "You're getting a bit too complicated for me."

*"Cher ami,"* said Ferenc, "this is almost the simplest thing about this operation."

"Do we trust the girl?"

Ferenc scowled. "Only so far." He held his hands about six inches apart. *"That* far we have to trust her or we have no plan at all. Understand, Jepthah, she's totally dedicated—but to what? Not to us, certainly. Not to the Pinays. Certainly not to the French Foreign Office. Sombody back there"—he flourished a hand in the air, pointing vaguely east—"is pulling her strings."

Jepthah looked mulish. "Why don't I handle this job alone? Why do I need the girl along?"

"You'd never find the place at three A.M. It would take you an hour, and you haven't got that much time."

Jepthah still looked mulish—in his particular Sabra way. He liked things to be plain and hard-hewn as the Mt. Sinai rock face. "I don't like any of it. Too many people—all going in different directions. This Russian, this Serge Vassily. Are you sure he's not dealing from the bottom of the deck?"

"He thinks he is. To the Chinese."

"Beware Russian diplomats bearing gifts," said Jepthah bleakly.

"Oh, I do! I do!"

"I don't understand the position of your old school chum, André de Quielle, in this."

Ferenc's face went stony. "His position is that of the French Foreign Office—totally self-seeking, cynical, corrupt, and—I think in the end—self-defeating."

Jepthah was startled. Moral outbursts were not in Ferenc's line.

134 •

"The French Foreign Office knows exactly where the money siphoned out of Pinay's bank is being spent—on naked terror. They don't care, provided the terror is not *here*. They feel the best way to ensure the terror doesn't hit Paris is by a measure of control, which is just another word for complicity."

Ferenc fell silent, awed by his own logic. He had not quite spelled it out that explicitly even in his own mind. It made a difference putting it into words. Dimly he began to understand why François Duvillard had kept the diaries. Because he had no friends, no intimates to talk to about his solitary plottings, he had to work out his own thought processes in the diaries, if only to be sure what they were.

"And Pinay?"

The name restored Ferenc to cheerfulness. "Pinay is a twentieth-century banker. His sole interest is to see the money is kept in his bank, and not some other bank. One hundred million francs is a lot of francs. The very size of the account makes it respectable. Pinay would be horrified if a bank robber tried to deposit the proceeds of a bank bust in his bank. But one hundred million deposited by a government for assassination—so much nicer a word than murder—washes the whole thing clean, if you understand me."

"I *don't* understand you," said Jepthah bluntly. What was Ferenc moralizing *for*? It was dangerous, this self-questioning. Jepthah's concern was strictly operational. The thing was too complicated by a mile and a half.

"Jepthah," cried Ferenc, "*I* didn't make all these complications. I fell into them. Duvillard was already deeply involved with all these people. I have inherited all this maze. I can't simply dismiss it. I'm playing *his* role."

"You look terrified." Jepthah blurted it out because it needed saying. And because he was worried. Ferenc needed all his strength for what lay ahead.

"Exhaustion," admitted Ferenc. "I've had to be here, I've had to be there—and in the remaining time I've had to read the diaries to understand what the hell I'm supposed to be up to." He was silent a moment, wondering how much he should confide in Jepthah. Jepthah could get the operation scrubbed if he felt Ferenc wasn't up to it. Ferenc didn't want that. He decided to say no more. Anyway, how to explain the emotional exhaustion of playing five roles?

Instead he said, "I'm going to grab a little sleep now, Jepthah, and I think you should, too. It's going to be a late night. I'll get Madame Blanche to put you in one of the upstairs rooms. There's a whole servants' wing up there—just as if the French Revolution hadn't taken place at all."

Jepthah paused at the door, his face full of unasked questions. He selected only one: "You realize what has to happen to the girl? I could handle that for you."

"No," said Ferenc.

# CHAPTER 19

Ferenc took his place in the ancient tonneau, sniffing its antique leather like the connoisseur that he was. Or that François Duvillard was—and increasingly he and François were indistinguishable. Old Jacques closed the monogrammed door reverentially with his gloved hand. Spryer than usual, he settled into the driver's seat.

The old car moved off, huffing and puffing a little. Ferenc looked out from beetled brows, seeking his tail—and not finding it. Ah, well. He settled back and drew toward him the polished worktable which was a peculiarity of the Isotta's rear seat. He put a map of Paris on the worktable and drew out a pad of paper and his gold pen. On the pad he wrote: "The Avenue d'Ail entrance." He pushed the little brass-headed button that lowered the partition between front and rear seat and dropped it on the seat next to old Jacques, who took it with his gloved hand without a word.

The car had been bugged by Frère's men that very afternoon. Ferenc had thought it best to leave it bugged, if only for his private amusement. At the Avenue d'Ail entrance, the car swept left into the Bois de Boulogne and made a stately, if solitary, promenade under the towering chestnuts, the enormous headlights cutting a brilliant yellow swath through the park greenery. On his neck Ferenc could almost feel the headlights of the pursuing car, far, far behind. It was a heavenly night for a chase, the stars gleaming like epigrams in the moonless sky. Ferenc wrote on his pad: *Faster*, and dropped it on the seat next to old Jacques. He could almost smell old Jacques's disapproval. The old chauffeur hated to go faster than twenty-five miles an hour. Nevertheless he picked up the pace, pushing the antique car up to forty miles an hour, an unearthly speed for the Isotta. The pursuing car fell away for a moment. Ferenc dropped another note: *Right on Rue Isambert.* The Isotta shot off right, past the Restaurant Voisin, its windows shuttered and its terrace tables empty as a blind man's eye. Northward the old car flew in the velvety night, its headlights splintering the blackness of the forest of Boulogne with rays of purest amber, as if conjuring up the trees by elf light. The car was groaning now, its fine old woodwork creaking; everything rattled a little bit in protest—the crystal flower vases in their silver holders, the burled worktable, the folding seats. Around the gentle curves the tires squealed in a well-bred way, not at all like the uncouth screech in gangster pictures. Ferenc dropped note after note: *Sharp right! Sharp left.* They went to the very top of the park and down another road to the very bottom. They crisscrossed and recrossed the crisscross, and finally, when the time came, the old Isotta shot down a bridle path just barely wide enough for it. The headlights snapped off, and the Isotta felt its way into the greenery in first gear, pulled behind a bush, and stopped. Minutes passed before the pursuing headlights rounded the curve of the road and swept past the hiding place.

Ferenc and old Jacques took to their feet then, striding through the noisy fall leaves, steering by the stars. No lights, Ferenc had warned. They slithered and slipped down the steep embankment on the other side of the granite statue of "Eros Reclining." At the foot of the little declivity, they paused to catch their breath. Old Jacques's breath was rattling like dry leaves, as if he'd long lost all the spittle that makes men's mouths workable. His old eyes were round with pure delight. Life was beginning to have meaning. Ferenc, his hands in his greatcoat pockets, head pulled deep into his collar, observed this reflowering of the ancient ego with mixed feelings. The old man could well become a very great nuisance.

He looked at his watch. Two A.M. Right on time.

Nicole felt her way down the Pinay back stairs carefully. She had memorized every foot of the way, especially the creaking fourth, sixth, and twelfth steps. Years of feeling her way around the pitch blackness of the Palestinian refugee camp, avoiding the heads of sleeping children, had taught her how to stay upright in the dark. It was pitch-black on the stairs, and she navigated them successfully —until the last step. It groaned. A new groan. Deep inside herself Nicole spoke a silent Arab curse. That stair groan had not been there the day before. She listened. Nothing.

In her bedroom at the foot of the stairs, Philippa was bolt upright in the soft blackness. She looked at the illuminated face of her watch. One thirty A.M. What on earth! In Philippa's circumscribed world there was only one reason young ladies stole downstairs in the middle of the night. But this one! Besides, she knew no one in Paris. Did she? Perhaps someone was stealing *up* to her room?

Philippa strained her ears. She didn't dare open her door and look. There might be a man there. She heard nothing.

For very good reason. Nicole had fled on stockinged feet down the main stairs, silent as a wraith, out the side door into the garden, fragrant with fall smells; there she slipped on her loafers and sped over the grass to the side gate in the great stone wall. She opened it with her own key that dear Philippa had given her that morning and walked quietly down the little alley to the street. There Jepthah awaited her, standing beside the Peugeot. Silently she slipped into the front seat. Jepthah closed the car door and got behind the wheel. Neither said a word.

Twenty minutes later the car was in the Bois. Covertly Nicole was studying Jepthah, without turning her head so much as a millimeter from straight ahead. She knew him as Hans Schutzanzug—a member of the German People's Liberation Army. Another one! The operation was already far too large.

Jepthah drove moderately, attracting no attention at all, if there had been anyone with attention to attract. The streets were empty. So was the Bois. The car fled through a deserted world, its occupants silent. Jepthah's jaws were clenched tight. He had never been this close to an Arab terrorist without killing him. It was emotionally devastating. He wanted to kill her or beat her or—or *something*. Instead, he was her ally, her coconspirator. Jepthah began to understand the maze of emotional complexities in which Ferenc was operating.

Inside her skull, Nicole was thinking quite different thoughts. German? He didn't look German. He looked like an Arab. Or even an Israeli. He didn't look European like François Duvillard or the rest of them at the Pinay household. He looked Middle Eastern. Very confusing.

Meanwhile, in another part of the forest, a mile across the Bois, Ferenc had nudged his ancient chauffeur to his feet. The two of them tramped noisily through the fall leaves to the covert, where, underneath a mantle of leaves, the thing lay. Ferenc reached his arms deep into the covering leaves and hauled it out. It wasn't all that heavy—a cylindrical object covered with burlap. Old Jacques probed in the leaves for the other object, which in its burlap covering looked like a basketball.

Ferenc slung the long cylinder over his shoulder and started back to the car. Old Jacques followed, holding the basketball object by its handle of string. They made an unconscionable racket through the leaves, but there was no help for it. Old Jacques had to be helped up the steep embankment, and when he had got to the top, puffing and blowing, he had to have a fairly long rest. Altogether, between the time they left the car and the time they got back, a good forty minutes had elapsed. Quite enough time, Ferenc thought.

Back at the car they took a very long time attaching the six-foot thing to the high suspension that yawned beneath the Isotta.

Then the searchlight cut through the blackness, scaring old Jacques half out of his wits.

"Stay right there," said the voice. Colonel Frère's.

Ferenc, flat on his back underneath the car, assembled his rubber Duvillard features into a smile of pure malignity. The flics pulled him out from underneath the car by the heels. Dozens of them, lining every avenue of escape.

*"Merde et diable!"* said Ferenc in his most disingratiating Duvillard manner. "You are very thorough, Colonel Frère. One, two, three, four . . ." he counted the flics with his fingers. "Twelve! I am terribly flattered that you considered me worthy of such an army!"

140 ·

Colonel Frère, dapper as ever, his Légion d'Honneur even more conspicuous than usual in the glare of the searchlight, stood impassive as two of his men rescued the cylinder from underneath the car. Two plainclothesmen stepped forward and took it from his hands—as if they were handling eggshells. Ferenc sat up and brushed the leaves from his tan gabardine jacket, watching as the plainclothesmen unwrapped the object. Reverently. Slowly. The atmosphere was churchlike in its solemnity.

"It's not, after all, a mummy, Frère," said Ferenc flippantly. "You don't have to bow down to it."

They paid no attention. Very slowly, as if it might explode, they unwrapped fold after fold of burlap. Underneath the burlap was a cardboard cylinder, and this was inspected for clues as if it were the Rosetta Stone. Then it was opened at the end, and Frère himself reached in and drew out—a golf bag. Complete with clubs, their heads swathed in numbered felt caps.

"What did you expect, Frère—a machine gun?" Ferenc smiled an infuriating smile.

The plainclothes flics were drawing out the clubs one by one, smelling them, turning them over.

"Golf clubs," said Ferenc. "I am a passionate golfer, Frère. You know that. Or you should—with all that intelligence·*apparat* at your command. The very last word in golf clubs, the Guichemont, all-aluminium club face, twenty-two percent lighter and twelve percent more resilient. Let me demonstrate."

He took the number 5 iron from Frère's hand. Then he took the basketball-like object from the flic who was holding it. "Golf balls," he explained, opened it, and took one out. He dropped the golf ball on the leafy forest floor, took a mighty swing, and sent the ball disappearing into the darkness. "Thirty-three percent more distance from the rough," he said.

Colonel Frère watched him, expressionless. "What are you doing digging up golf bags at a quarter to three in the morning in the Bois de Boulogne, Monsieur Duvillard?"

Ferenc dropped another ball and took another mighty swing and sliced it almost into the face of a flic. I'd better quit this, he thought. Duvillard was a much better golfer than that. He faced Colonel Frère.

"Leading you a merry chase. It's been great fun. I've been watching your men clambering clumsily all over the bushes around my house for two days now, Colonel. I thought they needed a little exercise. You, too!"

He leaned on the golf club, a picture of insouciance, thinking at the same time how Duvillard would have enjoyed all this and (he must confess) enjoying it himself. "Tell me, Colonel Frère, what are you looking for? Arab terrorists? Well, I have found the leader of the gang for you."

Ferenc yanked old Jacques out from the flics who had been holding him and put him in the very center of the searchlight, the ancient eyes streaming with water, the thin body bent like a bow, the mouth quivering. A very cruel, very Duvillard thing to do.

"There he is—the mastermind behind Munich, behind the Rome airport massacre, behind the murder of the diplomats at Khartoum, the travelers at Lod. Planned all of them! He's a very wicked old man underneath that palsied exterior."

Colonel Frère remained very cool under this bombardment of sarcasm. "You appear to have all the massacres at the tip of your tongue, m'sieu," he said. Very coolly, he walked away underneath the arching trees. Without a word, the flics followed. Ferenc and Jacques were left alone in the darkness.

It fell a little flat, Ferenc was thinking. Very cool customer, this Frère. Ferenc had done what he set out to do—to monopolize Frère's attention for two hours. But far from deflecting Frère's suspicions, he'd sharpened them.

Far across the Bois, Nicole was carrying the rocket in her arms like a baby. Behind her Jepthah padded along through the fall leaves, the rocket launcher slung over his shoulder like a shotgun. It was heavy, and he stumbled from time to time over branches hidden in the leaves. The pair struggled up a steep slope to the Peugeot on the grass beside the leafy Bois road. Nicole put the rocket on the front seat and helped Jepthah lay the rocket launcher between the two seats; it stretched from the rear seat almost to the windshield.

The car moved off, Nicole again cradling the rocket in her arms. The only baby I'm ever likely to have, she thought, staring down at it fondly. She was thrilled to her marrow by the presence in her arms of so much destruction. Jepthah could feel the heat of her exultation and forgave her. She was only seventeen. In the starlight she looked like a little girl with her first puppy.

142 •

Out of the Bois now, Jepthah drove straight down the Champs-Elysées, deserted of cars and people, swept around the Tuileries and past the Louvre, following the Seine, shining in the starlight. Far above the Ile St. Louis, he swept into the bewildering Clochard area, and here Nicole directed him, street by tiny street, the maze getting ever more tortuous and impassable to cars. It was easier on foot, Nicole told him, but the weapon was very heavy.

As the streets degenerated into alleys, Jepthah slowed the car until finally he was crawling along in second gear. At the Rue des Lignes, only two hundred paces away from the Rue Dragoman, Nicole told Jepthah to stop the car and turn off the lights. She rolled down her window and listened. Jepthah watched her quizzically. Her head was thrust forward, every inch of her alive, like a gazelle scenting a lion, the eyes huge.

From two hundred paces away, they both heard footsteps. *Click. Click. Click. Click.* Very fast. Who would be walking fast at that hour on the Rue Dragoman? A metallic click like the heel and toe of a flic's shoes. Nicole pressed her two hands together, fingers touching her chin, looking like a nun at prayer. She held the position for twenty seconds, listening to the footsteps. They stopped—and then they heard a different sound. A door opening. Then—*ka-bump*—closing.

Nicole put her mouth next to Jepthah's ears. "Wait!" she commanded. She put the rocket down on the back seat, slipped off her loafers, opened the car door, and slipped out. Leaving the car door open, she walked on stockinged feet noiselessly to the end of the street. Jepthah watched, eyes aglitter. He reached under his arm and took out the snub-nosed .38. From his side pocket he drew out the silencer and screwed it on. The girl had disappeared into an alley. Trouble, he was thinking. How do I know? I just do. So does she.

Nicole was in the shadow of the building, shielded from the street lamplight by the curve of the house. Diagonally across the Rue Dragoman from her was the hideaway. But empty? Nicole strained her desert ears. She swept the street with a long glance. No cars. Where were those click-click heels now? Who was the author of that too-measured tread? One didn't expect a measured tread at 3:00 A.M. in that quarter. A drunk, perhaps. Or a thief. Or a prostitute. The tread was too authoritative, too Establishment, for that place and that hour.

Nicole knew very well how to wait. She waited now, eyes on the house, ears at full voltage, for minute after minute after minute. She listened to her heart ticking quietly away and admired herself for her calm. She smelled the smells of poverty, so very like the smells of the refugee camps of her childhood. She could almost hear the stillness of Paris asleep.

A match flared on the very top floor of the hideaway, lighting up for a long three seconds two windows of the very room Nicole had been in that afternoon, outlining the venetian blinds against the blackness of the night.

Who might that be? Not François Duvillard. He was in the Bois de Boulogne, acting as decoy. Not Hélène Labuisse. She was in the arms of her lover, Robert Pinay. Who then?

There should have been no footsteps. And certainly no matches lit in that house. The situation reeked of treachery.

She fled back to the car on stockinged feet, her heart pumping wildly now from the adrenaline of her alarmed intuitions. Just as she reached the Peugeot, she saw a police car—even before she heard it—cruising slowly across the Rue des Lignes, and even from that distance she saw the stiff police caps on the driver and his companion. She leaped into the car. "Police!" she said, jerking her thumb to the rear. For a few seconds they sat motionless. Behind them they heard the car stop and then the nasty whine of a car in reverse, coming back for another look.

"Start the engine," said Nicole icily. "And give me *that*." She took the silenced .38 from him, watching the police car approach in her side mirror. "Be prepared to go straight ahead. I'll direct you."

"What about the hideout?"

"Flics," said Nicole. "We've been fingered."

The police car drew abreast and in a moment would cut across their front, blocking their escape route and giving the flics cover. Nicole poked a smiling face out of her window.

"*S'il vous plaît, Monsieur l'Officier!*" she trilled.

The police car halted exactly abreast of their car, a fatal violation of police procedure. The police driver looked at the pretty girl, his eyes full of questions, his face not four feet from Nicole's. She shot him right in the mouth. As the flic's head hit the wheel, it exposed the other flic, who was trying, too late, to get out of the car door. Nicole pumped three bullets into his back.

"*Allons-y,*" she said.

144 ·

The car shot forward. *Diable*, thought Jepthah. Two dead flics!

"Right at the next turn," said Nicole. She put her head out, listening for pursuit. How many police cars were there? Too much wind rushing past her ears.

"Stop!" she commanded.

Jepthah halted the car, wondering why he was taking orders from this seventeen-year-old. Two dead flics!

Nicole was straining her Arab ears for the sounds of pursuit. There were none.

"*Allons-y*," she commanded. "*Doucement.* We don't want to attract attention."

Jepthah drove out of the Clochard area like a nun on Sunday. Her idea was risky. But then, what one wasn't? Anyway, it was her risk. She reveled in it, loving it. Lips half open. Eyes like stars. How did we get mixed up with this crazy?

They drove through the sleeping city, windows down, listening. Twenty minutes after they had left the Clochard area they heard the first high feminine *hee-haw hee-haw* of a police car, clear across Paris from them.

Jepthah parked at the side of the Pinay house, near the alley, and took the heavy rocket launcher on his shoulder. Nicole cradled her foundling in her arms, eyes aglow. At the side door they listened a very long time. The great house slumbered, entombed in its bourgeois dreams. Nicole took off her shoes and slipped them into her side pockets. Jepthah tied his by the shoelaces around his neck. They crept, silent as cats, upward.

At the foot of the stairs outside Philippa's bedroom, Nicole pointed to the fateful steps—fourth from the bottom, then the sixth, then the twelfth—the worst one. She waggled a finger. He nodded, as if he understood. But he hadn't. It's one thing to be told where to step and quite another to have trod the course, as Nicole had done. She stepped nimbly over the fateful squeaks; Jepthah missed the first and the second squeak and by sheer overconcentration hit the topmost—the worst one—square on the nose. The stair screeched. The two stopped dead.

Inside the bedroom Philippa sat up again. She had not slept since the first time, and now she looked at her illuminated watch face as if timing the lovers. If that's what they were. This time curiosity overpowered fear. She got out of bed and opened the door a crack.

She thought she heard breathing. It was too much. She stuck her head out and caught the merest *soupçon* of a glimpse of—what? It looked like a man. Carrying something. On his shoulder. Philippa closed the door and sat on the edge of her bed, curiosity raging in her like lust. What *was* the girl here for? She wasn't her husband's mistress; clearly she wasn't a banker. What on earth! Philippa was devoured by curiosity.

Speculations raced through her mind like phantoms—each one eliminating itself by its wild improbability. Why was a man—if it was a man—going *up!* At that hour? He should be coming down. Shouldn't he?

Minutes passed. She fought her curiosity like a drunk fighting the desire for the day's first drink—and she lost. She threw her dressing gown around her shoulders, too much in a hurry to put it on properly, and stormed up the stairs—hitting all the fateful steps resoundingly. *Creak. Squeak! Squeak!* At Nicole's doorstep she hesitated only an instant. Then she let herself in, expecting—she knew not what.

Darkness. Boldly she snapped on the light. Nicole's clothes were in a heap on the floor. Nicole's dark curls were on the pillow. Philippa glanced around the room, one of the smaller bedrooms in her house. Two chairs, a tiny gem of a Louis Quinze desk, a great painted nineteenth-century cupboard. Was he in that? Or on top of it? Or under the bed? Philippa crouched swiftly and looked under the bed. Nothing. When she straightened up, she found herself looking into Nicole's round, questioning eyes.

"Madame?" said Nicole. She looked at her watch then—a very clever bit of playacting. *"Mon Dieu!"* she exclaimed prettily. And again, plaintively, as if asking explanations: "Madame?" Never explain; make the other person explain. She'd learned that lesson long ago—not at terror school but from a wiser teacher—her mother.

Philippa watched all this playacting, reluctantly admiring. She didn't believe it. She didn't, on the other hand, know quite what to do about it.

"I thought I saw a man on the staircase," said Philippa dryly. "I was worried about you, Nicole." Worry about this little kitten indeed! One might more sensibly worry about the soundness of her husband's bank.

"A man!" said Nicole, opening wide her seventeen-year-old eyes as if the creatures didn't exist.

"I couldn't have imagined it," said Philippa. Her curiosity was devouring her again. She opened the painted door of the armoire. It was full of Nicole's dresses—and nothing else. Philippa stepped back, nonplussed. What was she to do now? There was only one conceivable hiding place left—the top of the armoire. It was unspeakably rude of her, searching her guest's room this way, but she was powerless in the grip of her curiosity. She stepped, ladylike, on the small dressing-table chair and peered.

Nicole was sitting up now, her arms crossed over the Christian Dior pajamas that Philippa had picked out for her, and now she committed a tactical error. She laughed. She couldn't help it. The intense disappointment in Philippa's face when her eyes found nothing on the top of the armoire set her off. It would have been far better to have played the injured innocent. "Madame, you wrong me!" That should have been the play. But Nicole had been strung out on excitement for a very long time—the long drive in the Bois, digging up the heavenly weapon from its bed of dry leaves, finally the splendidly orgasmic killings of a pair of *cochons*. It had been altogether quite an evening, and now it was turning into a Feydeau farce. Philippa looking at the top of her cupboard for lovers. Nicole's aplomb came unstuck. She laughed. A serious mistake.

Philippa observed this breach in the facade of Nicole's innocence with intense satisfaction. She didn't know what Nicole was up to, but she felt, more than ever, she was up to something. And it wasn't a lover. It was something far more complex than that. How very satisfying it was to confirm one's basest suspicions! Life would be insupportable if there were any innocence anywhere. This was Philippa's credo. It bolstered her ego in those exceedingly rare moments when she felt she had lost her way. When, for example, a lover threw her over. Or, as had happened with Ferenc, had simply disappeared just at the moment when she thought things were going well.

Philippa stepped off the gilt chair, expressionless. For a moment she watched Nicole in the throes of laughter, like a lepidopterist observing a butterfly on a pin. Then she walked to the door and flipped off the light.

*"Dormez bien,"* said Philippa as if nothing had happened, nothing at all.

Nicole laughed and laughed. In the austere profession of terrorist, there weren't many moments of pure comedy. One had to enjoy them to the fullest when they came.

Four A.M.

Ferenc poured out a finger of Scotch whisky and handed it to Jepthah, who downed it with a gulp and sighed deeply, his nerves unclenching.

"She probably mistook me for a lover."

Ferenc swayed, fighting an intense desire to fall asleep right on his feet. "Where is the rocket?"

"On the roof of Pinay's house under a blanket of leaves."

"How did you get off the roof?"

"The usual way. The drainpipe."

"Is it solid?"

"Rock solid."

"Good," said Ferenc, fighting sleep with all his might.

"The girl's trigger-crazy, Ferenc. We've got to get rid of her. She'll blow us sky-high."

"Go to bed, Jepthah," said Ferenc, eyes glittering like a madman's with lack of sleep. "We'll work it out in the morning."

In bed again, Ferenc wondered who blew the whistle on the Rue Dragoman hideaway. Then sleep overtook him.

CHAPTER *20*

In the rococo office with its preposterous crystal chandeliers and its splendid Quai d'Orsay view of the glistening Seine, André de Quielle was reading the report of the Secretary-General of the United Nations as comedy relief: "A crime crisis occupies the center of the world's problems," the Secretary-General had written. Never had there been a greater sense of insecurity in human life. Even in Britain, that most law-abiding of all nations, crime rates were shooting up to a frightening degree, whereas in New York. . . . "Crime is not responding to present legal and judicial practices, and truly radical departures from outmoded and discredited approaches should be considered." Dear Dr. Waldheim! Nothing in there about terror. Crime in the streets of New York or even London, yes. But terror was a political matter, and any suggestions about novel methods for combating it would annoy the Arab delegates, to say nothing of the African delegates, and even a few South American delegates. No, it was far better to kick a few rich and powerful Anglo-Saxon asses. Power lay in the hands of the weak and sensitive.

The telephone rang. It was Colonel Frère, who operated from a rabbit warren of an office at the very top of the subprefecture so crowded with filing cabinets he barely had room to tie his shoelaces in, an afterthought of an office, he liked to say.

"André," said Colonel Frère, "we have just had a top secret from Beirut."

Under the crystal chandeliers of the French Foreign Office, one got all the hot air from the United Nations, thought André; it was the rabbit warrens, the afterthought offices, that got the meaningful stuff.

"Selim Seleucid has been kidnapped in Damascus," Colonel Frère said in his dry, measured voice.

"Selim Seleucid?" said André. "Am I supposed to know who he is?"

"Of course you are. He is the most far left, the most extreme, and the most uncompromising Palestinian leader of all. He was behind the slaughter at Khartoum." Colonel Frère uttered a dry cackle, which was as close as he came to laughter. "Our people in Beirut heard that Seleucid has been kidnapped by the Ashfi Hashad faction—*moderate Arabs*—in an effort to cool him down, at least until the Geneva conference gets under way. Moderation by kidnapping. I thought it would amuse you."

"It does indeed, Colonel," said André. Cooling a terrorist down by kidnapping him. What a delicious idea! Especially on top of the Secretary-General's suggestion that radical departures were needed in law enforcement. Would the Secretary-General approve of kidnapping?

Aloud he said, "Does it make our task any easier?"

"Probably not. What the Ashfi Hashad crowd has done is simply to sever the communications between these terrorist groups operating in Europe and their leader. We don't think that will necessarily stop anything. It will simply confuse operations—ours as well as theirs." Colonel Frère hated confusion. He had a severely logical Gallic mind. He hated an operation that resisted logic, and God knows, terror, which was his total concern, fought logic at every step.

"Colonel," said André, "those two dead cops in the Clochard area. Were they yours?"

"Yes," said the Colonel. He had failed. Twice in one evening. The operation in the Bois. The operation at the Rue Dragoman. One or the other should have borne fruit. Both had blown up in his face. It was bitter.

"I think we'd better have lunch," said André. "I have a wild idea."

The two women smiled at each other over the breakfast table, each daring the other to make something of it. "Any letters?" asked Nicole.

"None for you, I'm afraid," said Philippa, pouring the seventeen-year-old some coffee. "Were you expecting a letter?"

"From a girl friend at my school," said Nicole sweetly.

What school was that—the School of Bitter Experience? Philippa found the very idea of Nicole having a school chum bizarre.

Nicole was playing at being submissive, eyes downcast, sipping her black coffee, which she would have liked to have filled with sugar the way they did in Damascus.

"*Merde!*" the submissive young girl with the downcast eyes was thinking. No letter! She had her mission; she had her rocket; but Selim Seleucid was to have told her which plane to aim it at and the precise hour at which to take aim. She'd been in Paris three days. Time was running out.

In his severely modern office, Robert Pinay, who had little faith in the sanctity of the ordinary mail, was dictating a memorandum for the eyes of the Prime Minister only, to be delivered by messenger.

My dear Prime Minister:

A price of thirty-five francs a barrel is realistic only over the short term. The fifteen-year deal you are discussing with Saudi Arabia should remain flexible for the advantage of both sides. If the American quest for oil shale is successful, the price of oil could well be one-fifth what it is today within ten years. These long-term arrangements must contain the utmost freedom to renegotiate—or we will be beggared by our own expediency.

He paused to reflect. Of course, if Messmer continued with this lunatic long-term purchase at short-term prices, the Arab money pouring into his bank would be quintupled. All very nice. But the franc was already floating—or rather sinking under the pressure of these crazy oil prices. It was pleasant to contemplate a balance of 100 million francs growing to 500 million francs—but not if the franc was worth only one-twentieth its present values. The life of an international banker was just one knife edge after another.

One was, of course, self-interested—but where did one's self-interest lie?

In the Russian Embassy, Serge Vassily was reading *Le Monde,* as always, entirely for its style, feeling its substance was about as relevant as *Alice in Wonderland.* The security chief, a Russian as square-jawed and fish-eyed as Gromyko, dropped the *Figaro* clipping about the two dead French policemen on his desk. Vassily read the story and handed it back.

"The French don't handle these things very skillfully, do they?" he said. The security officer said nothing. Vassily had never once got him to commit himself about anything at all—even that it was a nice day.

The silver-haired Russian telephoned his friend François Duvillard. Duvillard was not the sort of person to litter the streets of Paris with the bodies of dead policemen. Not his style at all. But he might have some ideas.

*"Il dort,"* snarled that nasty old lady, Madame Blanche.

Vassily hung up the telephone thoughtfully. Sleeping late was not Duvillard's style either. For such an exquisite decadent, he had always been a surprisingly early riser.

At the Cochon d'Or, Colonel Frère nibbled the terrine and spoke of the philosophical implications of terror. Later he and André would get down to the hard facts. But philosophy was quite accompaniment enough for the delicious terrine.

"Muhammad Heykal, who is the Egyptian Walter Lippmann, has strongly urged the Arab states to make their own atom bomb. He says the Israelis have three atom bombs and the Arabs need their own simply as a bargaining counter. Has the Quai d'Orsay any policy—or even any thoughts—about Arab possession of an atom bomb?"

André sipped his wine. "The Quai d'Orsay has a policy for everything—even that," said André cynically.

"What is it?"

André laughed. "My dear Colonel, I have no idea. We have policies about all kinds of unlikely eventualities—if the blacks take over the United States, we have a policy. If the Communists take over Britain, or—even wilder—if the capitalists take over Moscow, we have a policy. If I cluttered up my mind with all these improbabilities, I'd be out of my wits."

Colonel Frère took a little bite of his toast with its precise pat of terrine, enjoying himself: "Is improbability so improbable anymore? Look at the nature of terror—the coups that have already taken place. Now just suppose this luncheon were taking place back in nineteen fifty-eight, and I said to you in the climate of the time: 'Just suppose a group of Arab terrorists would take over the American Embassy at Khartoum and gun down five senior diplomats, three of them American.' What would you have said then?"

"Ridiculous," said André.

"Yes, but it happened," said Colonel Frère. "In the light of current improbability, the possession of hydrogen bombs by the Arab states is not only *not* improbable but approaches probability."

A very French logician, thought André. "Do you like this wine?" he asked. "Too light?"

"Not at all," said Colonel Frère. "With terrine I don't like the wine to have too much body. It quarrels with the pâté."

Ferenc awoke in the huge canopied bed at 1:30 P.M., the latest he'd slept in years. For the first time since the operation started, he felt rested, his mind quick and springy again. He was a lightning waker, one who is in full possession of his wits the moment he awakes. The thought that flashed through his mind at the very second of awakening was the same one that had crossed his mind just before sleep blotted him out: Who blew the whistle on the hideaway on the Rue Dragoman? Only Hélène Labuisse and Nicole knew about it. At least in theory. Actually, could he be sure of that? No, he could not. Still, he had to work with what he had. Would Nicole have fingered —even if she knew how to do such a thing—a hideout she planned to use that very night? It didn't seem logical, but then nothing about that young lady was very logical.

Hélène Labuisse? Hmm . . .

Ferenc rang for breakfast, reflecting sourly that he was picking up all François Duvillard's bad habits, like breakfast in bed. Even the same kind of breakfast—croissants and black coffee in place of his usual cucumber and yogurt. He reached for the diary under his pillow and was reading it when Madame Blanche shuffled in with his coffee and croissants.

"Ask Schutzanzug to step in, will you, Madame Blanche?" he said without looking up.

Madame Blanche nodded, her eyes slits of hostility, and shuffled out without a word. A bad sign? Yes, very bad.

In the diary Ferenc read:

Biology is a true science with total control over its material. Yet the study of human behavior is as scientific as theology, which is to say, it's a branch of superstition. Psychiatry is as medieval as werewolves, and its practice and conclusions as lunatic as those in the madhouses of the Middle Ages. Is anything more idiotic in the age of lunar exploration than to continue our explorations of human identity with Augustan or Platonic motivations?

At the Cochon d'Or, Colonel Frère and André de Quielle had progressed with maximum enjoyment from the terrine to the soufflé, and the conversation from the hydrogen bomb to abnormal psychology.

"We have a whole literature on the behavior pattern of the terrorist now," said the Colonel, "some of it very interesting. Compulsive travel is part of the identity pattern of all terrorists—starting with Lee Oswald, that peculiar American who assassinated John F. Kennedy for no reason anyone has ever put a finger on. Oswald was always on the move—to Moscow, to Mexico, even in the United States. We have now clearly identified a whole series of terrorist behavior patterns. A further refinement of the travel itch is what is now called compulsive border-crossing by these schizophrenics—and they are all schizophrenics. Your terrorist is a case of total alienation, and he actually *likes* to be on foreign soil. He *likes* to be in a country whose language he does *not* understand. He feels safer and less vulnerable."

Coffee arrived, and the two Frenchmen settled down to more practical matters. "All our fears and consequently our thinking have been predicated on the possibility of a terror coup in France," said André. "I think we're wrong. We know now that there is a very grave split in the ranks of the Palestinians. Therefore we must look to a coup aimed at disruption of any force seeking settlement on any current terms of the Palestinian grievance because we know that nothing remotely satisfactory to a terrorist organization could be settled by anything along conventional diplomatic lines. Therefore it is precisely at those conventional lines the terrorist would strike." André, too, was a very logical Gallic thinker.

"And where might that be?"

"The most central of all diplomatic cities—Geneva. And the most conventional of diplomatic gatherings—a peace conference."

Ferenc was in the immense floor-level bathtub of François Duvillard, luxuriating both in the hot water and in his thoughts. "There are no villains among terrorists," said Ferenc. "Did you ever think of that? What do we get out of this, Jepthah—you and I? At best, the prospect of a very quick bullet or an even quicker explosion. If we're unlucky, we can look forward to some prolonged and painful torture before we expire."

"Oh, for God's sake, Ferenc," said Jepthah impatiently, "get on with it." Ferenc was full of words lately. It wasn't like him. Wallowing in that ornate bathtub wasn't like him either. Jepthah was an action man.

Ferenc smiled a François Duvillard smile. "I was just wondering why someone would finger our hideout. It looks very much as if someone is torpedoing his own operation, doesn't it? Now why would anyone do that, Jepthah?"

"Because he's got a better offer?" suggested Jepthah, a cynic.

"No," said Ferenc sadly. "Quite the opposite. It's not self-interest we should look for, it's self-sacrifice. Someone is offering himself—or more probably herself—upon the altar in the interests of pure naked ideology—the most dangerous and wicked of all the wellsprings of human behavior."

"I think we should blow town, Ferenc."

"So do I."

"Tonight?"

Ferenc got out of the bathtub and toweled himself meticulously. Little dabs here and there—under the arms, between the fingers.

Jepthah found this attention to detail annoying. The old Ferenc used to throw a towel around his middle and let the rest dry itself. He was becoming a little old lady.

"Tonight is a little abrupt," said Ferenc. "We must get the rocket off the roof."

"Let's get it off the roof then. We must be in Geneva in three days. That crazy Isotta won't go better than forty miles an hour." Jepthah had worked out the logistics in his head. He was for getting on with it. Dalliance was danger. Ferenc was dallying over everything now, his bath, his breakfast.

"Hmm," said Ferenc. He dried his little finger with the big white towel and thought about Nicole. "We must take the girl. Can she move that quickly?"

At the Cochon d'Or, the two Frenchmen were sipping Armagnac from huge glasses and trying to pick each other's brains on the subject of François Duvillard. This was where their collaboration broke down. André couldn't tell Colonel Frère about Duvillard's penetration of the bank because, of course, that involved highly sensitive bits of French foreign policy and its obsessional concern over Arab cash and its continuing presence in French banks and in French hands. One couldn't tell a cop that because a cop didn't understand economics, did he?

Frère, on the other hand, had been gripped with a suspicion about Duvillard so dazzling he didn't dare share it with anyone, not even his own superiors. Because it was still a suspicion, not a fact. Because he was a police officer with the most rigid concepts of his duties, he would share his speculations with no one until he had a little more to go on.

This made the dialogue a little opaque.

"Of course, everyone in our world despises François because they feel he is not *sérieux*." To be *pas sérieux* in Pompidou's France, at least in the circles which Frère and André were talking about, was to be beneath contempt. It was also to be beneath notice. Therefore, why were they even talking about this butterfly who should have been far too trivial for their attention? Aha! Both noticed the discrepancy of the other's concern, and both concealed their notice in light badinage.

"I have always had an idea that just possibly we didn't take François Duvillard at his true value for one reason."

Colonel Frère fingered his great brandy snifter. "And what is that?"

"Because he has no vices while appearing to have them all."

It was brilliant, Colonel Frère admitted to himself. He had never thought of it, and now that it had been presented to him he could not understand why he had missed it.

But André was not just giving things away. He was fishing. "Duvillard doesn't pursue girls, he doesn't drink, he doesn't gamble. He is not especially interested in money. Therefore, in the absence of triviality, there must be seriousness, mustn't there, Colonel Frère?"

"Your logic is without fault," said Colonel Frère, his highest compliment.

But André wanted information, not compliments. He wanted to know why Frère's men were surrounding Duvillard's house and tailing him everywhere, a bit of information Quai d'Orsay intelligence had gleaned in the last few days.

Aloud he said, "He is a man of very great intelligence. We both agree to that?"

André nodded solemnly.

"Then what," pursued Colonel Frère, "does he use his intelligence *on?*"

Now *he* was fishing. Obviously his friend André—to say nothing of the Foreign Office—had made some inquiries into Duvillard. What had they found out? André had no intention of telling him.

"*That* is the question," said André.

## CHAPTER *21*

In her little chamber under the eaves, Madame Blanche was curled over a piece of paper, her whole body contorted with malignity. She was writing a letter to the police.

"Messieurs," it began, "You will think me insane, but I have reason to believe that a very great gentleman in this city has been done away with and that his place has been taken by another."

How could she explain how she knew this? How to explain the intuitions of age and years of servitude? How to explain the missing bits of personality in a man otherwise physically a precise reproduction? Madame Blanche bent her whole body to the task as if that would make the explanation more plausible. It didn't. The letter sounded like so many letters the police of all countries get—crazy. To make matters worse, she dared not put her name on it. It was anonymous. That gave it even less credence. Still, police everywhere make a superficial investigation of anonymous letters to see if they fit with any known facts. Anonymous letters have played a very great role in solving crimes, especially in France, where the writing of anonymous letters has reached a degree of excellence unknown anywhere else.

In quite a different part of Paris, Nicole had eluded the infuriating vigilance of Philippa just long enough to enter a post office and dispatch a four-word cable inquiring about the health of Grandma in Zurich, who was not Grandma and not in Zurich. Selim Seleucid had told her to use this method of communication only for severe emergency. It was that. She had her rocket. She must have orders—otherwise she would have to proceed in other directions.

She paid for the cable and walked quickly out of the post office and down the street. She didn't want that nosy Philippa asking her questions about whom she was sending cables to, and she wouldn't put it past her to have followed her under the pretext she was protecting her against rapists. What a laugh! Nicole hopped into the first taxi. "Les Jardins de Luxembourg," she directed.

The Gardens were peaceful and lovely, and she needed a little quiet to think. She had to be on her guard with everyone—Robert Pinay, Philippa, François Duvillard (especially him), and now this new menace, Hans Schutzanzug.

She paid the cabdriver and strolled slowly under the yellowing leaves of the ancient trees of the Gardens, past the shrieking children and their starched nannies. Childhood? She'd never had one. An urchin, scrambling for food in refuse dumps. These children played games. Urchins played survival. Nicole watched a tiny girl in a sky-blue jacket, exquisitely stitched, that must have cost a hundred francs, jumping up and down for the sheer pleasure of it, chanting, "I hate *Maman!* I hate *Maman!*" with intense pleasure. Sheer self-indulgence. Hatred among the young was enormously enjoyable. She and her fellow urchins had been taught hatred as in the bourgeois world one is taught table manners. Hating Israelis was the *correct* thing to do. At the age of four, Nicole remembered, she and her brother used to chant, in a manner not much different from that little French girl, much more bloodthirsty words. Just what they would do to an Israeli if they caught one. Cut off his balls and stuff them in his mouth! Gouge out his eyes and stuff them up the other end of him! What bliss it had been—these lovely, bloodthirsty fantasies! Nicole watched now as the little mother-hater was taken in hand by her nanny and had her nose wiped and then scampered off to watch, round-eyed, the older children rolling hoops. French children's play had not progressed an inch out of the nineteenth century.

Nicole strolled on to the leaf-covered fountain, black with soot, where the naked recumbent lovers fondled each other with such chaste Victorian rapture. Nicole stared, enjoying the innocence of it. What a self-confident century was the nineteenth—no one would dare enjoy themselves like that today. Statues like that were considered hideously immoral because they were so bourgeois. Her group's idea of a good creative afternoon would be to blow that statue up. She sat down with her back to the naked marble lovers and thought about her lack of instruction. Always the loophole in Arab plans.

She caught a glimpse of a nanny looking at her, horror-struck. My God, my God, Nicole thought, thoughts are in my face again! Try to look seventeen, she told herself. The thought made her smile. Seventeen! Me! What an age to be blowing up airplanes!

Jepthah sat in the very center of François Duvillard's bedroom, a towel under his chin, looking like someone in a barber chair. Ferenc was working on his face. "The rest of you doesn't matter," said Ferenc. "You don't have to pass the kind of inspection I do. Thank God!"

"The old one?" asked Jepthah.

"He'll be in on it—he's already guessed me, so we might as well let him in on you. Anyway, we have no choice. He hated Duvillard."

"Why?"

Ferenc put the rubberized strip of cloth on Jepthah's nose, straightening it, lengthening it, adding something of François Duvillard's superciliousness. "Old Jacques has been with the Duvillards since before François was born. Jacques adored the little boy François. Until he went away to school. After that he treated old Jacques like a bug."

"A right son of a bitch."

"That's what everyone thought."

"Don't you?"

"Well . . . it's not that simple. François hated that kind of adoration. Hated to be loved, really. Considered it a violation. He treated the old man badly, humiliated him savagely, to keep him at a distance." Why am I defending the son of a bitch? He's indefensible, thought Ferenc. Because I can't play the man and not defend him?

He stepped back and surveyed Jepthah.

"How is it?" asked Jepthah.

"You'd pass in a dim light. That's all you have to pass in."

In quite another quarter of Paris, Hélène Labuisse was having a bad time.

"What happened?"

"I don't know," said Hélène Labuisse, terrified but trying not to show it.

"That's hardly a reply."

"The girl's cleverer than we thought and more ruthless."

"You're just guessing, aren't you?"

"It's the only way it could have happened. The hideaway had been staked out very quietly in the late afternoon. She *couldn't* have known."

"Where is the rocket? We cannot allow it to remain in the hands of a professional terrorist."

"Maybe she's got it under her bed. It isn't very big."

There was an immense silence. That was food for thought indeed.

"If we could find it in Robert Pinay's *house*. . . ." The tones were dulcet. That would be even better than the original plan. If Robert Pinay, respectable banker, were found with a Soviet rocket, clearly marked, and an Arab terrorist in full occupation, the flight of funds from his bank. . . . "If you could arrange that, Mademoiselle Labuisse, we would be prepared to overlook many things."

"Are you asking me to betray Robert Pinay? Is that it?"

"Quite."

She had no choice, really. It was Robert or herself betrayed. They were quite prepared to throw her to the wolves.

At just that moment, Nicole was returning to Robert Pinay's house from the Luxembourg Gardens. Philippa met her in the entrance hall.

"François Duvillard has just phoned you." Philippa's voice was light and dry. Things were getting beyond her. "He thought you might like to go to the opera with him tonight." It was ridiculous. François Duvillard hadn't set foot in the opera for decades.

"The opera?" trilled Nicole. "How delightful."

Opera! *Merde!* What was this about?

The most conspicuous car in Paris called for her at 8:00 P.M., and she posed the question the moment she settled herself in the deep leather upholstery of its tonneau. "What are we doing?"

"Being conspicuous. You look marvelous."

Nicole was in a white Voisin, very simple, very elegant, very expensive.

"The last thing in the world we want to do is attract attention."

"Not tonight." Ferenc showed his teeth in a dazzling smile, half turning so he could look her full in the face. "Try to look absolutely infatuated with me."

Nicole laughed.

They sat in one of the forward boxes in the baroque monstrosity of an opera house, Ferenc in black tie, she in her Voisin dress. It was opéra bouffe, Ferenc admitted. "But then that's what I'm supposed to be like. A clown with a sinister turn of mind. This kind of jape is exactly what Colonel Frère expects."

Through the gold curtains, across the preposterous cherubs and naked wooden ladies twisting about on the ceiling, Ferenc caught a glimpse of Colonel Frère's flic among the standees. Poor fellow had not had a chance to buy a seat, and the thing was a sellout. *La Bohème* always was.

"They're desperately poor." Ferenc was explaining the plot. "He's an artist, she a poor seamstress. They're in love."

"It's revolting," said Nicole, smiling bravely. "Revoltingly bourgeois. She should be shooting policemen, not wasting time falling in love," said Nicole, smiling away. "And we should be out of Paris now that we have our rocket."

"We are."

"When?"

"Tonight."

She was astonished. "But the rocket!"

"That's being dealt with."

Afterward they went to the Relais de Courcheval on the Seine, a tiny place, fashionable, ridiculously expensive, and Nicole ate chateaubriand as if she had been eating it all her life. Ferenc pointed out the celebrities. "That's Ferloff, a sculptor of sorts. Glues bits of feathers on drainpipes. Very famous."

Nicole eyed the heavily rouged artist who wore sequins on a pair of jeans and a skintight blouse with red penises stitched on it in red velvet.

"Is it a boy or girl?"

"I don't think he or she knows yet."

Later he said, "Tell me about yourself."

"There's not much to tell. I went to a convent near Lausanne in Switzerland until just the other day."

"You are a liar, mam'selle."

"Yes," agreed Nicole. "And so are you. You were never in the army in Algeria, m'sieu."

"Who told you that?"

"Philippa."

"You mustn't believe anything Philippa says."

"I don't—except that."

They got along very well on this level. "Where's our flic?" asked Nicole.

"Seated right behind me. Bald with gold glasses."

"It's not the same man."

"They change them from time to time. They have a union like everyone else."

"What is a union?"

Ferenc explained about unions. Nicole was horrified. "Capitalist sheepdogs. They should be blowing up the machinery, not negotiating their own enslavement."

"Absolutely," agreed Ferenc.

He took her to Kastel's, and they watched the dancers.

"Can you do that?"

"I can do anything that moves," bragged Nicole.

She threw herself into the dancing with a sinuosity that was thoroughly non-European. "Your stomach muscles alarm me," said Ferenc.

"Terror school. We had to crawl a mile on our stomachs."

Later he said, "You must try to look infatuated."

It was 2:00 A.M. He took her home in the most conspicuous car in Paris and kissed her lingeringly in the very center of the rear window.

"Has this to do with the rocket?" asked Nicole practically.

"Yes," said Ferenc.

At the door of the great Robert Pinay town house, he told old Jacques, "Have a little sleep, Jacques. We may be a while."

They crossed the pavement. He took the key from her hand, opened the door, and went in with her. The house was asleep, as it had been planned. In the darkness of the great hall Ferenc watched, well back from the window, as the pursuing car slipped past the old Isotta and turned the corner. But only just. Ferenc could see the flic who jumped out immediately. There would be others.

"Come," said Ferenc grimly. They tiptoed upstairs. Nicole pointed silently at the wicked steps—the fourth, sixth, and twelfth. Almost vengefully Ferenc trod on all three—*squeak, squawk, KEEEK.*

Nicole walked ahead of him, understanding none of it. Inside her door Ferenc stripped off his jacket, untied his black tie. "Get undressed," he whispered. Nicole hesitated only long enough to be sure that he was *sérieux.* If it were frivolity, she would have been enraged. If this was part of the operation, she was unquestioning. Ferenc *was* serious, almost solemn. Even in bed when he drew the naked brown body to him, he appeared almost devout, as if it were a ritual. Nicole put on her round-eyed look. "I am a seventeen-year-old virgin fresh from a convent school, m'sieu," she whispered.

"You are a liar," whispered Ferenc.

She smiled and put her brown arms around his neck.

164 •

# CHAPTER 22

Even while making love to the delicious brown body, Ferenc was a man apart. His ears were straining. He'd led them there in order to flush them into the open. And if they didn't make their entrance at all, what then? He would have been guilty of a frivolous bit of sex. In fact, worse. Sex with an Arab girl. It was shameful. Like her, Ferenc was a very serious terrorist. This bit of delectable Arab flesh in his arms was a part of a deception, no more, and even while kissing the parted lips, he was thinking that this is the difference between a man and a woman. The mind is always there; even in moments of rapture, my mind is shooting out thoughts—any one of which would horrify this seventeen-year-old. For she looked lost in the stars, mindless. Oh, my God, if I could lose myself like that. He kissed the mindless lips, thinking all the time, if I could only borrow a little of that total absence. Wondering even about Jepthah, if Jepthah was on the roof, if he, Ferenc, had succeeded in borrowing their attention long enough for Jepthah to slip through the flics surrounding the house, and if he hadn't, what then, all this while enjoying the sweetness of this very young flesh. . . .

Downstairs, Philippa refused Colonel Frère. "I did exactly that last night. I found nothing. It's a very small room."

"Do it again. That whole scene last night might have been staged to deflect attention from her—and from that room." Colonel Frère, like so many others, had once been Philippa's lover, and he shared an intimacy of mind with the lady. Otherwise he would hardly have dared thrust himself into the home of so eminent a banker.

"What on earth are you looking for?"

"I can't tell you that. I can tell only that it's of enormous importance." Behind Colonel Frère's insistence lay a confluence of information and intuition he could hardly explain.

"But why *here?* I cannot imagine anything in my home being an object of police suspicion."

"Our information came from a source too eminent to ignore—or to share with you, Philippa." Even more powerful were Colonel Frère's dazzling suspicions about François Duvillard, which he had shared with no one, and had not dared act on—until he'd got this incredible tip.

"Why have you laid this monstrous burden on my poor shoulders, *mon colonel?*" purred Philippa. "Why have you not approached my husband?"

Colonel Frère looked at the beautiful Frenchwoman and made a face. Philippa knew very well why he had not gone to her husband. He was terrified of Robert Pinay. He knew how powerful these bankers were and into what high places and with what devastating effect their telephone calls reached. Therefore when Robert Pinay went to visit his mistress (and how had his informant known so intimately that Robert Pinay would visit her that night and at that hour?) Colonel Frère had called on Philippa immediately. Philippa knew this was why she had been approached rather than her husband as well as Colonel Frère did. He tried a different tack.

"Your niece," he said, "what do you know about her?"

That undid her. It was not, in the end, Colonel Frère's urging but her own curiosity about the girl that overcame Philippa.

"If you insist," she said, leading the way.

Now she stood, appalled, in a blaze of light, confronting a pair of naked lovers. The last thing she expected. The night before, yes, but not tonight, not with François Duvillard, who did not make love to young girls or, for that matter, as far as anyone could tell, to anyone else, male or female (Philippa herself had tried many times), as if the act of love itself were a desecration. Philippa did not know what she expected—plots, concealments, subterfuges—anything but the naked simplicity of what confronted her.

For naked it was. For a long moment. Then Ferenc drew a sheet over himself and the girl, not rapidly, but slowly and casually as he imagined François Duvillard would have done, if François Duvillard ever got into situations like this. That long moment gave Philippa her second shock. That body! Philippa had never seen François Duvillard naked—she doubted anyone had—but that body flatly contradicted the François Duvillard exterior.

"Philippa," drawled Ferenc in his best Duvillard way, "why don't you join us? Your skill in these matters is widely renowned."

The moment he said it, he regretted it. François Duvillard would have taunted her in that way—but *not* with *that* remark. François Duvillard would have been horrified by anything so explicitly sexual about himself. A slip, a bad one. Ferenc could see the implacable hostility in Philippa's eyes turn to something infinitely more menacing, a look of thoughtfulness.

Nicole's eyes were on the ceiling, as if she were not part of this exchange. She had been summoned from unutterable depths. She looked at Philippa now, her eyes remote as Venus itself, and then committed a feline affront of monstrous guile. She drew the sheet over her head, blotting out Philippa, extinguishing her as if she were a bug. It was a total insult, and Philippa's jaw dropped at the enormity of it. The girl was beyond anything in her experience.

"Colonel Frère!" cried Philippa.

She had not meant to do any such thing, and Colonel Frère had not meant her to do any such thing.

"Oh, do bring in the Colonel," drawled Ferenc. "We could have a rubber of bridge." Much more Duvillardish, less nakedly sexual.

Colonel Frère stood at the doorway, intensely reluctant.

"If you'd like to look under the bed, Colonel, you might find the golf ball I lost yesterday." Badinage. A remark of such frivolity that

Ferenc could not have been capable of it at all. I am summoning up demons that are beyond my powers, thought Ferenc.

Colonel Frère went right to the heart of the situation. Speech itself was an indecency in these circumstances. He went to work, looking under the bed, in the armoire, above the armoire, on the sill of the window, below and around the sill. Very swift, very professional. That left only one place. Frère stationed himself next to the bed.

"I'm sorry, m'sieu," he murmured. He took the sheet off very swiftly, exposing the lithe brown curl that was Nicole—and nothing else.

"*Je m'excuse*," he said, and marched out of the room.

That gave Philippa one more chance to look at François Duvillard in the nude. No one in Paris was a greater expert on the male body than Philippa, and this one jarred her. It was all wrong for the part.

She walked out of the room.

"That one," whispered Nicole, "has seen something that surprises her. Were you her lover?"

Ferenc shook his head. He was François Duvillard, not Ferenc —and François Duvillard had never been Philippa's lover.

Ferenc leaped out of bed friskily. He reached out the window and tweaked the rope that led to the roof and Jepthah. He waited.

Nicole rose languorously, still far away, and opened the armoire. Not the blue wool this time. Once the pinnacle of elegance to her, now she found it painfully wrong. Three days in Paris changed a girl's point of view. She picked out the black trousers and a black sweater. Very inconspicuous for roof climbing. She ran her hands regretfully over the blazingly white Leroy bell-bottomed pantsuit. She'd never get to wear it now.

The answering twitch on the string came finally. Only then did Ferenc start to slip into his underpants. His outer garments were on Jepthah, who was at that moment on the rope leading down from the roof.

Nicole was packing her handbag—that expensive Italian soft black leather one which would be almost the only thing she'd take along from her shopping spree—with the tools of her trade. The .38 automatic, a huge wad of French francs, and her passports—three of them, all in different names and different nationalities. All those lovely clothes would have to stay behind.

Jepthah swung in on the rope and without a word began stripping off his clothes—a tough tweed jacket and trousers in dark brown, a black turtleneck sweater.

As fast as Jepthah took off the clothes, Ferenc slipped them on—the black sweater, the dark brown trousers, the jacket. Jepthah, meanwhile, slipped on the dinner jacket Ferenc had discarded. The two men bent over a diagram of the roof Jepthah had drawn. Jepthah pointed to where the stuff was, outlined the escape route over the next two roofs. Ferenc wanted to embrace his partner as they'd always done when they went their separate ways. He couldn't. What would Nicole think? Instead, he patted him on the shoulder. His lips formed *"Au 'voir"* without saying it.

Nicole was first out the window and up the rope, Ferenc eyeing her anxiously. Climbing up knotted ropes was no job for amateurs. She went up it like a monkey. He swung out on the rope after her as Jepthah held it close to the building.

Very dark and quiet on the roof. Every step seemed to make a noise in the stillness. They crept on all fours along the steeply slanted slate, feeling their way with their hands.

At the front parapet Ferenc peered over cautiously. Below him stood the ancient Isotta with old Jacques slumbering in the driver's seat. Ferenc looked for flics but saw none. They were probably around the corner. There must be police eyes on the old Isotta—or the thing wouldn't work.

They waited. Ten minutes passed. Then Jepthah in his Duvillard mask, wearing the Duvillard dinner jacket, strolled out of the front door of the house. Ferenc had thought of that one. There would be no point after Frère's discovery in slipping down the back stairs. Walk right out by the front door. That's the way François Duvillard would have done it, and that's the way Jepthah did it, walking boldly down the path, letting himself out of the wrought-iron front gate. At the Isotta he shook the sleeping chauffeur awake and slipped into the back seat. The ancient car moved off with massive dignity. After a long minute a black car stole out of the side street just to the south of the Pinay town house and crept after the Isotta. After a minute or so, another black car rounded the corner and stopped in front of the house. Colonel Frère came out of the mansion and climbed into the car, which moved off after the first one.

So far, so good. But there might be other flics. The pair on the roof crept on hands and knees, feeling for leaf piles. At the very rear was a series of gabled windows originally designed by Mansart for the servants' quarters. In the embrasure between two of them lay the rocket and the launcher under a mantle of leaves. The conspirators dug them out carefully. The girl shouldered the rocket, Ferenc slung the launcher over one shoulder and the rope over the other. Burdened with the weapons and the rope, they stole erect to the next roof, fifty feet away. Ferenc inspected it for movement and listened for sound.

The conspirators climbed the little parapet between roofs and crossed it with agonizing slowness, avoiding the TV aerials and the chimney pots. Twice Nicole slipped, each time coiling her body protectively around the precious rocket. What a hole that would make in Paris, she thought.

The blackness was a curse. But also a blessing. At the end of the second roof Ferenc looped the rope around Nicole and lowered her to the garden at the rear of the sleeping house, a full street away from the Pinay house. Next he lowered the rocket and launcher to Nicole below. Last came himself, and that was the tough part because they couldn't leave ropes lying around. He slipped the rope around a pipe that let out the smells from the lavatories. One end of the rope he tied to his foot; he scrambled over the parapet and lowered himself, paying out the rope with his hands. This used twice the length of rope, and it wasn't long enough. When the last of the rope was in his hand, he simply let go and fell the last story onto the soft turf. The rope slipped around the pipe and followed him to the ground. Ferenc coiled up the rope and slung it over his shoulder. Over his other shoulder he hung the rocket launcher. Nicole took the rocket in her arms, cradling it like the baby she liked to think it was.

A small wrought-iron door led to the street. There stood the Peugeot. Ferenc put the rocket launcher casually into the back seat along with the rope, then covered them first with the blankets and then with the baskets of food Jepthah had left. Ferenc and Nicole climbed into the front, and he headed the car north to the Etoile and then onto the Boulevard de Courcelles. He kept on the Boulevard, heading west and a little north, leaving the central city at the Porte de Pantin. On the N3 he headed west across France. At dawn they crossed the Marne and entered Châlons. Nicole slept most of the way.

Meanwhile, the Isotta was going in quite a different direction, south to the Palais de Chaillot, across the Seine, and then south through the sleeping city to the Porte d'Orléans with the two police cars in slow pursuit.

# CHAPTER *23*

Madame Blanche's anonymous letter to the police had reached its first destination, a police IN basket where a grizzled police officer, too old for his rank, read it for style rather than substance. It was as nutty as most of the ones he read, but he was struck by one thing. It was written on very expensive thick blue notepaper. Its little white crest and the posh address in the 16th Arrondissement caused the aging police officer to purse his lips in a peculiarly French way. He rose from his desk and took the missive to his commanding officer, who was very ambitious and five years his junior. This policeman, Moulin, was a snob. He was attracted instantly by the notepaper, even more by the name. François Duvillard! *Mon Dieu!* "Monsieur Duvillard is harboring a nut. He should be warned."

Madame Blanche opened the door herself. The sight of a police officer sent her into transports of delight. She responded, as was her wont, with a cackle of glee. This confirmed the officer's deepest suspicions. Clearly a nut.

172 ·

"Where is Monsieur Duvillard?" asked the police officer.

"He is gone!" giggled Madame Blanche, from the wondrous excitement of it all. "They are all gone—m'sieu, old Jacques, and Schutzanzug. All have disappeared. Hee hee."

Moulin was convinced he had on his hands not only a madwoman but probably also a triple murderess.

It was the dog that had not barked in the Sherlock Holmes story. Hélène Labuisse searched the newspapers and found nothing—the most alarming news of all. For if the police had searched Robert Pinay's house and found a Russian rocket, that bombshell would be spread over every front page. Unless the police were keeping it quiet for their own reasons, which was infinitely menacing.

Hélène Labuisse was not immobilized by terror, as so many are. Fear had an aphrodisiac effect on her. She had enjoyed the attentions of her lover, Robert Pinay, enormously the night before, precisely because she had betrayed him and because it might very well be the end of the affair. What she felt now, though, was not fear; it was stark terror—and it galvanized her. She was a veteran of a score of betrayals, and in the movement the difference between betrayer and betrayed was largely a matter of speed of foot. Above all, she had to get out of this flat instantly. She tossed a coat around her shoulders and let herself out the front door, padded down the back steps, and left by the rear door. They might be watching the front.

Once on the street, she almost ran, coat flying, to the nearest underground, the most anonymous transport in Paris. She was headed for the vast rabbit warren of police offices on the Ile de la Cité, the last place in the world they'd look for her.

Colonel Frère had been struck by a thought at around Fontainebleau. It was already broad daylight, and the sun glittered on the ancient Isotta's polished brightwork. In the rear of the car the figure the Colonel pursued sat erect, altogether too visible. Something was very wrong.

Colonel Frère took up the microphone of his police radio. "Bossert," he commanded, "I'm turning back. I rely on you."

"Shall we take him into custody?" inquired the officer in the other car.

"No," rasped Colonel Frère. "Report back when he comes to roost."

In the Pinay household Philippa sipped her coffee with a bitter smile. The time had come for a little talk with her husband. The visit from the police—even though it had only been Colonel Frère, whose importance she underestimated as women so often do underestimate husbands and lovers—had been a shock. She'd shoved it aside because there was so much else to think about. Her seventeen-year-old niece (if she was a niece, which Philippa greatly doubted) found in bed with a man. And such a man—François Duvillard, who had never been known to engage in such activities. Philippa was an intensely loyal wife, although not a faithful one. Robert should be told. She reached for the phone and started to dial the number. Her maid came in to pick up the breakfast tray. "Is Mademoiselle Nicole awake yet?" inquired Philippa, still dialing.

"Mademoiselle Nicole is not here," said the girl.

Philippa stopped dialing. "*What?*"

"Mademoiselle Nicole is not in the house, madame. No one has seen her this morning. She has disappeared."

At Châlons, Ferenc left the sleeping Nicole in the car, watching her carefully through the glass of the *boîte* as he telephoned Tilsit in Tel Aviv. It was 5:00 A.M. in Tel Aviv, and Tilsit was sour.

"It's a farmhouse in the wood behind St.-Germain-du-Bois on the Saône," said Tilsit grumpily.

"Is it safe?" asked Ferenc.

"Nothing's safe," growled Tilsit. He didn't like this flight. "Your mission was to change French policy. What are you doing in Châlons?"

"We had to get the rocket out of Paris," said Ferenc. "Somebody's blown. Do you know who?"

"No."

"Check out a woman named Hélène Labuisse through the Embassy. She's Pinay's girl, and she's poison all around. The best way to change French policy is to blow Pinay sky-high. If the French knew what their own bankers are up to . . ."

Tilsit's voice was weary: "We can't blow Pinay up—yet. He's financing the purchase of the patrol boats"

Jesus, thought Ferenc savagely. The Israeli government in bed with Pinay, too. Out the window he saw the head of the sleeping Nicole. And I'm in bed with an Arab girl. Confusion on confusion. He was weary to his toes, asleep on his feet. Some of it must have got into his voice. Tilsit said: "Are you all right?"

"Just," said Ferenc. "Can you communicate with this farmhouse when you know when and where?"

"I'll get to you," said Tilsit. "Don't get too fond of the girl."

"I'm not fond of anyone, including you," growled Ferenc, and hung up. He walked back to the car. Through the car window he studied the sleeping girl. Black eyelashes on that golden skin. She looked about twelve. She slept as if there were no tomorrow. Do I trust her to drive? thought Ferenc. No, I don't. Wearily, he clambered back into the car and studied the map. St.-Germain-du-Bois. He made a rough calculation in his head. Twelve kilometers. Could he risk a nap right there? No, he couldn't. The rocket and launcher in the back seat under the blankets and the food would be hard to explain if they were stopped at a roadblock.

He drove through Châlons, where nothing stirred. In the country the sunlight glinted on the Marne. The air was fresh and hopeful, as morning air always is. To keep awake, Ferenc used an old trick he'd learned in the French Army—flicking his eyes from right to left, taking in the countryside in a wide sweep, trying to pick out the details and flashing them to his brain for identification and comment. There's a white farmhouse on a green hill. Sheep farm. How many sheep? Three. No, four. He counted the trees on hillsides, told himself the colors of the autumn leaves, named the kinds of trees—oak, beech, birch—tried to give precise dates to the châteaus, always holding his mind to the identifiable present, the right-now of the landscape, keeping it from slipping—as it wanted so desperately to do—into the dark recesses of myth and fantasy, constantly opening his eyes, clenching the lids open.

He wanted—oh, how he wanted—to stop for a cup of coffee. The villages were awakening now, and the cafés were spreading their colored umbrellas on the sidewalk tables. But he dared not stop with that deadly basketball in the rear seat. Twelve kilometers. The end of the earth. The girl slumbered on.

It was a tawny, secretive village, St.-Germain-du-Bois, a French village like any other. Ferenc drove through it, the weariness vanishing now that he was so near. He wound through the turnip farms and plunged into the wood. The farmhouse was in a patch of trees with the river running through its lower meadow. Ferenc pulled the car directly into the empty barn, out of sight. The key was under the horses' water trough outside the barn, where Tilsit said it would be.

Ferenc let himself into the stone farmhouse. A bare pine table in the kitchen. Homemade, like the two chairs next to it. A coal stove full of old ashes. The tiny bedroom adjoined it, a brass bed occupying most of it. The whole farmhouse was scarcely the size of François Duvillard's bedroom. In the lone bureau dresser were a couple of sheets, rough, heavy, intended for long wear, much of which they had already had. In the kitchen Ferenc opened the lone cupboard. Coffee, sugar, tea, a few plates.

Nicole entered the kitchen, pressing her elbows into her stomach, her eyes huge and sleepy. Silently she inspected the kitchen, then the bedroom. She opened the dresser drawer, found the sheets, and started to make the bed.

Ferenc went back to the barn and took out the rocket and the launcher. He laid them on the hay pile in the loft of the barn and covered them carefully. He'd like to have locked the barn door, but there was no lock. Israeli counterterror couldn't afford a lock for the barn door, he decided whimsically. His mind was getting thick and heavy again. Full of nonsense. He strode stiff-legged back to the tiny stone dwelling and carefully locked the door from the inside. In the little bedroom Nicole's clothes were already on the floor and the black head was on the pillow. The eyes were closed, but they opened when Ferenc came in and watched mournfully, tenderly, while he undressed.

What's real? thought Ferenc. He climbed naked into the bed, kissed the unsmiling girl on the lips, and fell asleep. Nicole lay on her back, looking at the ceiling, thinking: I want to live. Heresy to a terrorist.

# CHAPTER 24

Colonel Frère's voice was frosty. He'd had a tiring night. "I must ask you the source of your information, André."

André de Quielle looked out the gorgeous Quai d'Orsay windows to the swirling Seine, muscles standing forth clearly on his jaws. "Did you search the house, Colonel?" he asked tight-voiced.

"We gave it a number two search," said Frère. "We could hardly subject your cousin's house to a number one." A number one meant tearing the furniture apart. Hardly the thing to do to all that priceless Louis Quinze furniture. "A rocket and rocket launcher are not exactly rolls of microfilm, André. You can't hide them in bedposts. I must have the source of your information. If there is a Russian rocket and rocket launcher capable of shooting down airplanes in the wrong hands anywhere in the Paris area, it is a police matter."

"You don't know what you're asking, Colonel." It meant tearing up the whole Foreign Office intelligence community he'd spent three years building. "There are very delicate foreign relationships involved here. We can't have the police stamping around in areas involving our allies in matters bearing on foreign policy of the most sensitive sort." (Some of which André totally disapproved of.)

"My branch," said Colonel Frère, "was set up by order of the Prime Minister." The French government, like all governments, was scared to death of terror organizations and had set up special police branches to combat it in such haste they conflicted jurisdictionally with the long-established and more traditional authorities. This was one of those conflicts of authority. Normally, no one could override the Foreign Office in matters sanctified by foreign policy, which, after all, was wrapped in the authority of the President himself. Colonel Frère's temporary office overrode these limits, which showed how terrified of the guerrillas the French government was.

Under normal circumstances, with that inherent arrogance career foreign officers feel toward all lesser mortals, André would have stood his ground. But he was badly shaken. "You found *nothing?*" said André.

Colonel Frère played his trump card. "We found your cousin, François, in bed with a girl."

André exploded with incredulity. "You found François! In bed! With a girl!" Each mouthful an expletive of disbelief. "Colonel Frère, I'll be in your office in ten minutes."

Colonel Frère hung up his own telephone and sat back, feeling slightly mollified. Only slightly. He didn't like wild-goose chases.

The Sergeant stood before him then. "A Mademoiselle Labuisse to see you, Colonel," said the Sergeant.

The Colonel let her in himself and put her in a chair, apologizing for the smallness of his office. "A very great pleasure, Hélène," he was saying, "but . . ." He spread his hands wide to express his mystification at her visit.

"I wish police protection, *monsieur le Colonel,*" she said.

Nicole was the first to wake up. She had, after all, had that long sleep in the car. She opened her black eyes on the stone walls of the farm cottage, deliciously languorous. Next to her she felt the warmth of the other. Colleague? Colleague and lover. That was the way it should be. Love and flight. They went together. All her short life, flight had been associated with pleasure. Starting with flight from the refugee camp, her life had been a series of flights; always life had been better. I am a true revolutionary, she was thinking. Flight is my element, like the birds. It's my greatest happiness, fleeing.

She rose now, shivering in the autumn cold, and dressed quickly to get warm. Her black shoes with silver buckles were under the bed, and she sat on the edge of the bed to slip them on, looking the while at François Duvillard. She couldn't see much. He lay on his stomach, face buried in the pillow. She would have liked to have run her fingers over his face, but there wasn't enough face to caress.

Nicole slipped into the little low-ceilinged kitchen, closing the door after her; she lit a fire in the stove with straw and wood chips she found in a wicker basket. Outside the door were chunks of log, and she piled on a few and watched the flames shoot out the round hole in the surface before putting the iron lid on it. Reluctantly, because she liked the smell of the leaping flames. She sat on the top of the stove, feeling it warm her bottom until it got too hot. Then she searched the cupboards. Coffee. Tea. She was famished. At the bottom of the cupboard in a heap was a rough string shopping bag. She hung it on her arm and sallied forth.

The sun was high, an autumn sun, diffuse and brilliant. Nicole explored the terrain, partly because she'd been taught always to know the area a terrorist beds down in, mostly for pleasure. The patch of woods in which the farmhouse stood was thick with fall leaves and fell away sharply to the flashing Saône. She walked to the water's edge and searched for fish with eager, inexpert eyes. Fishing was something she had heard of, as an Eskimo might hear of palm trees, something people did elsewhere. Improbable. She was a desert girl, and she'd never seen a fish that wasn't lying stone-cold in a basket.

The bank across the river rose much more sharply than on her side of the stream, and it was densely wooded. Automatically she looked for a narrow spot where a girl could—if she was in a hurry—get across easily and vanish into the woods. Flight again. She smiled her urchin smile. If you teach a terrorist a foreign language, *flee* should be the model verb. Not I am. You are. He is. But I flee, you flee, he flees, we flee. They fled. We were fleeing. I have fled. I will flee. Present, past, and future indicative. I should have fled. I should flee.

She walked back past the farmhouse, down the rocky track to the road. She could see the village to her right through the trees. She walked on the left side of the road, keeping her head down, listening for cars. There were none in either direction. In the village she went from shop to shop, her face closed in, meeting no one's eyes, her own fixed on the *charcuterie,* the *pâtisserie,* the *boulangerie.* She bought long rolls, a terrine, eggs, a chicken; she bought lettuce and butter and slices of ham; she bought Moroccan oranges and French peaches and apples from Normandy; she bought cheeses from the district and from Auvergne and from Provence; she bought sugar and chocolate and finished by buying a round black sinful chocolate cake, hungry at the very sight of it.

It was a very heavy string bag, but she carried it easily over both arms, eyes on the road, mind faraway in Damascus. Where was Selim Seleucid? And where were her instructions?

The farmhouse was warmer now from the fire, though still damp. Nicole pulled back the ragged curtains to let in light. She peered into the bedroom and found the sleeper still inert, and closed the door softly. Then she stood stock-still in the center of the room and did a terrorist thing—she listened. She almost stopped breathing and turned her ears on all the way. It was a very silent French country-side. She could hear the sleeper in the next room breathing; she could hear the Saône rippling over the rocks; she could hear the hiss of the fire; she could hear her own heart beating. She was memorizing the ordinary sounds so that if at any time an extraordinary sound crept in there, she would be fully alert. It was an old terrorist exercise, and she enjoyed it in a deeply feline way. Three days in the city dulled the ears. One turned them off in the city in sheer self-defense. Now in the country she turned them on again, reveling in the subtlety of the country noises. A cowbell tinkled half a mile away. Birds cheeped distantly, unlike any birds in her experience. She was listening for the sounds of danger and being seduced by the sounds of the country wind.

She found a skillet and fried ham and eggs in it. She made coffee thick with sugar in the Damascus way. She cut herself slabs of the French bread and wiped her plate clean with it. She ate a peach and drank a second cup of coffee, thick with sugar, and felt deeply content. She stretched her brown arms over her head in a long stretch, pulling her body taut, becoming in the process deeply aware of her body, all of it, from the black, curly mop of her hair to her tough, muscular toes. She felt gloriously female and full of blood.

What in hell is the matter with me? I am in love, that is what is the matter with me. *Mon Dieu,* in love! With that supercilious, decadent, worthless Frenchman! How very deplorable! And yet he was an Arab, too, in a very distant way. Not altogether an effendi. She was trying to justify it, was she? Anyway, it wouldn't interfere with her as an operative; it would sharpen her. Because she would be even more totally dedicated to her purpose, even more concerned with his safety. . . .

Safety! It was a jarring note. No terrorist could afford concern for anyone's safety.

Her hatred flared like a match. Love, she thought bitterly, is a bourgeois fairy tale. I am a revolutionary, nurtured on hatred, the proper fuel for such a one as me. Love is a sin, a vice, a depravity. That is what she thought, again and again. But even when she was thinking it, she was not believing it.

She felt deeply, blissfully happy, and happiness was not an emotion a terrorist should spend much time either contemplating or experiencing. Happiness was an illusion created by the privileged classes for the subjection of just such a one as herself—an Arab girl who had sprung from the very loins of deprivation. Happiness was an orange they gave you to shut you up. So she thought. And even while thinking it, happiness flooded her inextinguishably.

She fed the fire with more blocks of wood. She washed her dish and cup. She sat down again at the plain bare table on the hard chair, arms over her head—why is that such a physical expression of exaltation? she wondered—at the same time lifting her shoulders, her whole body light as a twig. She put her feet on the table, hands under her head, and tilted her chair back, eyes on the ceiling, enraptured in spite of her most earnest efforts. I am too young, too young! If I were older, I would be more sensible.

When at four in the afternoon Ferenc rose, still fogged with sleep, she was aloof. She made him eggs and ham and fresh coffee and sliced bread, keeping her eyes away from him in mortal terror that her sin would be found out. Ferenc ate like a wolf, waking up slowly.

After he finished, she faced him, hooding her thoughts. "What do we do now?" she asked.

"Wait," said Ferenc.

# CHAPTER 25

The ancient Isotta Fraschini had proceeded at its stately pace down N51 to Orléans, where it picked up the Loire. Where love was invented in the twelfth century, thought Jepthah, lolling in the tonneau in his François Duvillard disguise. What a place for a police pursuit! At Amboise he checked in at Le Choiseul, the best hotel in town. The flics would be flashing their badges and throwing their weight around at the desk, wanting information about his telephone calls and even his meals. He made no phone calls, but he ordered up a superb meal to be served in his room—the grilled salmon with the *soufflé meringue aux fruits,* washed down with Vouvray, the local wine. He was pretty sure it was flics serving the food. Might as well make their mouths water. He turned in to the big fourposter bed very early. It was going to be a long night, and he might as well get some sleep.

"I will tell you where the money comes from only if I am promised complete immunity."

Colonel Frère rubbed his face, heavy-eyed. He flicked the inter-office squawk box. "Come in, Pierre," he commanded. To the woman who sat before him rapier-straight, he said wearily: "I can't do that, Hélène, until I talk to the magistrate."

The Sergeant stood before him. "Take her away," said Colonel Frère.

"You are not taking me to the cells," said Hélène Labuisse, rigid with fear.

"Would you rather we let you loose on the streets?" asked Colonel Frère.

"They can get at me in the cells," said Hélène Labuisse, her eyes round with terror.

"Not these cells," said the Colonel. "Take her away, Pierre, to the top-security cells." To Hélène Labuisse he said, "We're quite interested in keeping you alive."

André de Quielle leaned against a filing cabinet, his French good looks unruffled. A true Quai d'Orsay foreign officer, betraying nothing. After the Sergeant had led the woman away, André said in his most neutral tones, "You must understand what is at stake here, Colonel Frère. A certain power is financing terror—and I think you know who I mean. . . ."

"I know who you mean," said Colonel Frère.

"Yes, but perhaps you don't know quite how deeply committed this head of state is to a policy of terror. He financed the Young Palestine League in five acts of naked terror. He laid out the money for the massacre of forty-two people at Fiumicino Airport in Rome. They skyjacked the British VC Ten and burned it at Schipol Airport in Amsterdam. They have failed twice—to assassinate the Israeli Ambassador in Cyprus in November, 1973, and again to assassinate Henry Kissinger in Beirut—but they are still trying. We have so far avoided any of these horrors either on French soil or to French officials."

"You have bought off the terrorists, have you?" said Colonel Frère, trying without very great success to conceal his contempt.

André remained a diplomat, very suave. "Colonel Frère, these are crimes only in the sense that war is a crime. I deplore them as deeply as you. But when a head of state is the . . . shall we say, perpetrator, then the matter has removed itself from the realm of the police. You cannot, after all, arrest a head of another state. It's difficult enough to arrest the head of your own state, as the Americans have discovered."

"Terror is my domain," said Frère, not yielding an inch. "You Foreign Office people must yield a few of your secrets. Because the fact is quite plain—you are being betrayed from within your own organization, André."

The terrible thing, thought André, is that I'm afraid he is right. Aloud, he said: "Might I suggest an alliance, Colonel Frère?"

Colonel Frère pointed to a chair.

"These are the wild men of the Palestinian terror organizations," began André de Quielle carefully. "Next to the Young Palestine League, Black September is a bunch of nuns. In actual truth they broke away from Black September because it was *too* moderate, improbable as that sounds. The appalling truth is that these last two terror attacks—the murder of diplomats at Kaffir and the blowing up of the airplane at Dubai—were all part of a fight for power between *rival* terrorist organizations. The Young Palestine League has been able to pull off these coups because it is financed by oil revenues from a certain head of state."

Colonel Frère moved impatiently. "This is all old stuff, André."

"Ah, but wait," said André. "The two rival terror organizations are headed for direct warfare. The stake is—as you know—whether the peace conference at Geneva takes place or not. Both sides are planning a massacre of the *other*. That we know. We don't know where or when—and it's just possible neither organization quite knows its own plans yet."

That was better. Colonel Frère let the facts fall into place in his mind, trying to fit them with what he knew.

"You already know," said André, "that some sort of terror coup was afoot and that a female terrorist was somewhere in Paris." He drew a deep breath and then, with the utmost reluctance, revealed his hole card. "What I'm telling you is this, Colonel Frère. That the Ashfi Hashad group of old Black Septembrists whom we so jokingly called moderates have got wind of at least *some* of the plan of the Young Palestine League and are planning their own little massacre of the *other* terrorists. Not a quiet little assassination in some side street, but a big operation designed to capture world headlines at the same time as their rivals are eliminated. And since the Young

184 ·

Palestine League terrorist is in Paris, the massacre could very well take place here."

Colonel Frère brooded over this intelligence in silence, letting it fall into little slots in his brain along with the other facts.

"We don't know how much the Ashfi Hashad group knows," continued André heavily. "They have had Selim Seleucid in their hands for several days now, and they are wringing information out of him bit by bit by some rather ingenious methods because he is a tough old desert warrior and doesn't yield easily to torture. Now, Colonel, your turn."

Colonel Frère moved things around his desk—pens, papers, letter openers. Then, reluctantly, he showed *his* hole card: "The Ashfi Hashad group is being financed by the Chinese. Their sole interest is to embarrass the Russians, whose arms are being hawked around by that same head of state whom we all know and love. The name of the Chinese connection is one of the facts that Hélène Labuisse is withholding from me, trying to get total immunity, which between ourselves she is not going to get. I strongly suspect the Chinese connection of being your informant on Robert Pinay." He paused, shoving things around his desk. "Your turn," he said politely.

André sighed and yielded. "Fourchet," he said tonelessly. "He's the head of Foreign Office counterintelligence, a career civil servant of twelve years' standing."

Silence again, each man pursuing his own will-o'-the-wisp. "I'll have him picked up," said Colonel Frère.

André regarded him with steadfast, troubled eyes. "I don't think you'll find him, *mon Colonel.* I've already tried."

Colonel Frère played with the objects on his desk, putting the paper cutter on the inkwell, the pencil crosswise on the paper cutter, frowning with concentration.

"Why would a man like that—with a secure future in a brilliant profession such as yours—risk everything to become an acolyte of Chairman Mao?" Frère was the very model of a French civil servant; he assumed everyone's aspirations were like his own.

"Oh, Colonel, you are asking me to solve the riddle of the sphinx. What propels the Kim Philbys of the world to conspire against everything their training and background and even their own self-interest would dictate that they fight to uphold?"

"We must discuss this at lunch sometime," said Frère. "I think we should have a talk with the woman. Would you like to come along?"

"Certainly," said André.

In quite another part of the rabbit warren, the police officer Moulin was in a perplexity. He had ordered Madame Blanche locked up, pending . . . well, whatever he decided. The French police are not hampered by the superstitions of Anglo-Saxon jurisprudence. The police are not required to charge you or discharge you. They can just lock you up, pending their investigation; pending, in short, the confirmation or nonconfirmation of their suspicions. The woman was clearly nutty. Saying again and again that François Duvillard was not François Duvillard! What lunacy.

Moulin undertook the search of the Duvillard town house by himself because he didn't quite dare tell anyone what he suspected. This delayed things a great deal.

Lack of confidence was not one of Philippa's weaknesses. She faced the two men, Colonel Frère and André de Quielle, with enormous élan, seated them in her drawing room like the splendid hostess she was, inquired about their health with that piercing concern that the great ladies of society can assume about totally imaginary subjects, and when they asked about Nicole, she lied to them, smiling, serene, casual, offhand.

"Oh, she's in the shops again. She's not been in Paris very long, you know, and she's entranced by our fashions." Philippa smiled at the two men. She'd been to bed with both men, and that gave her assurance, which she needed. For Philippa had called her husband about Nicole's disappearance. She told him also about the visit of the police the night before. She was a very loyal wife and had discarded the solemn vows of secrecy she had made to Colonel Frère the night before as lightly as she would a bit of cleansing tissue. Her nest was threatened, and in her bourgeois world this was the holy citadel to which she owed her ultimate loyalty. Her husband had been alarmed—and that in turn alarmed her, for few things alarmed Robert Pinay. "If they come back," Robert said to her, "tell them nothing." When Colonel Frère duly appeared on her doorstep—unaccountably with André de Quielle—Philippa told lies so skillfully, urbanely, and suavely that Colonel Frère, who was expert at the detection of liars, swallowed it all. It was just a question of waiting until the girl came home.

That delayed things until the next day, when the game had changed irrevocably.

## CHAPTER 26

In the medieval splendor of his hotel bedroom, Jepthah woke at 2:30 A.M., having set the alarm in his own skull for that hour. By the light of the moon he peeled off the scars and skin and hair of François Duvillard, resuming his own physiognomy with a sense of deep relief. He crept out of the room into the empty corridor and stole down the back stairs, silent as a shadow. The lobby would be full of flics, so Jepthah continued straight down into the cellar. There must be a cellar door to let in all those vegetables. There was. There should have been a flic watching it, but Bossert was shorthanded, and there wasn't.

As he slipped out through the patch of market garden at the rear of the hotel, Jepthah caught a glimpse of the ancient Isotta gleaming in the moonlight. Poor Jacques, thought Jepthah.

Six hours later Jepthah was on a bus to Geneva. The flics hadn't even missed him.

Nicole and Ferenc walked in the woods across the Saône from the farmhouse, arm in arm like French lovers, Ferenc told her. Anglo-Saxons would hold hands, he said. Arab lovers, she told him, would not touch at all. They loved with their eyes. "It seems not very much," she said, "but it can be quite emotional—lovemaking with a glance. Quite satisfying. Europeans would not understand it."

"They did once upon a time," said Ferenc. "Not so long ago. Love over the fan. Love across a crowded room or perhaps just a look behind the back."

This was not a serious conversation. Ferenc had said they must not attract attention, and the best way not to attract attention was to act like French lovers. French lovers loved woods and streams and open places. Love *sur l'herbe*—you found it in French painting and in much of French literature. It was part of the stratagem, this dialogue. Love was part of their disguise.

"We are not lovers," said Nicole, "we are conspirators. Is that it?"

"Perhaps a bit of both," said Ferenc. They were lying on the top of the hill on the other side of the Saône in a grassy meadow that sloped steeply and offered a good view of the village. He kissed the girl on the lips with exquisite pleasure. Seventeen, he was thinking, and an enemy. That's what is giving me such delicious pleasure. It is perverse, it is a wickedness. I am a monster practicing a perversion, and that is why it is so tumultuous a sensuality.

Her own thoughts were hardly thoughts at all. Just bliss, overwhelmingly nonmental. She was in love. Still, it was convenient—what a word!—to play this as a game. She could keep her secret and enjoy her emotion, have her cake and eat it. She ran a finger along the line of his lips.

"This love on the grass," she said. "Could you demonstrate it a little more fully?"

"No," he said. "The village can see us as well as we can see them. The idea is to appease curiosity, not to arouse it. Kissing on a hillside in full view of the good bourgeois is as far as French lovers would go. Anything more advanced would be clearly foreign and an object of great suspicion, and we mustn't arouse that." He kissed her once more and then rolled over and lay on his back, hands under his head.

They contemplated the blue autumn sky and watched the birds

wheeling in the sky for a very long time. Tension between them had vanished, and talk was unnecessary. They pursued their own thoughts.

After a good ten minutes Nicole broke the silence. "Waiting is not my game. I have never been one who waits. I am more at home in that little peasant farmhouse than in all that splendor at the Pinays'. I am a child of the refugee camps."

"I cannot imagine you in tatters," said Ferenc.

She smiled faintly. "Can you, François, imagine tatters at all? Tatters are outside your experience."

She rolled over onto her stomach and told him about life as an Arab urchin, watching him to see what he would think. "It's what being an animal is like. You wake up in the morning at first light, ravenous, and it is what life is, filling your stomach—well, not filling it, just getting something into it—and it is *all* that life is. There is nothing else. Just finding enough to eat. Well, of course, this is what a bird does. A bird must eat half his own weight every day, and he must start at first light, or he will not make it. That is what being an Arab urchin is like—like one of those birds." She laughed bitterly because, of course, it wasn't like that at all, watching him carefully, this decadent, elegant lover who had never known an hour of deprivation.

He looked back at her sympathetically, his greatest bit of acting.

"But of course we had our amusements," she said, her eyes veiled. "Hating Israelis. Hatred is the sole entertainment of those who have nothing. Hatred has taken the place of religion as the opiate of the masses," she said. She explained some of the games Arab children played, which largely involved unspeakable tortures they would inflict on an Israeli if they ever caught one; she told him of the curses of Arab children against Israel and Israelis, some of which were poetic in their unimaginable horror.

"*Ma foi*," said Ferenc mildly. "Young children should not be permitted such obscenities. They are damaging their own souls." He drew the girl to him and kissed her to shut her pretty lips. He was shaken to the core.

"Come," he said, pulling free and sitting up, "we'll explore the woods. We can't just lie here all morning. It's bad for our characters."

190 ·

She snapped her fingers. "That—for my character," she said, and wrestled with him, delicious sport that made her dizzy with pleasure.

Oh, God, thought Ferenc, this is the way men lose their souls—and was instantly stabbed with the thought that it was a very François Duvillard idea, not a Ferenc idea at all. She was very strong, solid steel wire, all of her, and the best way to resist a girl like that, thought Ferenc, was not resist at all. He gave up the struggle and lay passive on his back, looking up at her soberly.

"Oh," she said, disappointed. "I won. I beat you."

"Yes, you won," said Ferenc. "You are very strong."

She made a little face and felt her biceps. "Too strong for a girl," she said sadly. "We had to climb on ropes up a cliff, not using our legs, just our arms. Like a monkey." She became piercingly aware of all the hard muscles in her boyish body and bitterly ashamed of them. "Come," she said, "we'll walk in the woods," and tried to pull him up by the hands.

"No," said Ferenc perversely, "it's very pleasant here. Why walk in the woods?" He pulled hard, as she pulled him, and she fell on top of him.

"You're impossible," she cried. "One minute you want to walk in the woods and the next you want to lie on the ground."

"*You're* impossible!" retorted Ferenc. "One minute you want to lie on the ground! The next you want to walk in the woods!"

They bickered about this delightful triviality for a full ten minutes. Then they walked in the woods for an hour, trying to pretend they were mapping escape routes in case they needed escape routes, but unable to stick to the subject very long. At twelve thirty they returned to the peasant farmhouse. Nicole grilled kidneys in the Arab way, with two kinds of rice and chicken livers. She drank watered yogurt, Ferenc drank wine. Afterward they went to bed and made love all afternoon. After all, they had to kill time somehow.

In Paris that morning, Colonel Frère was staring appalled at a thoroughly cowed Moulin. The comedy of police errors had shuddered to a halt.

"Why didn't you report this?" said Colonel Frère, keeping his voice steady. He'd like to have wrung the man's neck. Madame

Blanche's letter, the first ounce of confirmation of the Colonel's dazzling suspicions, lay before him. "What were you investigating?" said Colonel Frère tonelessly.

"That she . . ." Moulin stopped in full flow. The idea that Madame Blanche had murdered her employer seemed to shrink in possibility.

"That she'd killed him?" inquired Colonel Frère. "Well, I think somebody did. But not her."

The Pinays were having lunch together in the small breakfast room just off the main salon, a very unusual occasion. They hadn't lunched together, *à deux*, in years.

"Colonel Frère wishes to talk to Nicole," said Philippa, helping her husband to some salad. "A hard-boiled egg, *chéri?*"

"No, I think not," said her husband. "I worry about cholesterol. What does he want to talk to her about?"

"I don't know, *chéri*. What is there to talk about?" Philippa looked straight into her husband's eyes with a little smile. She had dressed very carefully for this occasion. Lunching with one's own husband! What a novelty! It was also, she felt, the moment of truth. "I think, *chéri*, it is time you confided in me just who Nicole really is and what she is doing here. Or rather, *was* doing here?"

"You think she's not coming back?" asked Pinay gravely, eating his salad. "Her clothes are still here."

"There is an air of finality about that room. I don't think she is coming back, and I ask myself, Why? What has she to fear, *chéri?* What is it all about?"

"It would be better that you not know, my love," said Pinay. "The police can be very tiresome—but if you know nothing, you know nothing. Might I have a little more of the camembert?"

192 ·

# CHAPTER *27*

Jepthah listened, lying full length on the hotel bed, the telephone tucked under his ear. On the other end of the phone, all the way from Tel Aviv, Tilsit spoke in parables. He didn't trust the telephones of Geneva.

"Abraham is having trouble with his flocks," said Tilsit. "Youth and age are at each other's throats."

Youth was the Young Palestine League. Age was Ashfi Hashad, both Palestine guerrilla factions. "Why don't we just fold our tents and steal away in the night?" asked Jepthah. "If they want to cut each other's throats, by all means let them."

"It's not that simple," growled Tilsit. "Tell the boy David that Goliath is wrestling with himself—and to back away for a bit."

"What about Bathsheba?" asked Jepthah.

"She hath transgressed," said Tilsit. "So be careful because the Philistines will kill her if they can get their hands on her. Tell the boy

David to search in his own heart for the truth which will set him free." In short, use his own judgment when to dump Nicole.

"It shall come to pass," said Jepthah.

"Keep in touch," said Tilsit.

"Yeah, verily," said Jepthah, and hung up.


The confrontation at the Pinays' was naked because Colonel Frère was in no mood for silken words. His telephone call to Amboise had filled him with cold rage. The quarry had fled, and furious as he was at Bossert and the local police for letting it happen, Colonel Frère could not avoid the thought that the situation was largely of his own making. He should have ordered the man picked up. He hadn't, and it was a grave mistake.

It was in a black mood that he listened to Robert Pinay weaving his fantasies about the flibbertigibbet activities of a seventeen-year-old girl. As Philippa had predicted, he didn't believe it. But even Philippa was astounded by Colonel Frère's response to this nonsense.

"You are a liar," said Colonel Frère.

Things must be even worse than I had imagined, thought Philippa, for so correct a bureaucrat to fling at her eminent husband so offensive a word. For the first time she thought of her own safety. It was just the beginning of a very long process of disengagement, the first tremors of disloyalty, when a wife thinks, "My interests are no longer identical with his interests," followed shortly by the even more clamorous thought, "My interests are sorely threatened by being identified with his interests." None of this showed on Philippa's alabaster countenance, on which she had spent nearly half an hour of great effort.

"The Colonel forgets himself," said Robert Pinay.

"We have Mademoiselle Labuisse in custody," said Colonel Frère. "She has told us everything." Not quite everything.

Behind the alabaster mask of Philippa, strong juices spurted. If I leave Robert, where then? she was thinking. And what shall I take? The silver, of course, but will he let me get away with the dining-room chairs, which were his grandmother's?

"Among other things, Mademoiselle Labuisse has told us all about your relationship with François Duvillard," said Colonel Frère. Then he threw his lightning bolt. "But what she doesn't know—nor do you—is that François Duvillard is *not* François Duvillard. The François Duvillard you have been sharing your secrets with, Monsieur Pinay, is an impersonator."

That staggered them all—not least, Philippa. In her mind's eye flashed again those naked flanks she'd seen in bed with Nicole. She'd seen those flanks on someone—but on whom? Philippa had a very long list of naked male flanks to run through.

The nightmares were the worst in years. Ferenc was wielding the Gauleiter, as they used to call the long electric needle, on Nicole's naked flesh, and she was screaming so piercingly that it penetrated to the very marrow of his spine. Even in his nightmare he knew it was a nightmare. "If I can only wake myself up, this will all go away," thought Ferenc as Nicole screamed and screamed and he struggled to wake himself. It was like swimming through a sea of molasses to the surface.

He awoke with a shudder—to find Nicole's round eyes four inches from his own. "You were groaning and thrashing around. What is the matter?"

"Nightmare!" said Ferenc, and held the muscular, boyish body to him in contrition for what he had done to it in the dream. He was always defenseless after his nightmares, vulnerable to passion. He caressed the golden Arab face, seething with despair, the remnant of his nightmare.

"Nightmare?" said Nicole, who had never had one. "What was it—the nightmare? Tell me."

Ferenc just shook his head, robbed of speech.

"Tell me!" urged Nicole. "It will help you rid yourself of the demons!"

"Algeria!" said Ferenc darkly. "Algeria is the nightmare of France." He held her tight to him, shaken by the revelation. He'd never said such a thing before, but having said it, it was true. Algeria *was* the nightmare of France, and those who had participated were condemned to everlasting nightmares in expiation. Ferenc sat bolt upright.

"We are condemned to relive it in our dreams until we die! We were commanded to torture by our sergeant. Torture detail for the day—like cleaning the latrines or doing kitchen duty. It was a duty —to make someone scream for four hours—then you were relieved."

Ferenc buried his face in the comfort of the young breasts. He'd forgotten altogether that while Ferenc had been on torture detail in Algeria, François Duvillard had not, and that he had admitted as much to Nicole.

Nicole had not forgotten. She held her lover's head on her breast, flat on her back, and looked at the ceiling, her mind full of questions. This was no time for questions. Her lover was horror-stricken, she caressed his head, trying to banish the nightmares with her fingers, trying at the same time to banish the questions.

Presently they were both blinded by desire so sharp, so agonizing, it blotted the mind like morphine.

Afterward Ferenc slept, still as death. Nicole lay on her back, her mouth a little round *O*, and relived every thrust, every kiss. It's like dying! Like dying! Flames licked at her body in retrospect, almost more shattering than in truth. She was engulfed, torn from her moorings. She felt whole, a woman altogether, a complete human. Before this, I was a blob of nothing. I am alive, and how very peculiar to be made alive by something that feels like dying!

She cradled her sleeping lover's head on her breast, sitting up slowly so she could look down on him, staring at him transfixed, as if she could, by the very staring, unlock the riddle of the universe. She wished he would wake up so she could drown herself in his eyes, submerge herself in his flesh, die with him again.

Time passed. I should sleep, thought Nicole. I will be dead on my feet. I should sleep, and I have never been more awake. Presently the flames receded; the mind reasserted itself, and the questions came back. She kept them at bay by simply staring at the sleeping face on her breast, a sight that drowned questions.

Nicole stared with compassion at those sleeping eyelids, framing unspoken endearments.

Eyelid! It seemed ajar, that eyelid! One end of that eyelid stuck out from the flesh in a most unnatural way. Nicole took the bit of flesh in between finger and thumb. It felt like any flesh, but dead, certainly not like the rest of that piercing body. She lifted the fragment ever so gently. It came off in her hand—the whole eyelid. Underneath lay quite a different eyelid, younger, firmer, thinner, less—the thought fled terror-stricken through her mind—depraved.

Nicole sat up, an involuntary movement, her soul wrenched with . . . what? Terror? Like finding a stranger in bed with her. The head lay in her lap now, and Nicole bent over it in a long arch, her heart pounding. Terrified, she thought. I'm terrified! Slowly, slowly she lifted the sleeping head and put it down on the pillow. She put a bare foot down on the stone floor and stood by the side of the bed looking down at this . . . stranger, her naked body shivering with cold in the 2:30 A.M. autumnal air. Like a sleepwalker she turned from the bed and slipped on her black trousers and her black sweater.

She sat on the bed gently, so as not to waken the sleeper. Ferenc lay on the pillow, face up. With exquisite stealth, as if she were walking through mine fields in terror school, she lay down on her stomach, head supported on her elbows, scrutinizing the face inch by inch. Now that the left eyelid had proved false, the right looked equally bogus. Nicole, subtle as a safecracker, felt the right eyelid with the tip of her forefinger. False as a houri's kiss! With her dextrous fingernail she separated truth from falsehood and examined the revised face, lips pursed. Now the whole physiognomy seemed wrong. Nothing fitted with anything else. Nicole lay, chin on her hands, staring at the sleeper, looking for clues. Those lips that had sent tongues of flame through her, could they be . . . ? Nicole ran her fingertips over them and felt underneath with her fingernail. Ah! It was a shrill bleat of unspoken despair. The lips, too!

The lips presented a far more complex problem than the eyelids. To remove the false ones without disturbing the sleeper, Nicole called on all her guile. The probing fingernail was gentle. For minutes on end she worked at the corner of the lips so gently that no movement at all could be seen. When Ferenc moved a little in his sleep, she desisted for minutes until his breathing resumed fully and steadily. Then she went back to work, tirelessly gentle. It took an hour to loosen the fake lips. Then she went to work on the brow—all those tiny, decadent wrinkles that more than anything else were the expression of François Duvillard.

Suspicion grew like a fungus in her darkest recesses. Slowly. Then not slowly at all. She was herself a conspirator, a liar, a player of roles. The unimaginable was imagined, and once imagined. . . .

She stood back from the bed, staring at the sleeper, the beloved. . . . Beloved! She went to work on his scanty luggage, found the gun—well, everyone had a gun, but she searched it for clues, found none, and then searched again. When she found what she feared to find, she uttered an Arab scream of despair, her whole body contorted into one savage howl. Like that earlier shriek of despair in the hotel room, it was totally silent. . . .

"In essence, our moral position . . ." began André.

"I am not interested in moral positions," snapped Colonel Frère.

". . . was one of acquiescence rather than one of active initiative," concluded André firmly. "You had better be interested in moral positions, Colonel, or otherwise you will not understand anything at all about this business, and it will lead you into serious miscalculations. At stake is the very destiny of advanced industrial nations like ourselves. At stake also is the very existence of Israel, which has been led into adventures it would not have dreamed of authorizing except under the threat to its survival. At stake also is the moral position, which verges on holy war, of at least ten different groupings of Arabs. Terror, my dear Colonel, is conducted on a very high moral plane, and if you don't understand that, you don't understand anything."

"*Mon ami*, I had no intention of arresting you," said Colonel Frère. "Why are you defending your part in this sleazy operation?"

"I am not defending myself," said André angrily. "I am explaining the position of the French Foreign Office in a very difficult time. I am telling you, Colonel Frère, you must not arrest or question or in any way disturb Robert Pinay—at this time. You have no idea how delicate these negotiations are."

The man with holes for eyes was at that moment passing through customs into Switzerland. He was bearded now and looked quite different from his Foreign Office appearance—except for those eyes. His passport was under the name of Finisterre. He was met by a limousine, which took him to a grand stone house whose sweep of lawn extended clear to the shores of Lake Geneva. Fourchet was conducted immediately to a room at the very top floor few of the other United Nations staff ever entered.

A slim young Chinese with intelligent eyes named Lin Chiu poured him tea and listened sympathetically to the recital of misfortune. "We managed to get a photograph of her," said Fourchet. He opened his attaché case and handed Lin Chiu a photograph.

It was of Nicole snapped while she was shopping in the Faubourg St.-Honoré. "Not very clear, I'm afraid, but you can identify her."

"Very young," murmured the Chinese, "for such a mission."

"It's a very young outfit, the Young Palestine League."

"Where is she now?" asked Lin Chiu.

Fourchet spread his hands wide in a peculiarly Gallic gesture. "We don't know. But we know where she will be when the plane arrives—even the very spot at the Geneva airport where she will stand. We don't know—nor did she—what airplane she will be aiming at."

"I think I may help out there," murmured the Chinese. "We have just received a list of the Arab delegations—with their flight numbers and arrival times." He handed it to Fourchet. "And what about Mademoiselle Labuisse?" he asked sympathetically.

"That's been taken care of," said Fourchet, absently studying the folder.

They found Hélène Labuisse hanging from the light cord in the maximum-security cell.

"You will have great difficulty explaining to me the moral position of Hélène Labuisse in this affair," said Colonel Frère to André de Quielle.

"Hélène was a woman of fashion—ideological fashion," said André. "She went from Marxist to Leninist to Trotskyite to Maoist—the way Philippa changes her clothes—depending on what was in that year. She foundered finally in her own internal contradictions, as the Marxists say about us."

"We must discuss it at luncheon when this is all over," said Colonel Frère.

"If it is ever over," said André. "We are in the midst of a revolution whose end is nowhere near in sight."

"Who is winning?" asked Colonel Frère ironically.

"Oh, the People," said André. "The People always win in the end, Colonel."

## CHAPTER 28

Ferenc woke slowly. Normally he sprang out of sleep, fully alert. Sleep was an abomination, a situation to be got out of as quickly as possible. This time he hated leaving sleep, he slept dreamlessly. Very unusual.

The first thing that struck his eyes was the patch of autumn sunshine on the stone floor. Then Nicole's feet, already shod in the silver-buckled shoes, standing in the splash of sunshine. All very odd. His eyes traveled up past the black-trousered leg and saw the gun in her hand, the little automatic she carried in her handbag as other girls carry eye shadow.

Finally the black, blazing eyes. Lips drawn up in a snarl. Not a human expression at all. Ferenc said nothing, gathering his wits. What the hell! Nicole seemed beyond speech. Feral. Malignant. Ablaze. She was breathing as if she'd been in a race. Great gulps of air entering that feral jaw, teeth bared like an outraged orangutan. Simian. Not beautiful at all. His beautiful golden Arab an avenging demon.

He was too much a professional not to know. Without touching his face he could feel the absence. My wrinkles, my scars! I've been stripped of my identity. This is the great fear we all have at the very bottom of our heart when we fall asleep; we will awake, and they'll have taken it all away while we slept. All the loot. Our loved ones. Then, the final indignity, our very own self. We'll awake a frog. And we don't know how the other frogs will accept us.

There was a great silence in the room. Ferenc didn't dare speak. Nicole seemed to have lost the power, although her mouth hung open as if speech were in it, but frozen solid, unable to get out.

What the hell! thought Ferenc, as awake now as he'd ever been, his body beginning to coil like a spring, his mind bursting. What did I do wrong? And that other thought of a terrorist when things go wrong: Whatever I do must be done in the next second and a half.

"I should have killed you in your sleep!" The sibilants hissed like snakes.

"Yes, you should have," said Ferenc calmly. "You'll find it harder now."

The professional in him said that he was talking to another professional. That was what the bared teeth, the gasping breath, the blazing eyes were all about. She was trying to stoke the fires of hatred to ignition point—and very high it was—when she could pull the trigger on a man looking her in the eye. Not just any man, but a lover. How long had she been standing there? How late was it? Without taking his eyes from hers, Ferenc tried to tell time by that splash of sunlight. It must be ten o'clock at least. How have I slept so long? Because we made love, and it drained me to the bottom. Because I didn't have any dreams. He felt rested. Oh, fine! Nothing like getting killed when fully rested.

"Israeli!" spat Nicole. It started with that long sibilant hiss of *Is;* then the lips drew back in a snarl for the *rae,* the top lip curled upward like a mad dog's, and the final *li* was an exhalation of hate.

Ferenc, his eyes latched on to hers—he couldn't break that gaze if he tried—could see a lifetime of hate. Not simply in the eyes. In every ligament in that thin, muscular body, tight as a wire, all of it, curved forward like a scimitar, the gun held at arm's length.

Still, she hasn't fired that thing, has she? The longer she doesn't pull that trigger, the harder it's going to be. Provided I don't give her an excuse. He lay as he'd wakened, naked under the sheet, Ferenc now, not François. Does she recognize me as the man who took a shot at her in a Paris street? Heaven help me if she does, but I don't think she does. His neck was bent slightly on the pillow, but only slightly. He was still in full sleeping position. Except his eyes were open. And he wished they weren't.

His golden Arab girl snarling like an ape! My God! My God! How did she find out? What have I done wrong? I must make a move, thought Ferenc. If only to say something. Roll under the bed? No, she was as professional as he was. She wanted an excuse. Don't give her one.

"I. Hate. You." Each word a full sentence.

But a false note. She was more expressive of hate, unspeaking. Was she saying, *I love you?* Why hadn't she killed him when she found out? Jepthah had told him she'd killed the two flics as casually as she'd squash a bug. If she hated him, she'd have killed him and been long gone. Was she saying, *I hate me for loving you?* Was that it?

Here it came again, the lips contorting like an ape's. "I—hate —you." Trying to heat herself into flash point.

Ferenc made his move.

"I love you," he said. Very simply, without emphasis. It was the only option open.

"You . . ." A howl of despair. "You lie!"

Why does she care if I lie? thought Ferenc. And parenthetically, underneath all his other thoughts: Do I lie? Does anyone tell lies in circumstances like this? Why did that particular move pop up just then? But all this under, as they say in music, like the left hand in jazz improvisation doing something the right hand wishes it wouldn't. Where do I go from here?

"How do you think it's been with me?" Inspiration! The only thing to say! "Loving an Arab girl! How do you think it's been with me?"

That smote her. She had been rigid as a post since he'd opened his eyes. Now she moved. Fractionally. Her shoulders straightened an inch from the scimitar curve. The eyes widened a millimeter. Not much. But something.

"My mother died!" Nicole was whispering now. "Deprivation! Malnutrition! Lice! Despair! That's how you killed her, murderer! You stabbed her in the throat with despair! Assassin!"

Her eyes were full of tears like a human. The animal in her was ebbing. Her mother? How do I give her back her mother? Mothers are dogma, an incantation. She's retreating into ritual.

"If you kill me"—Ferenc was whispering now, too, matching her mood—"I'll be a lump of bleeding flesh. Not a person anymore. A lump, gathering flies. Staring eyes, mouth dribbling. Not your lover anymore."

Well, it was a gamble, but then what option had he? How sensual was she? How much would she mourn the loss of him? Anyway, he had to get her off the subject of her mother.

Her face was full of scorn. "You think you are irreplaceable, you Israeli thug!" She uttered a bark of laughter that was not laughter at all. She came a step closer, back arching again, eyes glittering. "Do you know how many lovers I have had, you Jewish pig? Roomsful! *Roomsful!* All of them better than you, you excrement!" The eyes full of tears again. But with rage? With something.

Is she trying to make me jealous? thought Ferenc. By God, she's succeeding. He felt a wave of fury against every last one. If there were any. For one second he lost control and let slip an uncalculated, unrehearsed thought, his first: "You're lying."

She laughed a real laugh—scornful, bitter, but nevertheless honest-to-goodness mirth. "You think you were the first? Ha!" The eyes sparkled with malice. "You're jealous."

That pleases her, thought Ferenc. "Yes," he said. "I didn't think I was the first. But I don't believe—roomsful."

Roomsful of men. Terrible image. He could see, in his mind's eye, a roomful of naked men, taking turns with Nicole. Terrible.

"Roomsful!" repeated Nicole, gleeful now. "Roomsful! And I enjoyed every last one better than you."

I can read the lie in her face, thought Ferenc. Goading me, is she? Well, this is better. He faced the gun with more confidence. He took a chance and sat up in bed, pushing the pillow behind his back. Never taking his eye from her. "Why didn't you shoot me when I slept, Nicole? You would have saved yourself all this talk."

Without a flicker of hesitation, she answered him. "Because I wanted to see what you looked like truly, you Israeli filth. I wanted to look in your Israeli eyes and spit in your Israeli face. Murderer! I wanted to see the difference in you—impostor!" She was walking now, back and forth, from one side to the other of the narrow room. She was relaxed, brandishing the gun for emphasis, shrugging. She looked to Ferenc infinitely desirable. He'd never seen her in this scornful, contemptuous, bitter, savage mood. It made her older. It also made her tumultuously sexual. He could feel her clear across the room. Before, she'd been a slim, fetching teenager. Now she was a volcano. In a burst of clairvoyance he thought, I'm feeling her because she's feeling *me*. This doesn't happen to one alone.

"I loved the *other* one," crooned Nicole, taunting him now. "Not *you*, you Israeli shit. *Him!* He was a man."

"He was a son of a bitch," said Ferenc coolly. A very interesting son of a bitch. He didn't say that last bit aloud.

"He was a magnificent lover," laughed Nicole. "Unlike you, you Jewish filth."

Is she trying to make me jealous of me? thought Ferenc. "It was me all the time," whispered Ferenc.

"It wasn't," said Nicole angrily. "I would never fall in love with an Israeli pig. It was him! François! Not you!"

She was slightly insane, thought Ferenc. She really thought of François as another person. Dangerous waters. "It was me," he said silkily. "Not François Duvillard at all. It will come as a very great shock to you, Nicole, but François Duvillard didn't like girls. Or sex."

"It's a lie!" exploded Nicole. Now the gun arm dropped altogether. She was truly shaken, unbelieving.

"I'm afraid not," said Ferenc. If I sprang now, he thought. The gun's hanging down. She could never get it up and squeeze off a shot. The moment passed.

More moments passed. She stood there, her eyes clouded with thought, deep inside herself. Ferenc lay relaxed against the pillow, watching. A fly buzzed at the window, and faraway Ferenc could hear the wheeze and click of a mowing machine working in the autumn fields. Nicole sighed heavily. She looked spent, dazed, her body slack. She'd been up all night, and the strain was showing. Presently she drifted to the window and stared out, unseeing, her back to him. An open invitation. He did nothing. He couldn't. She's unstrung me, he thought. Or perhaps François Duvillard has unstrung me. I should make a move. Why don't I?

Presently she sat on the bed, her face woebegone. "What's your real name?" she asked quietly.

"Ferenc. What's yours?"

"Chantal."

204 ·

"Very French."

"My mother was Lebanese. They're very French."

The gun hung between her knees now. She stared at the floor.

"You really were in the French Army, torturing Algerians?"

"Well, anyway, I wasn't murdering your mother."

Nicole gave a mournful laugh. "No, not Mother. She was starving to death in Syria."

"Did you like your mother?"

Nicole made a face. "Not much. I loved her, but I didn't like her much. She was a slob." Silence. "And *your* mother?" asked Nicole politely, ironically.

Ferenc gave a little grunt and thought about his mother. "Well. French. Bourgeois. She set a good table." He made it a questionable virtue. "I was the oldest and the most discontented."

"Where did you live?"

"Paris."

"You left Paris to go live in Israel!" Nicole was incredulous. "Why?"

Why indeed? "Algeria, mostly. Guilt. Romance. New country. There are not many new countries." Then Ferenc asked a question that had been bothering him. "How did you . . ." He paused, a little shy. "Where did you acquire all that elegance? All that chic? The education?"

She laughed scornfully. "They sent me to school, the organization. The elegance is as bogus as your face. We are both impostors."

She tossed the gun away on the floor. It slid across the stone floor and came to rest under the window.

Ferenc looked at it blankly. "Hadn't you better put the safety back on?"

"*Merde!*" said Nicole. She picked it up and inspected it. "I had the safety catch on all the time. What would they have thought at terrorist school?"

She sat on the bed again and handed the gun to him, mockingly. "Now you shoot me."

Ferenc held the gun in his palm and contemplated it like a relic of some ancient religion—preposterous. "It's too heavy for a girl, this gun."

"I'm very strong," said Nicole. "Go ahead, kill me." Taunting him.

"I should, you know," said Ferenc. He held the gun at arm's length, pointed at her head, squinting down the barrel. "I'm a very good shot, you know."

"Well, you could hardly miss at six inches. Go ahead, pull the trigger."

Ferenc screwed up his face ferociously, eyeing her down the barrel. "The Young Palestine League killed twenty-two of my countrymen in one mad massacre alone at Lod Airport. You are a member of the Young Palestine League."

"Yes," said Nicole, sitting up straight as a post, defiantly, "and I missed being selected for that mission by an eyelash. I was deeply disappointed when I wasn't. Go ahead, shoot, you fearless Hamossad l'Tafkidim M'yuchadim thug." She laughed.

"How did you find out about that?" Sighting down the barrel.

"Microdots," flared Nicole. She turned her back on the gun and strolled over to the little wooden dresser where, for the first time, he saw the few things he'd taken scattered. She held up the precious microscope with its concealed camera. He hadn't wanted to take it, but he feared he might need the microdots one more time. Nicole unscrewed the microscope top and drew out the little camera, which she held in one finger like a bug. "You didn't think we knew about microdots, did you? You didn't think I had enough brains to take this thing apart, did you? You underestimate us. You *always* underestimate us." She glittered with rage. "Go ahead, shoot me, you murdering Israeli pig!"

She glared right down the gun barrel at him, and he glared back, and it was all pretty ridiculous.

After a while he tossed the gun on the little wooden dresser. "Oh, Nicole!" he said.

They looked at each other sadly. She kicked her shoes off and climbed into bed with him, clothes and all. "I'm cold," she whispered.

He put both his arms around her without looking at her.

"Now what do we do, Ferenc?" she asked hopelessly, using his real name for the first time.

"I don't know," said Ferenc. "I don't know." He made a wry face. "We're Romeo and Juliet. What a comedy!"

"Who are Romeo and Juliet?" asked Nicole.

## CHAPTER *29*

Philippa threaded her way through the lunchers at the Relais Plaza, throwing little smiles, little coos that translated loosely into *"Bonjour,"* at the fashionable, the movie stars, Mrs. Henry Ford here, Catherine Deneuve there. André was sitting in a booth against the wall, watching these fashionable mewings with detachment. He'd been summoned. For what purpose, he knew not. Philippa inserted herself sinuously next to him, still waving hellos out there to the multitude.

After the small talk, it came: "André, have you seen Ferenc recently?"

André's movements became slow motion. He'd been eating his club sandwich, sipping his wine at, say, 33 revolutions per minute. Suddenly he went to 15 RPM, like a record slowing down. Why had Philippa brought up Ferenc? Ferenc had not been absent from his mind since he had failed to keep his lunch date, days before.

"I didn't know you knew Ferenc."

"I knew Ferenc—very well."

"Oh, *that* well!"

"Don't be coarse, *chéri*. He's disappeared."

"Yes, I know."

"Where," asked Philippa, "do you think he's disappeared *to?* Tel Aviv? It was all so unexpected. I saw him at your cousin's party."

"Yes, so did I." Warily. André was concentrating on her every inflection. With Philippa every trill had meaning within meanings.

"In fact, I got him the invitation."

"Why should you do that? Ferenc knows my cousin as well as you."

"Yes, it was very curious. Ferenc didn't want to call him. I haven't seen him since."

Nor have I, thought André, of his best and oldest friend.

Philippa looked at the Ghislaine watch on her elegant wrist. "I must fly." She began the business of extracting herself snakelike out of the curved seat. Then she stopped momentarily, eyes on the most distant part of the room. "André, have you any idea who the impostor was that Colonel Frère was talking about?"

"No, I haven't," said André, suddenly angry. He reached across the table and grabbed her escaping hand. "Have you?"

"Not a suspicion!" Eyes wide, the picture of innocence. "Darling, not an idea! André, you're crushing my poor little hand!"

"Why did you join together those two things?" said André coldly. "Ferenc? The impostor? Why?"

Philippa faced him with arched eyebrows. "Ouch!" she said distinctly. André let go of her hand. She stood then, slim, elegant, slipping on her gloves. "Ferenc has gone Israeli on us, hasn't he? Israeli. Arab terrorists. They go together, don't they? Good-bye, darling. It was sweet of you to take me to lunch."

She threaded her way out of the crowded restaurant, throwing little kisses here and there to the right people.

An hour later, André was seated opposite Colonel Frère in Frère's small office. The Colonel was building his edifice of pens, pencils, paper cutters. "Old Jacques has made things even more complicated. You'll find this hard to believe, but the interrogators think now that the man we followed in the car is not the real impersonator but a man impersonating the impersonator." Colonel Frère permitted himself a Gallic smile of exquisite irony.

André's heart was cold. "Have you any idea who ... either of them might be?"

"I thought you might help out there. Your foreign intelligence is much more complete than ours. Does your intelligence group have anything at all on the membership of"—Frère picked up a piece of paper and read from it, stumbling over the Hebrew—"Hamossad l'Tafkidim M'yuchadim?"

"Hypersecret counterterror organization. Surely you don't think the Israelis are mixed up in this. This is an Arab operation."

"Why would the Arabs want to plant a provocateur in a Hassimi bank that has had deep Arab financial and familial involvement for two hundred years?"

"Oh, my God, Frère, you know as well as I do there are Arabs and Arabs—two dozen factions, all cutting each other's throats."

Frère was stupefied by the passion of this denial. He said silkily, "Have *you* any idea who this impersonator might be, André?"

"No." He was in the grip of an acute clash of loyalties.

Colonel Frère let it drop. "What news from Damascus?" he asked.

"Selim Seleucid is dead. But not before Ashfi Hashad wrung his withers. They know who the girl is, and they know what Selim wanted her to do—and where. What they don't know—nor do we—is where she is now."

"The operation is Geneva? You're sure?"

"Fairly sure. And if it's Geneva, it's out of your territory, Colonel, though not out of mine."

"Not out of mine yet," said Frère grimly.

Jepthah said nothing about finding Ferenc as Ferenc, and not as François. The absence of comment was itself a shriek of disquiet, especially to Ferenc. Jepthah was not noted for chatter, but he would have noticed. He should have said something. He said nothing, munching on his roll, eyes on his plate. Nicole washed dishes in the tumult of silence that followed his arrival. He'd arrived five minutes before, walking from the bus stop. Nicole and Ferenc had been in the little kitchen only ten minutes themselves. Before that they'd been in bed. Had Jepthah arrived, perhaps, earlier and taken a spy around? Perhaps peeked through the bedroom window? It would be very like his cautious mate to circle the place, spy out the land, before making a public entrance.

Nicole gave Ferenc a look of concern and questioning. We're allies, are we? thought Ferenc in a spin of emotional confusion. Against Jepthah? My partner? Which one?

Jepthah sipped his coffee, eyes on the table.

"Did you have any trouble?" asked Ferenc finally.

"No," said Jepthah.

Silence again. After a bit, Nicole put the market basket on her arm. "I'll get the food for lunch and supper," she proclaimed at the door of the little farmhouse. Ferenc nodded, eyes on Jepthah, and she slipped away to St.-Germain-du-Bois.

The silence clung like early mist. "How's Tilsit?" asked Ferenc finally.

"He's all right."

It was like pulling teeth.

"Well, what did he say?"

"We're to wait. The Palestinians are at each other's throats. Let them kill each other for a while. When they stop, we wade in and help start the killing again."

Silence again.

"Would you like to take a walk?" asked Ferenc.

The two men walked up the wooded hillside to the point overlooking St.-Germain-du-Bois on the other side of the Saône. Ferenc flopped on the turf. Jepthah leaned against a tree, chewing at the inside of his face.

"What's going on between you and the girl?" Jepthah flung it at him like a Hebrew curse.

"There's only one bed," said Ferenc. "These things happen."

"How much does she know?"

"Nothing she didn't know before," said Ferenc. The lie clanking like steel in his mind. How can I explain to Jepthah? I can't.

"Tilsit says dump her—when you see fit."

Ferenc lay back flat on the grass and looked at the sky. "Do you know how to arm, aim, and maintain a Russian Grail rocket and launcher—and hit anything with it?"

"No."

"Neither do I. She does. We need her. At least until Tilsit makes up his mind what we do next."

Jepthah continued to chew on the inside of his face. He wasn't liking it, thought Ferenc. The hell with him! Am I changing sides? No, it was the only way. Jepthah was stupid about some things.

After a time, during which neither spoke, Ferenc said, "I had to take François Duvillard off. Colonel Frère has by now alerted all the flics in France for François Duvillard."

"I don't think so."

"It was my decision," said Ferenc harshly. "It's my hide."

Jepthah had no answer to that.

Presently the two of them went back to the farmhouse, walking well apart.

## CHAPTER *30*

It was an uncomfortable time.

They supped that night in pools of silence in which an occasional pebble of conversation was flung, making a few ripples. No more. They were all by nature silent people. Terrorists all. There was a tremendous mistrust in the air, a condition short of distrust. It was, instead, a misplaced trust, none of them knowing where their own loyalties lay, a state of emotional anarchy. It was not that they distrusted each other—although that lay just over the horizon—but that they distrusted their own judgment, their separate intelligences pointing them one way, their instincts another.

Nicole washed the dishes. The two men played gin rummy with ferocity. "Down for two!"—a snarl of defiance. Or: "Gin!"—a snarl of triumph. One way to release their feelings—a card game. Nicole watched the game at Ferenc's elbow, a blatant choosing of sides that made Ferenc even more savage in slamming the cards down. He hated being two against one. Against Jepthah, his comrade, his partner. He'd have hated it even worse if she had chosen Jepthah's elbow—or not chosen any. Emotional chaos. A game one couldn't win, thought Ferenc. But then had he ever had a winning hand in this game?

They listened to the news on the car radio. There wasn't any. At least there was none about them—about the disappearance of François Duvillard. About a Russian rocket. That was all right. Or perhaps it wasn't.

They resumed the game, Ferenc 1,100 points ahead. At 11:00 P.M. Jepthah rose from the table. "Continue tomorrow," he said briefly. "I'll sleep in the barn."

"Why?" asked Ferenc.

"The hay is more comfortable than a stone floor."

That was unanswerable. Jepthah departed.

Nicole and Ferenc were alone for the first time since Jepthah had come. They felt acutely embarrassed by this sudden freedom. Ferenc picked up the cards and put them away in their box. Nicole fiddled, putting away dishes that didn't need putting away. They went to bed unspeaking, stripping naked and climbing in swiftly because it was cold. It was a small bed, and the bodies couldn't avoid each other long. It took little contact to set them ablaze, and the kissing started, eyes closed. Like taking to drink, Ferenc thought in the brief seconds when he did any thinking, a postponement.

Afterward they lay coiled together—pretzels, not spoons. She opened her mouth to speak, and he closed it with a kiss. He put his finger against her lips and in her ear whispered, "Say nothing." Pointing vaguely barnward. Jepthah might very well be reconnoitering, hateful thought. Hateful because it meant his mistrust was growing into distrust. Even more hateful because it meant Jepthah's mistrust was growing into distrust, too. If he were reconnoitering.

Nicole put her lips against his ear and whispered so low he could barely hear, "I was only going to say I love you."

Ferenc grimaced. Into her ear he breathed, "He suspects. He mustn't *know*."

They lay then, nose to nose, eyes locked. "Does he know I know you're Israeli?" Into his ear hole. A bat couldn't hear it.

Ferenc shook his head. Into her ear hole: "I think he suspects. He mustn't *know*."

Because if he *knew*. . . . Ferenc didn't like to think about that.

In a whisper Nicole repeated the anguished question she'd asked before: "What are we to do?"

There was only one thing to do, and Ferenc did it. It was international, interdenominational, and nonideological. And exhausting. Afterward they slept.

Nicole woke at two. The silence of the French countryside at night. Nothing stirred. Ferenc breathed. That was all. She lay on the pillow, drinking in his face with her eyes. There was so little time. She memorized every line of it, every beloved curve of it. She was astonished with love. But clearheaded with love, too. There were tasks to be performed, notwithstanding love. In fact, because of love. Otherwise . . .

She slipped out of bed and into her clothes, silen' as a fish in water. Barefoot she crept out of the house and into the barn. Just inside the barn door she stood on naked feet and listened as only a terrorist can listen. She was listening for the sound of a sleeper's breathing, and in the stillness of the night there *must* be the sound of a sleeper's breathing or there must be no sleeper. There was no sound. Nicole stood motionless a full half hour. Only then did she risk her pencil flashlight. There was no one on the haystack, no one in the barn. She turned off the flashlight then and felt in the darkness for the rocket and launcher in the haystack. They had not been moved.

Nicole slipped out of the barn, hugging the shadows. She plunged silent as moonlight into the woodland, ducking from shadow to shadow, swiftly now, because there was no time, almost running. He'd be on foot, too, so she had to be careful. Even sticking to the shadows she made it to the village in ten minutes. There he was, where she thought he'd be, in the telephone kiosk. Getting his orders.

Nicole turned and fled, openly now, straight down the road, because she knew where he was, back to the farmhouse. Silently she stripped. She felt in her handbag and drew out the .38 automatic and slipped it under the mattress where it couldn't be detected, next to her pillow where she could get to it swiftly. Only then did she creep back into the warm bed.

Ferenc was rumbling with nightmares, thrashing and groaning. Nicole lay on her side, one arm under her head, watching, eyes huge. She wanted to be in his nightmares. Ridiculous. And harrowing.

When the groans grew fierce she clenched her teeth in an agony of sympathy, trying to share the pain, resentful of being left out. It grew insupportable finally, and she woke him up, holding his head to her breast ferociously. She kissed him and murmured endearments and caressed the horror-stricken body. But she didn't tell him about going to the village. One nightmare at a time, she thought.

The next morning the autumn sun burned like fire. The air was vibrant with the sound of mowing machines in the fields. Nicole fed the men rolls and coffee. The silence was ferocious. The men got out the cards, and Nicole swept the stone floor with the peasant broom made of sticks, watching Jepthah all the time from underneath her eyelids. It was autumn hot, and the little farmhouse with the stove lit was stifling. Nicole opened the door and leaned against the doorpost, looking like a French peasant girl with her broom in her two hands, fierce, independent, smoldering with some inner fire. I'm divided, torn, she kept telling herself, but the fact was she had never before felt so whole, so undivided. She loved making the coffee, washing the dishes, sweeping the floor, all the tiny domestic chores that stifle so many women. To Nicole they were a liberation from the drudgery of skulking about rooftops, shooting flics, being shot at. Oh, Nicole would have given her immortal soul to have spent the rest of her life right there in that tiny farmhouse sweeping floors with a broom made of sticks. What sentimental slush, she thought fiercely, I'd be bored out of my skull in a week. She turned and contemplated the two men, slamming down their cards with their war cries: "Down for six!" "Gin." Nicole's gaze focused on Jepthah. The enemy. It brought back to the surface of her mind the realities of her situation. She put away the broom and went into the little bedroom, and under the pretext of making the bed, slipped the .38 in her skirt band. Then she fastened a scarf over her black curls to make herself conform a little more closely to French peasant appearance. It was risky, making all these trips to the village, but she had to get to the post office.

"I'll get the food," she proclaimed to the card players, who didn't even look up.

In Paris at that very moment Frère was issuing an order to provincial police in a circle radiating from Geneva to be on the lookout for a group of two men and a girl. Any such grouping of strangers that was clearly out of place in any French village should be reported to police headquarters in Paris. There was a fairly accurate description of Nicole included, but the description of the two men was wildly misleading.

In the village Nicole scribbled a postcard, a long one, to the letter drop in Zurich. It had to be long because it had to contain the address and a post office box. In the post office she bought a postbox from the postmistress under the name Madame Ferrand, the name on her other passport, and paid for it. That way a glance at the box from the doorway would tell her whether a message had arrived. She wouldn't have to ask at the window. The letter, she thought, should be in Zurich the next morning. She had no way of knowing that Ashfi Hashad had wrung from Selim Seleucid the Zurich box number.

The tension in the cottage was so thick as to be almost audible. Everyone pursued his separate thoughts, and the trouble was each was thoroughly aware the others were doing this. No one met any-one's eyes, and this tore Nicole's insides. She wanted most desperately to look into her lover's eyes because she had been torn from the moorings of her dedication. Death was no longer an irrelevance. She was afraid.

Of Jepthah. Nicole had had time to examine the implications of that 2:00 A.M. telephone call on her walk to the village. If not about her, what then? Whatever it was, he was not sharing it with Ferenc. She was sure of that. They'd had plenty of time to talk when she was in the village. Intuition told her they had not.

After lunch the situation got worse. Ferenc arose from the table. "I'm going to the village," he announced.

"Is that wise?" asked Jepthah. "We should stay out of sight."

"I must find out," said Ferenc. Then he corrected himself. "We must find out."

"I'll stay here," said Jepthah, sweeping up the cards.

Nicole sought Ferenc's eye in sudden panic.

"You stay here, too, Nicole," said Ferenc.

Alone with Jepthah? So be it. She was a terrorist again, cool as spring water. Me and Jepthah. So be it. As Ferenc left the farmhouse she rose instantly and started clearing away, keeping her hands ready, never turning her back to Jepthah, who unconcernedly started playing solitaire on the wooden table. Nicole washed the dishes, her face half turned so that Jepthah was always in the corner of her eye. She could feel the .38 in her waistband. Where was his gun? His back was to her, and she inspected his whole frame, looking for bulges. It would be there somewhere.

She took off the apron and made a decision.

"I'm going for a walk," she announced, and slipped out of the farmhouse very quickly. She pelted for the safety of the barn—she didn't want her back to him any longer than necessary—and once around the corner of the barn, she watched the doorway of the house through a slit in the stones. Jepthah appeared in the doorway, his eyes questing. Nicole didn't hesitate. She tore down the hillside and crossed the Saône, soaking her legs to the knees, and disappeared in the woods. If he was going to saunter to the barn—and he wouldn't dare run because he didn't know where she'd gone—she'd be in the protection of the woods before he'd rounded the barn. She was better in the woods than he was. He was a city terrorist. She was a country girl.

She'd reconnoitered the woods very carefully for just such a pursuit, though not knowing it would be Jepthah she'd be fleeing from. But then so had he. She'd seen him glancing about, memorizing the best rocks to lie behind, the thickest trees to hide behind. She lay behind a clump of boulders, her eyes on the stream. Presently Jepthah appeared and crossed the Saône slowly and carefully. He doesn't suspect, thought Nicole, smoldering with fury. They underestimate us! He thinks I don't know. The .38 was in her hand, and she could have gunned him down, but she didn't want him in the stream. She didn't want him where there'd be questions. Up in the woods would be better, where she could hide the body.

She froze. He was looking right at her. No, above her. Over her head. She twisted around, concealing the gun instinctively. Fifty yards away two French peasants were standing, their eyes on her, dark, sullen eyes, full of questions. It was their gaze that had attracted Jepthah's attention, thought Nicole. If he was any sort of stalker, he would suspect she was lying there, attracting that brute stare. She held her finger to her lips and smiled at the two peasants. Make them think it's a game. Had they seen the gun? If so, the game was up. They stared at her a long, agonizing moment, then went back stolidly to chopping wood.

Nicole twisted her head back to look at the stream. Jepthah had disappeared. Damn! He was in the woods now out of sight, and he knew where she was, and she didn't know where he was. She'd lost her advantage.

Tilsit was being very genial, much too genial.

"How's Jepthah?" he inquired.

"Fine," grunted Ferenc. Why shouldn't he be?

"And the girl?"

"Okay." What was all this social chitchat?

"Have you searched the girl yet?"

"Searched . . ." Ferenc choked.

"She's got the instructions on her for that rocket. With those you won't need her, Ferenc. We've decided to complete her mission for her. It's Arab against Arab. Ashfi Hashad against the Young Palestine League. That's her mission. It's to our interest that she complete that mission, but she probably will mess it up completely. Anyway, she's hot—very hot. The Ashfi are wise to her, and they're looking for her. It would be much easier to complete the mission without her around our neck. I told Jepthah all this, Ferenc."

"Did you indeed?" said Ferenc, and hung up.

He left the phone booth running. Damn, he thought, if I'd only brought the car. It'll take a good ten minutes on foot. He left the village at a dead run, which attracted a great deal of attention because no one ever moved that rapidly in St.-Germain-du-Bois.

It was not the only thing that attracted attention. Two telephone calls to Tel Aviv had not gone unnoticed in the little telephone exchange, which had only two phone operators.

"You should report it to the police!" said Victoire in a blaze of excitement. She was blond and twenty-two.

"Hmpf," said Emma, who was forty-five and had been at the exchange for twenty-three years. She had herself thought of phoning the police, but now she couldn't. At least not while Victoire was there. It would smack too much of taking orders from that snip.

# CHAPTER *31*

Nicole ran like a frightened deer deeper into the woods, ducking from tree to tree, making no bones about noise. Not yet. She fled directly away from him because he had not yet had time to circle and come in at her rear, and she wanted to make sure he didn't have the chance, to use her speed now because he had the advantage of position. Anyway, he would be slowed by stealth; he'd be watching and listening. Let him see and hear her and see what he could do against her speed and those trees. Later the roles would change.

Six quick bursts of speed, six changes of direction, then Nicole went to ground like a fox. Crouched behind the bole of a huge sycamore, shoulders hunched forward, eyes bright, ears pricked. She'd changed from stalked to stalker. He would not now know where she was, and he couldn't blunder about as she had. It was quiet and hot in the woods. Sunlight dappled the forest floor. Listening intently, Nicole could hear the distant clatter of a threshing machine. She lay in the bracken with the .38 in her palm. A butterfly flew past her nose, and bees droned insistently. Overhead a bird twirred and chuckled. The air was clear as crystal and sparkled in her lungs like champagne.

She felt unutterably glorious. Everything in her raced—pulse, mind, heart. Fear had fled when she took to her heels, taking the initiative away from him. Kill or be killed. The greatest game of them all.

To her right, a sudden uproar of rooks, screaming in unison. Something had alarmed them. Coming from that way, was he trying to encircle her to her right? She slipped quickly, under the cover of the noisy rooks, to her own left, going from bole to bole, swiftly, not worrying about noise under the racket of the rooks but keeping low, very low. By the time the rooks had calmed, she had moved a full seventy yards in a gentle curve. She was behind a log now, listening and looking. He must be, she figured, about sixty yards away, lying to her right—and facing diagonally away from her. She was now encircling *him*, if her calculations were correct. But she couldn't count on that. They were very clever, the Israelis. It was not good to underestimate them. It was not good to lie in one place too long either. She listened and looked, listened and looked, head to earth, mouth opened. Nothing. He was listening and looking, too. Grounded. She moved like a wraith to her right, keeping low, clinging to the shadows, her mind sparkling. Her teeth bared in sheer feral pleasure as she crept through the bracken on hands and knees, stalking. . . .

The farmhouse was empty as Ferenc had expected, hoping he was wrong. He paused to catch his breath, leaning against the doorway, heart thudding. His eyes examined the ground. It told him nothing. Footprints going in every direction. Nicole would have taken to the woods, if she'd been given the chance. And if she hadn't been given the chance, Jepthah would have taken the body there. Ferenc closed his eyes, nauseated by the run—and by his thoughts. His brain beat like a pulse. The French police at our heels, the Arabs on Nicole's scent—and now Jepthah . . . We don't need this! Ferenc leaned on the doorpost, his eyes wild. He was nearly at the end of his emotional tether. He trotted, beat, around the barn, down to the water's edge, forded the Saône, and plunged into the woods.

After a hundred yards he came to rest, leaning on a tree. It was a

220 ·

big wood, and he had no idea which direction they'd taken. Then came the uproar of rooks. Dead ahead. Ferenc plunged on grimly, bolt upright, making no effort at concealment.

In the vast police headquarters on the Ile St.-Louis in Paris, the first reports of unusual trios of two men and a girl seen in villages in a semicircle around Geneva were beginning to come in. Or rather pour in. There are lots of villages in the semicircle outlined by Colonel Frère, and so suspicious is the French provincial mind that in almost every last one a trio of dubious nature, just answering the police description, had been sighted. A corpulent police sergeant of too many years on the force began leisurely sifting through them. Two men and a girl in a tent at St.-Abbas-sur-Jourville. What fun! thought the Sergeant. Two men and a woman had checked into *one* room in Cruseilles where heaven knows what they were up to. The husband is watching, thought the Sergeant lecherously, while the wife performs with the other man. So it went, all these clues a more accurate reflection of the closed minds of French villages than of the presence of intruders—two men and a girl at a farm long deserted near St.-Germain-du-Bois. The girl looked Arab, but then the whole point was that the girl they were looking for didn't. Provincial police reading their own suspicions into the facts. Two men and a woman seen bicycling together in a very suspicious manner near Divonne. How did one bicycle in a suspicious manner? wondered the Sergeant, putting it on the pile with the others. . . .

In the great mansion on the shores of Lake Geneva, the man with holes for eyes was bent over a map of the airport. "She'll be in here somewhere, but it's a very large parking lot and we must guard every exit to see she doesn't get out. It would be best to plant our own people in there."

"That is what we must *not* do," said Lin Chiu gently. He sipped his tea affably and delivered a small lecture on the nature of counterterror. "Think of it as chess defense, rather than chess offense," said Lin in his unhurried tones.

They squabbled equably then about the nature of terror and counterterror, a very civilized argument about its proper place in society. Without losing sight of their immediate problems, they debated quite seriously—one Western man, one Oriental man—the *etiquette* of terror, the proper way to hold one's knife before inserting it, as it were.

In the end, the Chinese won the argument, not because he persuaded Fourchet of the rightness of his views but because he outranked him, which is how political arguments are usually won.

"Philippa, these things are under investigation. I can't tell you who the impostor was. . . ."

"Because you don't know," said Philippa, putting in two lumps. She always remembered how many lumps her former lovers took. "And I do."

Colonel Frère's nostrils flared. "Philippa, if you are withholding information from the police. . . ."

"Only intuitions!" Philippa smiled her most winning smile. "I don't believe that's illegal—withholding intuitions."

"I have no information about the purpose of the impostor," said Colonel Frère, sipping China tea from the Sèvres cup, his bottom perched on the very edge of the Louis Quinze chair in the enormous main salon of the Pinay household. "Only suppositions."

"But that's all I have," cried Philippa radiantly. "Let us put our suppositions together, Colonel, and just possibly we'll have the foundations of a working theory."

And what do you want a working theory for? thought Colonel Frère. Just to play with? A game. Perhaps the most deadly bourgeois game of all—finding out who was doing it to whom for the sheer pleasure of knowing, a full-time occupation to very many women in Philippa's social bracket. It was a status symbol to be the first to possess a bit of gossip, but then of course, Frère was aware, the whole thing was a game being played by governments and would-be governments for reasons of ostentation not much different from that of Philippa. It was a status symbol to blow up airplanes and grab headlines. The bigger the headlines, the greater the status.

Colonel Frère said carefully, "I suspect the impostor was a member of an Israeli counterterror organization."

Philippa was flooded with happiness.

"Ferenc," she said—and refilled the Colonel's cup.

Nicole's chin hugged the forest floor, her eyes questing through the fern, her body flattened on the earth. She was only inches high in the bracken, and she had a 50-degree arc of vision. Protecting her rear were her ears. If anything stirred back here, she'd hear it. Jepthah should be dead ahead if he had not changed position, but then he might very well have circled her a bit more than she allowed, say, 15 degrees at the outset. He must be in an arc of 20 degrees ahead and to her right. She listened.

*Cromp. Cromp. Cromp.*

Jepthah wouldn't be thrashing around like that. She couldn't shoot with strangers about. The *cromp* was approaching on a diagonal, as near as she could calculate. *Merde!* She couldn't lie indefinitely ass to ground. Jepthah would be circling, circling. Her whole strategy was based on superior stealth and, above all, superior speed. Her eyes, three inches off the earth, darted back and forth, back and forth, over an arc of 90 degrees. The *cromp* was closer now. That way.

Ferenc.

He was walking slowly through the trees, eyes on the forest floor, looking first this way, then that way. Searching. Searching for whom—me? Jepthah? No effort to hide. Bolt upright. And what to do? Call out? And let Jepthah know where I am? Let *him* call out!

Ferenc stopped now, slowly turning, his eyes examining every bit of ground on a wide arc. He stooped and inspected the earth. *Merde!* He's tracking! Me? Or Jepthah? Nicole lay breathless, watching through the fern. Ferenc had straightened now, his head bent almost straight down and moving slowly in an arc to her right. My trail? Or Jepthah's?

Hers. There could be no doubt. He was arcing in the very curve she had taken, following the fern and underbrush she'd crushed in her wake. Soon he'd be right over her—if she let him. She wouldn't let him. Jepthah was watching, too, she was sure of it. If she permitted Ferenc to seek her out, she'd be grounded. Jepthah would have dead aim, using Ferenc as a stalking-horse. Now, he didn't know where she lay. It would take a full two seconds for him to bring the gun up and around, after he'd recovered from the first shock. It was a game she'd played many times in terror school. Human reactions were limited in speed. If you flushed a partridge—or a human —it took a full second and a half for it to register on the mind and react to the muscles. Nicole had already picked her angle of flight.

She sprang out of the bracken, a blur of speed, at a 25-degree angle from Ferenc, crouching low, and disappeared headlong behind the bole of a great tree. The shot came, as she knew it must, from a bush ahead and about 10 degrees to her right, so she'd figured him almost exactly—and he hadn't figured her because the shot was a long time coming. She had no idea by how much he'd missed. But she knew pretty well where he was. He knew where she was, too. But not for long. The tree was now between her and Jepthah—but Ferenc was on her side. Her eyes now were pinned on Ferenc's anguished face, and his eyes pinpointed exactly where Jepthah was. She'd counted on this happening. When the shot came, she was absolutely certain his eyes would automatically go to the spot where the shot came from—and since he was upright he had a much better area of vision than anyone else. She had used Ferenc as a bird dog.

There was only one other thing, and she tensed for it. She watched Ferenc's mouth open. This was the minute distraction she needed.

"Nicole!" wailed Ferenc. "Jepthah!"

Before the second name had sounded, counting on the momentary paralysis following that first shattering call in the silent forest, Nicole sprang like a lynx straight at the bush behind which Jepthah lay hidden, the automatic spitting bullets ahead of her, her arm held straight out ahead of her, all eight bullets shattering the forest stillness.

Jepthah never had a chance.

Nicole stood near him, the empty gun at her side, her eyes stony. A splash of blood stained the fern. Jepthah lay on his back, eyes open, his face twisted with pain.

Ferenc was beside him in a rush, on his knees, his fingers feeling gently for the wounds.

Jepthah spoke in a husk of a whisper. "She's poison, Ferenc! . . . Her own people . . . They'll kill her . . . you, too. . . ."

A gurgle of blood through the mouth from the punctured lungs, and Jepthah died.

Then it was very still indeed in the forest.

Ferenc's mouth was twisted, his eyes blind, as if eagles were eating his liver. Nicole had never seen such torment on a face before, and he came from a people where woe was common currency, where grief was theatrical. But nothing like this. Ferenc's mouth hung awry like a gate off its hinges. His eyes were flecked with insanity.

She felt terribly alone, left out altogether in this desolation, as if he had no space left in his heart, even to blame her. It was a grief close to madness because what had happened had to happen. It had been in the cards all along, and Ferenc had prevented himself from knowing what he should have known only because he didn't want to face it—and that is the most unspeakable woe of all.

Ferenc unclenched Jepthah's fingers from the gun. He crossed the hands on the chest. With his kerchief he cleaned the blood from around the mouth. He smoothed the muscles of the face and closed the eyes and straightened the head. He put the legs together. Now Jepthah was in the attitude of a medieval knight, a figure in stone on a sarcophagus in a twelfth-century church.

Ferenc, on his knees, wept.

CHAPTER *32*

Colonel Frère picked up a photograph that had been face down on his desk. It was Ferenc in his French Army uniform. The Colonel looked at the photograph a long time, unable to make up his mind. He didn't trust Philippa across the street. Paying off a faithless lover, perhaps? Who knew what was in that subtle, viperlike brain? To issue a general alarm for this face on the basis of that woman's whims!

It was 1:00 P.M. and deathly still in the forest. It was the sacred hour of luncheon. The peasants were bent over their noon repasts in their cottages. The body had to be dealt with, and that was the best time to do it. Nicole kept watch from a fork in a tall tree that gave her a view of the village and of the two nearby farms. Ferenc returned with the farm spade and dug the grave under the fern. A shallow grave because there was not time for a proper one and he didn't want a great mound of earth. The foxes would be after it within a matter of days. A shallow unmarked grave. Then the foxes. What else could a terrorist expect?

Ferenc's mood had passed from a frenzy of grief into a sullen fury, largely at himself. He and Nicole had exchanged hardly a word. "I'll get the spade," he'd said. "I'll stand watch," she'd said. When the task was done, Nicole came down from her tree and helped to restore the forest floor to its innocence, putting little bits of humus over the blood spatters, erasing the signs of digging.

They walked single file back to the Saône, she leading. Ferenc followed, trying to hate her. He couldn't. He'd squandered his supply of emotion for that day.

Not so Nicole.

The elation of killing had ebbed, and now her lover had left her emotionally deserted in a desert of silence. He simply wasn't there. He was an empty room. It was desolation.

They made their way back to the farmhouse. He sat unseeing at the table. She stood, hands behind her back, eyes on him. But he wasn't there. If he'd rage or accuse, she thought, I could defend or explain. This nothing was unbearable.

She put her basket on her arm and went to the village. I have lost my way! I have lost my way! The thought was unbidden. But it came clamorously. I have been so overwhelmed with my lover that I have lost my way. I must find it again. She ritualized then. I am a dedicated member of the Young Palestine League, and I have been deflected from my aim by this effendi, this Israeli gunman. It is worse than a betrayal; it is stupid.

She was shuffling along in the dust, lips moving, eyes lost. So odd a spectacle that a policeman watched in amazement. Very peculiar. Headquarters had asked for strangers behaving oddly, and here was a stranger behaving very oddly indeed. But he had already written his report, and it had been scorned by Paris. He was not going to do it again.

The post office was next to the *épicerie*, and she glanced through the door at her box, expecting nothing.

There was a letter. She stared, astounded. How could that be? To get to Damascus and back so quickly. She opened the box with her key, took out the heavy letter, and almost scuttled out of the post office. A letter! A letter! In her emotional emptiness it was a sign from heaven.

It would be in code, of course, but the code book lay in her pocketbook. She couldn't wait to read it. She needed so desperately something to occupy her, to fill the desert of her mind. Quickly, almost maniacally, she walked to the tiny village square, sat on a park bench, and opened the letter. She brought out the code book openly, something she'd never have done if her emotional state had been less dire. Painfully, she began to decipher the message.

It was the arrival times of the planes to the peace conference in Geneva, all twelve of them. Day after tomorrow! So soon! I have forgotten! I am a traitor and a fool. I have a mission for my people who are in danger of being betrayed by this peace conference, in mortal peril of a treacherous compromise.

She became aware of Ferenc, his presence piercing to the very core of her new emotional fire storm. Ferenc was in the telephone booth next to the *épicerie*. Telephoning! Her lover! Her enemy! Nicole put the letter and the code book into her handbag. She took up a position next to the telephone box, listening to whatever she could hear, without making the slightest effort to conceal her presence from Ferenc.

"You hung up," said Tilsit. The voice all the way from Tel Aviv was steely. Perhaps it was the connection. Or perhaps not.

"A flic," lied Ferenc. "Listening. There's no privacy in this village."

"Where's Jepthah?" Tilsit's voice was solid ice.

Ferenc had not expected the question, and he committed an unpardonable error; he hesitated. "Back at the farmhouse," said Ferenc finally, the lie echoing in his brainpan like a tin drum.

A pause.

*Click.*

Ferenc's mouth fell open. He stared at the receiver, horrified. Tilsit had hung up. On him! Ferenc. He couldn't believe it. He didn't want to believe it. He jiggled the receiver handle ferociously. "Operator! Operator!"

"M'sieu?"

"We've been cut off."

*"Moment!"*

The operator went off in pursuit of the other operators on the long road from eastern France to Tel Aviv. Ferenc glanced at Nicole standing rigid beside the telephone box, glanced away, unseeing, uncaring. Cut off! That must be it. Tilsit would not have hung up on him because that meant . . . an enormity that Ferenc was simply not prepared even to speculate about. He'd been cut off, that was all. Some mechanical fault, no more than that.

From outside, Nicole, a steel ramrod, watched, divining much, so instinctual had she grown where Ferenc was concerned. Disaster had struck. She could tell in every lineament. She even guessed, brilliantly, what disaster.

The operator returned. "You have not been cut off, m'sieu. The other party has terminated the call. Do you wish us to get him back?"

"Yes."

He had to get Tilsit back because not to get him back was a desolation that could not be borne. Ferenc had turned his back on France and become an Israeli citizen without a frisson of feeling. He had embarked on counterterror almost lightheartedly. After Algeria, he had told Tilsit, there were no terrors. After Algeria there was no conscience. After Algeria nothing was unbearable.

Except this, being cut off from the organization. To the terrorist the organization is all—mother, womb, country. It is the source of instruction, information, faith, hope, to say nothing of money, arms, and shelter; it is the fountainhead under whose protection the most evil—cleansing evil, Ferenc had always said—deeds could be committed; it was the confessional, the Law, the Prophet, and the inspiration. Cut off from it the terrorist became mortal man, hunted, reviled. Worse, he became the victim of his own conscience. Ferenc had to get Tilsit back on the line if he was to rescue his immortal soul from perdition.

All of it showed on his face. He was a man without a country, without a God, as he listened to the ringing in Tel Aviv, 1,500 miles away. Ringing, ringing. He looked like a man possessed. Across the street, in the little park, the policeman watched the ravaged face of the man in the phone booth, the rigid body of the woman beside him. They were a strange pair, and if he had not already turned in his report, he would certainly have reported this peculiar behavior to Paris.

"No answer, m'sieu."

Ferenc strode from the phone booth like a block of wood, past Nicole, as if she were a tree.

In the telephone exchange, Victoire blurted, *"Three* phone calls to Tel Aviv. Surely the police should be told." Emma set her mouth stubbornly. The girl would be off duty in four hours. Then she would voice her own suspicions to the police.

He was seated by the plain wood table, rudderless. Like me, thought Nicole, before I got my mission. She put down the shopping basket and went to the barn, her mind seething. From the haystack she retrieved first the rocket, then the launcher. She wiped the wisps of hay carefully off them, placed them on the ground, and wriggled underneath the car. The launcher was the problem. It was so long it had to be slung inconspicuously from underneath. They might look under there but they probably wouldn't. If they looked, one had simply to shoot one's way out of the situation, that was all. She was very relaxed about such things, now that she had her mission. She found the toolbox and wired the launcher diagonally over the suspension but not interfering with it. The rocket she wired in the cavity made by the driver's seat. If it went off, well . . . She smiled grimly.

And now, Ferenc. He was basic to her plan because she couldn't drive.

She found him where she'd left him, staring at nothing, legs sprawling outward.

"We must get out of here," said Nicole. "It's too dangerous for us to stay here any longer." She sat next to him and took his two hands in both of hers and looked at him. "We have attracted the attention of the police, and that is dangerous."

"Yes, the police," said Ferenc. He uttered a jarring laugh.

"Ferenc!" said Nicole, not liking that laugh.

"I've been cut off," roared Ferenc. His fist crashed down on the table, making the coffee cups dance. "Do you know what that means?"

"Yes," said Nicole. "I know what it means."

"You shot him like a dog," howled Ferenc, "and now I've been cut off. Cut off! Cut off!"

"He was tracking me like an animal," stormed Nicole. "He shot first."

He cursed her in Hebrew; he shouted a flood of Israeli curses, obscenities, noises, opening the floodgates.

She responded coolly in Arabic, matching him curse for curse in her own tongue. They stood, the table between them, shouting in their respective languages, having their first quarrel. More than a quarrel, a thunderstorm, in which poured forth their separate chauvinistic rages, their frustrations, and their sexual entanglement in one long howl of bilingual fury.

Out of the proliferation of Israeli curses came the Israeli word for whore that even Nicole knew, and perhaps it was the very truth of it that stung. "I hate you," screamed Nicole, and flung herself across the table at him, fists upraised; then it became physical because the force of her rush upturned Ferenc and the table and they all went down in a heap. Ferenc in his fury struck out with his fist at her jaw. Her head went back sharply against the overturned table, and then Nicole lay still.

Ferenc lay on the floor next to her, breathing throatily, fury spent. Nicole looked twelve years old, a child cocooned in innocence. Ferenc studied her face as if it were all that was left for him on earth, as indeed it was.

Reason returned, and it is not always a blessing.

Ferenc picked Nicole up from the floor and put her on the bed. He stretched out next to her and tried to make order of his anarchic situation. Tilsit had cut him off. That meant Tilsit had known or guessed about Jepthah. How had he done that? He must have ordered Jepthah to ring in by a certain time—and when he hadn't, Tilsit knew something had happened and that I was lying. If I'd said he was injured or even that he was dead, I'd have managed, but when I said he was at the farmhouse, he knew. That and my hanging up on him before. Oh, yes, he knew.

They'd come after him. He wouldn't be allowed to wander loose, not with what he knew. He had to be silenced. Ferenc knew that. It's too dangerous for us to stay here long, Nicole had said, and she couldn't know how dangerous it was. She had been cast out, too. Outcasts, both of them.

He became aware that her eyes were open, looking at him mournfully. He put his arms around her then because she was all he had left to put his arms around.

"We are like little children," he said ironically. He felt like François Duvillard again, experiencing total cynicism, which left him free of earthly anxieties. "You know François Duvillard—the man I was playing—was a multifarious fellow, far more complex than I ever was. He taught me many things, much good it will do me now, but one thing he practiced like religion was freedom from commitment. He found commitment itself—any commitment—a sin, in fact the only one. Everything he did was a noncommitment. He was betraying France, uncommitting himself to his country, by relaying her banking secrets to that Russian smoothie, Serge Vassily, and betraying Vassily by informing on him to André de Quielle, and at the same time uncommitting himself to his family—a very important uncommitment in France."

Nicole listened, uncomprehending, as if he were talking Greek. "I have my mission," she whispered stubbornly.

"Oh, yes, your mission!" said Ferenc ironically. "Your mission is my mission. My camel is your camel. Lead on, my prophetess."

Nicole didn't like this irony. She didn't understand.

"What is your mission?" asked Ferenc.

"To blow up an airplane," she said defiantly.

"Oh, yes, of course. That was my mission, too." He looked at her tenderly. Should he tell her she was an outcast, too? We are doomed, my little Arab, he was thinking, but why say it aloud? He felt infinitely tender, playful almost, removed totally from all commitment. Except to her? Well, that was not commitment exactly. That was purest pleasure in the François Duvillard sense (except that François Duvillard didn't like girls, but it was in the way he would take girls if he did like girls). Ferenc kissed the delicious Arab girl as François Duvillard would have tasted a peach—for purest pleasure.

She struggled weakly. "We must not do this now, Ferenc. We are in the most awful peril."

"But that is the greatest pleasure of all," said Ferenc—or François Duvillard—playfully, ironically. "In a moment of almost total peril. Because then the senses are most completely awake!" He undressed her, talking this way, lightly, caressingly, bewitching her, hypnotizing her.

She listened, drowning in this heresy, a butterfly on a pin. Her valiant lover, she thought, misunderstanding everything, to dare to love in the face of the most terrible dangers. She fell in love again, totally, hopelessly, bottomlessly, for all the wrong reasons (as if there are any right ones). And he fell in love, too, totally and without reservations, because he had been torn from this moorings and what else was left?

It was passion beyond passion, wonderment and surcease everlasting. Well, not quite everlasting.

Nicole awoke first, flooded with the immediacy of danger—as if she could almost taste it. Her eyelids blinked open, and she was gripped instantly by terror. Darkness had fallen, and that increased her feeling of dread. She woke Ferenc, if only not to be alone in this pool of dread. He shared it instantly as if they were one.

"We must flee this place, Ferenc," she said.

"Yes," said Ferenc.

They dressed quickly, silently. Ferenc picked up his black bag with his gun, his passport, his money. She dropped the .38 that had torn Ferenc's world apart that afternoon into her handbag. Minutes later, without speaking, they crept out to the barn, circling it first for enemies and intruders. Inside, Nicole knelt and showed Ferenc the rocket and the launcher, suspended from the car. He nodded. They climbed in without a word, and Ferenc backed the car out of the barn without lights and drove it to the main road. There he drove without lights for half a mile until he couldn't see a foot ahead of him. Only then did he switch on the headlights. At the next junction he turned off onto a tiny track well off the beaten way but still pointing toward Geneva.

## CHAPTER 33

"*That* woman!" sobbed Philippa. "Of all women."

Robert Pinay sat in the small Du Roc armchair in the Pinay salon, watching this demonstration blankly. He was too old for circuses. Philippa accusing him of infidelity! It was like a lion accusing a lamb of ferocity.

"My dear," he remonstrated gently, "your lovers would fill Napoleon's Tomb twice over."

"She was found hanging in prison," sobbed Philippa.

"Yes, it was too bad," said Robert, his bland stare uncomprehending. "Still . . ."

"She had betrayed France," said Philippa, as if she were singing the "Marseillaise." "And you helped her."

"Oh," said Robert, a long "oh," comprehending finally why he was being discarded, feeling at the time a stab of fear. Philippa had some information he didn't have, obviously. She was not one to walk

234 •

out lightly on wealth and position. But if the position were threatened, she'd be off the mark very fast because afterward it would be more difficult. One couldn't desert a husband who was down without losing almost more than one gained. But to desert a husband just *before* the ax fell, ah, that would be widely admired, even when completely understood.

"Oh, well," said Robert Pinay suavely, not giving away anything at all, "there are betrayals and betrayals, aren't there?"

Colonel Frère was philosophical: "The fact is, my friend, that the Arabs practice terror from conviction with great glee—and do it badly. The Israelis are idealists who practice terror reluctantly, but with great skill. It presents them with a moral dilemma. They do something well that they'd rather not do at all, whereas the Arabs do extremely badly something they would give their souls to do well."

The Colonel was in full flood, trying to soften up André. "The perfect terrorist, in short, would be one with an Arab conscience and an Israeli intelligence. Then you would get the will and the idea perfectly blended—and God help us all if that should happen."

"Colonel Frère," said André, "entirely apart from Ferenc, do you think it conceivable that an Israeli man and an Arab girl could collaborate on anything, much less a terror mission?"

"We have considerable reason to believe that an Israeli man and an Arab girl are together, for what reason we don't know. But we both know there is enormous dissension in the ranks of the Palestinian terror movements, and it is certainly conceivable that Hamossad l'Tafkidim M'yuchadim would do everything it could to exploit these divisions."

"You're dreaming," said André stubbornly.

It was almost the end of the camping season in the mountains, and the Camping Marbouche was delighted to find one last customer for their bungalows before closing up for the winter. The idea of holing up in a camping bungalow rather than a hotel, which the French police keep under surveillance far more completely, was Ferenc's. He was French and he knew about the French passion for *le camping*, which no Arab girl could imagine. It was more than the *coup d'intelligence israélienne* which Colonel Frère so feared; it was a *coup d'intelligence française* because Ferenc was thoroughly French. The last place the police would look for them would be a campsite.

They were bent now, unlikely conspirators, over a map of the Geneva airport. "There," said Nicole, "is where *they* want me to stand. Parking lot six. You can easily understand why. There is a clear line of fire to the approaching aircraft—and it is the only one of the seven parking lots that has it. You can also see why they wish me there. It would obviously have the heaviest security there. I could shoot down the airplane, and I would be immediately gunned down myself—mission accomplished, and me out of the way."

They were seated in the tiny, scrupulously clean kitchen of the little camping bungalow, the map stretched out on the Formica table between them. The refrigerator gleamed, the stainless-steel sink glistened, everything shone. Ferenc looked at the dark, passionate head bent over the map. "And where do you propose to mount your attack instead? Every other parking lot is shielded from the field by buildings."

"I would not like to be in a parking lot at all. I would like to be on a roof."

Ferenc uttered a sharp bark of laughter. "Yes, I imagine you would. Every roof will be covered with security guards. The Swiss are insane about roof security."

"There are many roofs," said Nicole stubbornly. "Look at that one—hangars for business and private airplanes."

"How do you propose to get up there?" said Ferenc ironically, in his François Duvillard manner, playfully.

Nicole unfolded her Arab urchin smile as broad as an umbrella and wrapped her brown arms around his head. "You are so much brainier than I am," she whispered, "and you have seen so much more of the world. I count on you, my bold, brilliant Israeli lover, to come up with a plan that will outwit those stolid Swiss burghers."

It's as if we're discussing strategy for a game of billiards, thought Ferenc, his lips on those satiny arms. He found himself admiring her total absence of conscience in this matter of gunning down an entire airplane. "And why should I do *that, chérie?*" murmured Ferenc, kissing the brown arm because it was there.

"Because we are shooting down Arabs, *chéri*, not Israelis, and

236 ·

that should make you radiant with happiness, my love, my heart, my blade, my own." She kissed him on the lips, holding his head between her two hands, in a hurricane of bliss. Could there be anything on earth so wonderful as planning the massacre of 126 of her country's enemies with her beloved Ferenc!

Oh, yes—oh, yes, thought Ferenc, a rudderless ship. If I did that, perhaps Tilsit would speak to me again—knowing full well that it would not happen. Not now, not ever. But because hope springs eternal—besides, what else was there to do, now that he had been cast adrift in the arms of this bewitching urchin?

"I have an idea," murmured Ferenc, afire now with passion. "But later."

Nicole struggled weakly. "We haven't much time, Ferenc. It's tomorrow! It's tomorrow!"

"I know," said Ferenc. "We haven't much time. That's why we had better not waste it with talk."

Afterward, they lay in a sea of contentment in each other's arms, the very desperation of their predicament contributing to their happiness.

"Do you think you have a plan that will work?"

"Yes."

"My angel!" She kissed him. "Do you think we will survive it?"

"No."

"My angel." She kissed him again, and they both laughed.

Because of course neither of them really believed they would expire on the morrow. No one ever does.

"Chérie," said Ferenc playfully. "Don't you find it odd that our missions coincide, that you and I can so cheerfully collaborate on extinguishing a hundred and twenty-six people—our aims and arms and lips united in joy?"

"Insha-Allah!" murmured Nicole rapturously.

"The will of God?" said Ferenc incredulously. "He must be a very peculiar God, your God."

"It is not good to question the will of God. You will get us into trouble." Her eyes were sparkling.

We are in a state of hysteria, decided Ferenc. Nothing else could explain this euphoria. Euphoria over what?—a massacre of 126 people, followed probably by our own? Why is this cause for rejoicing? Both of us rapturous. Wouldn't François Duvillard be enchanted, wherever he is. Ferenc enfolded the delicious brown body in his arms. I must be insane, he thought; it's because I've been cut off, I've been cast aside. I'm in a state beyond shock.

I've heard this is what happens to people when they enter prison. Stripped of everything—their goods, their fair name, their freedom—they feel a delicious euphoria—because they float in an irresponsibility they have not known since they left the womb.

Colonel Frère played his trump card.

"There are six planes arriving at Geneva tomorrow, any one of which could be the target. There is a planeload from the Young Palestine League, which are a bunch of wild-eyed fanatics stuffed with oil money who hate Ashfi Hashad and are hated in return. There is a planeload of Israeli specialists on their way to the peace conference. Both top secret . . ."

"What do you want of me, Colonel?" asked André harshly.

"I want you to go to Geneva and prowl around that airport looking for Ferenc, your old friend."

"And if I find him?" asked André.

"Just say *bonjour,*" said Colonel Frère.

Ferenc bought the Land Rover from a dealer in Marbouche, a transaction that would not reach police ears until long after it was all over, and paid from Nicole's great wad of French francs. From Camping Marbouche he rented a trailer, a tent, a camping stove with bottled gas, folding tables, chairs, and all the other debris the French find indispensable to camping. Nicole bought food, lots of it, enough for a week of intensive camping, and they both shopped for camping clothes, heavy sweaters and boots and socks. Nicole put the lot in the camp washing machine, boots and all, and when it came out it was all suitably aged.

They packed the rocket launcher at the very bottom, crosswise in the trailer, and over it came all the camping kit. At the bottom of this array the rocket launcher looked like just another bit of gear. Ferenc left the Peugeot sitting on a side street in Marbouche where sooner or later someone would find it, not nearly soon enough.

They left at dawn, dressed in their camping clothes, and crossed the border into Switzerland at St. Loup, where a sleepy French customs official paid scant attention to the campers. They were well into the mountains west of Geneva, and by 9:00 A.M. they had made camp in the woods on a little plateau away from the road. They had a bit of time to kill, and much still to do.

CHAPTER *34*

Colonel Frère showed his photograph.

"Ah," said the Swiss Inspector Verlag, studying the close-cropped curly hair, the almond-shaped face, the huge black eyes. "The international face. It is astounding how many faces there are like that now—French, German, Hungarian, even American. You might say that all seventeen-year-old girls—the pretty ones—look like that at some time. Later the girls become their nationality—French, Spanish, Swiss, whatever—but when they are seventeen, *that* is their nationality."

"She's an Arab—from Damascus," said Frère.

They were in an office in the main terminal, the jets screaming in at intervals, but it was quiet behind the double-glazed windows.

"There are six planes today that might be the target, all somehow involved with the Middle East, either coming from there or having something to do with the conference," said Verlag. "But you realize that with terrorists anything at all could be the target—women and children, Olympic athletes, innocent bystanders, they shoot anyone."

"The plane is the target," said André, speaking for the first time. "The motivation behind the deed is exceedingly complex. We think one set of Palestinian terrorists might be shooting down another set of Palestinian terrorists in a test of strength."

"On Swiss soil?" said Inspector Verlag in tones of horror.

"You will insist on holding these peace conferences here," said Colonel Frère.

"It's our third biggest industry," said Inspector Verlag. "Money is our biggest, and skiing is the second. Cuckoo clocks are well down the list now." The Swiss had simmered in quiet Swiss fury over that wisecrack by Orson Welles in *The Third Man* for twenty-five years.

The crisscross of political intelligence that day was truly remarkable. Israeli intelligence passed on the story that Serge Vassily had been dealing with an impostor in Paris (not saying that it was an Israeli impostor) to the CIA in return for some of the CIA spy plane and satellite favors during the late Arab unpleasantness. Armed with this, a CIA operative had a little talk with Serge Vassily, who was persuaded that defection was a good deal better for his future than Siberia. President Sadat told Qaddafi personally by telephone that if the Libyans couldn't hang onto their missiles better than they'd been doing, there'd be no more, Sadat himself having caught hell from the Russians for letting Qaddafi have such dangerous toys in the first place. The Saudi Embassy discovered that the money it was supplying the Young Palestine League was being spent in China on Trotsky-ites, a heresy almost beyond imagining to the feudal Arabians, and that source of money was cut off, sending the Young Palestine League a few weeks later into the arms of the Russians, who were far stingier with their money and far more particular on how it was spent. In Beirut the Popular Front Deputy Leader Yezid Alwah drew up plans to kidnap the Saudi Ambassador in London and pin it on Yasir Arafat, who, the other guerrilla organizations felt, was getting far too much oil money, to the detriment of the rest of them. On a higher level, Henry Kissinger was offering to clear and widen the Suez Canal in exchange for Syria's throat, diplomatically speaking, of course. And the Russians were pushing Assad of Syria into greater activity in the Golan Heights, if only to tarnish Kissinger's image as peacemaker.

Ferenc drove the Land Rover west on the mountain road, picking up the lake at Montreux, and drove down the north shore because the south shore lay in France. They wouldn't expect them to come from the east. Inside the cab on the floor, behind the heavy curtains, Nicole cleaned and loaded her .38, which had remained dirty since she had shot Jepthah. She inspected Ferenc's two .45s to see that they were clean and loaded. Murderous things, she thought, with a quiver of distaste. You didn't have to blow a person to bits, after all, just kill him decently dead. After that she lay back, full length, her head on a folded blanket, and studied the back of Ferenc's neck as if it were a secret garden of delight, memorizing every hair. She was in a state of sexual shock, not such a bad thing considering their destination. She considered their destination, rehearsing it emotionally, testing herself for the tremors. It was the paralysis of fear that was the dread of all terrorists, which is why they operate in groups. Where one man might seize up, a group never did, so powerful is social feeling. One is truly more afraid of disgrace than death among one's peers. With a lover the feeling was even more powerful. In fact, anesthetic. She felt nothing in her midriff, the seat of terror.

I'm a fool, she thought, trying it out for emotional content; I will be dead in three hours—no, four—torn apart by bullets, probably very painfully, and what do I feel? Nothing but elation, not in spite of it, but because of it. Ferenc says that at seventeen I am too young to comprehend death, which is why I inflict it so lightly. This is why, he says, all armies are composed of young people, and terrorist activists are younger yet. In Ireland, he says, the IRA is using children now, and of course children were being used in Vietnam on both sides for a long time. He is very wise, Ferenc, and very brave because he is not young and it hurts him to kill people. He was brought up to think it wrong, evil, all of that. Whereas I—well, I wasn't actually brought up in the sense that he was brought up. I was brought up to think there was only one wrong and that was Israel who expelled us from our land and who murdered our people, and here I am in love with an Israeli and how can I possibly not be torn by self-revulsion over that?

I should kill him, as I killed Jepthah. I could do it easily from right here, but why? We'll both be dead soon enough. Even that thought, the death of Ferenc, her lover, her prince, didn't disturb the elation. Death has no reality. It's like discussing the universe, billions of stars, billions of miles apart. You can't comprehend that. You know it's true because they say it is. But death! I am so full of life I cannot comprehend not being alive. It's impossible, death, a figment of someone else's imagination—a thought so comical that she uttered a bleap of laughter.

In the driver's seat Ferenc was concentrating hard on practical details, running over the plan bit by bit to see if he'd left anything out. By God, he thought, we might even manage it and get away clean. Right there, reality closed in. Get away where? To blow up a planeload of Arab terrorists and lay the blame on another bunch of Arab terrorists would be no mean coup, just possibly enough of a feat to win Tilsit's forgiveness for Jepthah, but the only way he could reenter that gate was to take his gun and blow a gaping hole in a curl-framed face—and right there, imagination boggled. Ferenc went back to reviewing more mundane details of the immediate plan, looking for holes. There were plenty of them.

He glanced at his watch. Noon.

The long sleek chartered 707 screamed its way to the main terminal and then whistled to a halt. Inside was a mixed bag of Arab diplomats and Palestinian characters of varying shades of respectability. Ibrahim Salid, the bedouin intellectual, was there, in converse with Sheikh Akbal of Kuwait and the Algerian Ambassador to Beirut. Across the aisle and barely on speaking terms were the Arab League leader Hassam Arfallah and two of his best men. Hassam was, by diplomatic standards, a firebrand, but by Selim Seleucid's lights a dangerously, almost treasonably moderate Palestinian, a man who spoke of compromise where there should be no compromise. This whole planeload of Arabs, though the differences among its 126 occupants were immense, represented compromise, any form of which was treason in the eyes of the extreme left of the Palestinian liberation movement.

When Hassam Arfallah stepped out on the gangway, he was amazed. "München," he said to his companions. "Why are we in

München?" The others were equally astounded. It was only when they were herded into the VIP lounge that Sheikh Akbal explained. "We are being held over for security reasons. A conspiracy has been discovered to attack this airplane. We are being held here while countermeasures are being employed against the terrorists."

# CHAPTER 35

"We wish to hire a plane," said Ferenc pleasantly to the young man at the desk marked Inquiry. He had changed into tweeds and looked, he hoped, rich. They were in a flat edifice almost a mile distant and at right angles to the main terminus. Outside the plate-glass doors at the rear of the building Ferenc could see a Lear jet warming up. What a terrible life the rich lived! All those possessions one must constantly use, or what are they for? How exhausting! I'm thinking like François Duvillard, and this is no time for aestheticism; this is the time to be Ferenc, master terrorist—and even *that* thought is too much Duvillard. No time for irony. Terror is not a humorous business.

"You can't mean today?" said the young man with subdued astonishment. He was accustomed to the vagaries of the rich, and Ferenc had counted on this. "The planes are booked well in advance."

"Indeed," murmured Ferenc, counting out Swiss 100-franc notes. "We thought there might be a cancellation and that a person in a position of central responsibility like yourself would be sure to know where the cancellation might occur." Ferenc had counted out ten 100-franc notes, which he folded carefully and then put carefully into the young man's palm and closed it over the notes. Ferenc and Nicole had not one but four plans—A, B, C, D—and they were going to try them all simultaneously, settling on whatever promised to work best. This was plan B.

"I'm not sure . . ." said the young man. "You mean immediately?"

"Not quite immediately," said Ferenc. "These things take time, I know. But by four this afternoon, before the light begins to fail, we wish to be off. The young lady and I wish to go fishing." The inflection indicated that the last thing in the world they were interested in was fishing.

"You have a destination?" said the young man, gripping the comfortably solid wad of notes more firmly. "One must have a destination."

"Lugano," said Ferenc pleasantly. Lake Lugano was no great distance from Geneva Airport as the crow flies, but a crow could never get over those mountains. Nor could you get there in a hurry by any known means of conveyance—road, rail, pogo stick—except light airplane. It had a little field for the Lear jets of the millionaires who lived on the lake. "The fishing, I hear, is excellent."

The young man looked at Nicole, who stood a little apart, wrapped in enigma, her best uniform. This man was too old for her, thought the young man, but they got all the young ones. Glamour and money. "There are six private plane companies. If you'll just have a seat. . . ."

He indicated the row of banquettes opposite his reception desk and picked up the telephone. Ferenc sat on the banquette and stared idly out the plate-glass window. He could barely see the main runway where the big jets came in. The building they were in was entirely for private business planes and light charter craft. These took off from a grass runway on the other side of Geneva's single northeast-southwest runway. A long, long taxi. Still, they might manage it.

The young man was on the telephone now. Reconnoitering for plans A and C, Nicole drifted dreamily right out of his line of vision toward the stairs. There was no one about. She climbed the open unbalustraded very modern Swiss staircase to the second floor, which was the top. She wandered down the corridor past charter offices with glass doors. No one paid any attention. The staircase leading to the roof was at the end of the corridor. Nicole ducked up it swiftly. There was a glass door leading to the roof, and through it Nicole counted three security guards. Insane about roof security, Ferenc had said. They were indeed. She scuttled down the staircase and prowled the corridor in search of the ladies' room. Ladies' room frequently had very good views. The second-floor ladies' room didn't. It faced east, and while you could see the main runway by craning your neck, you could not possibly fire a Grail rocket from that angle and hit anything.

Nicole descended to the first floor and found the ladies' room there in exactly the same position. Damn! So much for plans A and C. She returned to the main lobby. There she found Ferenc in conversation with a grim-faced Swiss. He had the wad of notes out again, but this time it didn't seem to be working so well. The Swiss were almost immune to bribery; they were too rich to be corruptible, thought Nicole indignantly. No country should be permitted to have so much money that it scorned it. It made a mockery of socialism, she thought furiously.

Ferenc had on his cool, ironical look, and he was putting away his money while still talking, showing him something else. The Swiss seemed to be slightly less imperturbable. He bowed from the waist, slightly but deferentially, and went away.

Nicole approached Ferenc, wearing her most *jeunesse dorée* look—young, spoiled, beautiful, vaguely sullen. "The loo is out," she said, low, because the young man was thirty feet away still, though occupied on the phone. "Wrong angle. The roof teems with flics."

They sauntered then to the plate-glass wall at the rear and looked out at the parked private jets. "He didn't seem to like the money," murmured Nicole. "What does he like?"

Ferenc stared out stonily. "Snobbery. I showed him one of my better passports. I'm Prince de Marignac, one of the oldest families in France. He'd know all about that. All Swiss are hotel men at heart, serving the old European aristocracy. He's going to see if a plane can be arranged."

He looked very handsome, her Ferenc, thought Nicole, staring out of this plate-glass window, so bored, so languid, at a moment when life was anything but boring.

"You're the Prince de Marignac," said Nicole, "but who am I? Brigitte Bardot?"

"No! No! You're the Marquesa de Cabriol, a Spanish girl who is someone else's wife, which is why we are in such a hurry."

*"Merde!"* said Nicole bitterly. "I'm a revolutionary. I'd rather you pass me off as a chambermaid."

"Oh, some Spanish aristocracy is very left," said Ferenc soothingly. "Haven't you heard of the Red Duchess?"

"If we can't use the roof or the ladies' loo, what then? Plan B or D?"

"A bit of both," murmured Ferenc lightly. "It's not the way we were trained to operate, but it's not such a bad way. It's very difficult to spike a plan we haven't yet fully formulated ourselves."

The Swiss was back now, still deferential. *"Monsieur le Prince,"* he said. "You understand security is very tight because of the peace conference."

"Oh, yes," said Ferenc.

"It will be necessary for monsieur to show himself to the police at the main terminus. I'm very sorry."

"Oh, bother!" said Ferenc, as if it were the most minor annoyance. "But it would not do for the Marquesa to be seen with me, you understand."

"Of course. The Marquesa can stay here."

Nicole listened with a sinking heart. She didn't like it. "If you'd let me have a few words with the Marquesa," said Ferenc.

"Certainly, m'sieu." The Swiss moved away.

"Calm down," said Ferenc. He could see the rising panic in her, and this would never, never do. "They don't know my face, only François Duvillard's. By this time they may very well know yours. I'll be back as soon as I've finished."

"I don't like it," said Nicole. "I don't like it one bit."

"We're past the point of no return," said Ferenc. "We must go forward, unless we cut and run, and where would we run to?"

"I don't like it."

"Have you any other suggestions?"

"What will I do while you're over there?"

"Get the gear on the plane. I've told them it's our fishing tackle and you want to handle it yourself. I'll take the car and leave you here with the trailer."

"Improvisation," said Nicole bitterly. "I don't like it. The great virtue of the plan was we avoided the main terminus where all the flics are while this got us into the airport from the back door. Now you are going in the front door."

"We have no choice."

They were facing each other.

She looked like a distraught elf, thought Ferenc, her lips and eyes all round *O*'s. "We haven't much time," he said gently, and kissed her, a not implausible bit of show for the young man behind the desk. He took her by the hand and led her out of the building. Together they climbed into the Land Rover and drove around the hangar to the concrete apron where the Lear jets were—and the Apache twin-engine they were chartering. They met the young pilot named Kenneth Rivers and shook hands. He and Ferenc unhitched the trailer from the Land Rover.

Nicole picked up the "fishing tackle," now in its canvas covering. The rocket was stowed in the launcher now. All one compact piece. They were at the very bottom of the airport complex, at the very end of the single Geneva runway. Automatically, Nicole made her mental calculations. The *piste bétonée pour l'envol* was 3,900 meters long, and from where they stood about 150 meters farther than that. The rocket's range was 3,500 meters, and it was not very accurate at extreme range. They would have to move up sharply, preferably a whole kilometer closer than this.

"I'll be back as soon as I can," said Ferenc. He leaped into the driver's seat, spun the Land Rover around, and shot around the edge of the hangar. Nicole followed him with her eyes, feeling intolerably alone in this vast open space at the end of that long runway.

The young pilot was stowing the gear in the baggage compartment. "Would you like to put that in with the luggage?" he asked.

"No," said Nicole.

He flicked a glance at her and then looked away, reluctantly. He had heard the scuttlebutt already. A young married Marquesa running off with a French Prince. It turned him on fiercely; young adultery is a powerful aphrodisiac to innocent bystanders, acting like the smell the lower vertebrates emit in heat.

"There's a coffee shop inside, Marquesa," he said, "if you'd like to . . ."

"No," said Nicole abruptly. She moved away from the plane, the rocket and launcher slung over her back like a golf bag and looking not unlike one, its thirty-pound weight tugging at her shoulder.

The young man looked cast down, then slightly mutinous. Nicole decided she'd better quell that. "I like to watch airplanes," she said.

"You're not supposed to be wandering around on the apron," said the young pilot, sullen now at the put-down. "There's a big security alert here. Because of the peace conference."

"How exciting!" said Nicole. "Will they shoot me if I wander too far?"

"They might. There are police up there." He pointed to the hangar roof. "The Swiss Army is all over the field. The Jordanian mission arrived without proper clearance the other day. They made them land over on the grass there. Troops surrounded the plane and kept them there until they were all screened. The Swiss don't like Arabs much."

Nicole gave her silvery *jeunesse dorée* laugh. "Nobody likes an Arab—except another Arab."

"They don't even like each other much," said the young man.

In the main hangar Ferenc had a bad half hour with the Swiss police. They had set up a procedure designed to catch terrorists, full of snares and hard questions, and they seemed instead to have caught a philanderer with someone else's wife. They didn't like it, but they didn't quite know what to do with it. They could clamp down and forbid the charter, but the trouble was—the breakdown point in all too-rigid police procedures, which almost invariably succeed in doing exactly the opposite of what is intended—that they had, in an excess of caution, already clamped down for hazy reasons on a score of charter flights that had turned out to be entirely innocent. The charter operators were screaming murder. The police therefore were reluctant to bang down the lid again without reason, on simple suspicion. They had no reason. Ferenc carried off the swindle with his best François Duvillard manner: He was merely running off with another man's wife—something that happened every day even in staid Switzerland. Grimly they stamped the precious seal on the papers in quadruplicate.

Ferenc left the police office, trying not to look as if he was in a hurry. They had chewed up half an hour of his precious time, and it had taken him half an hour to get there and find the office. He looked at the airport clock, 3:20 P.M. Forty minutes to touchdown. Twenty minutes, at least, to get the Land Rover out of the parking lot and back to the private plane hangar. *Merde!* He strode down the corridor and skipped down the stairs rapidly and out across the great main hall of the airport building, full of travelers arriving and departing. Full also of police and security men.

"Saul!"

He had almost run into her, a slim, pretty Swissair hostess, smiling just like in the ads. Saul! Who the devil was Saul and who was. . . . But he knew he knew her.

"Darling, it's Ariadne!" she said. "Don't you remember me, you naughty man? You never called me."

He smiled mechanically. "Ariadne," he said. "How very nice!" Good God, the Swissair hostess he'd spent the night with, whose name wasn't Ariadne any more than his was Saul.

"I've been back to Tel Aviv three times. But no Saul." She made a little mouth to show how sorry she was.

"I'm sorry, love. I have to go. I'm catching a plane."

"Well, you don't need to hurry. They have closed the airport."

"Closed the airport?" said Ferenc stupidly. Closed the airport!

"Some sort of security alert. They are scared to death of Arab guerrillas. Nothing goes out, and the incoming planes are all being scrambled and delayed, and, oh, what a mess! Nobody knows when anyone is arriving—or departing. So you can buy me a drink, no?"

Closed the airport? Ferenc brought himself up sharply. He was staring stupidly at the pretty Swiss right there in the middle of this vast concourse with cops all around. He gripped her by the elbow.

"Where's the bar?"

"Over there. Come."

Thirty-five minutes, he saw by the clock. But if they're scrambling the arrivals! "How long will the airport be closed?" he asked. If the airport were closed, they'd be left standing in the middle of the

· 251

grass runway—unless. . . . Then an even more clamorous thought struck. Scrambled the arrivals! Then they wouldn't know when the Arab charter job was arriving at all!

He plunked her down at the bar abruptly. "Order me a double Scotch," he said. "I'll be right back. I've got to make a telephone call." He departed almost running.

"Saul," wailed the hostess. "That's not the way to the telephones."

He was in the main terminal, walking rapidly but not too rapidly with all those flics about. Where was the way to get to the parking lot, parking lot 6? Ah, that way. He strode toward it, brushing through the travelers roughly. Glanced at the clock. Another three minutes gone. There should be no hurry now, but there was, there was! Nicole would keep her eye on the clock, and heaven help any jet that came over the horizon at 4:00 P.M.

The public address system was announcing the clampdown in three languages. *"L'aéroport est fermé,"* said a lovely, lilting feminine voice, a seductive close-down.

He was just at the door now leading to the parking lot when he saw André, a hundred feet away, staring at him, dismay in every line of that handsome French face. He was standing next to a uniformed Swiss policeman.

André! Hell and damnation! For only a quiver of a heartbeat Ferenc stared like a transfixed rabbit at his old friend, then he pelted through the door, his mind in flames.

André stood frozen. But the Swiss policeman had been alerted by this exchange of glances, the wordless electricity of a gaze. He had Ferenc's photograph in his hand, and he looked at it, something he would never have done if it had not been for that exchange of looks between two old school chums. André had fingered his friend just as efficiently as if he'd cried out.

"It's our man," said the policeman, and took off in pursuit.

At the private plane apron the young pilot had loaded the little Apache and he was busily warming up the twin engines. On the apron Nicole looked at her watch. Three thirty-five. Where in God's name was Ferenc? She was shivering now from the cold autumn wind cutting across the open space. That and premonitory dread.

She took a deep breath, another, and another. Oxygen. She needed lots and lots of air for her thudding heart. And her screaming mind. If they'd caught Ferenc . . . ?

She stared, huge-eyed, across the vast space of jets, aware suddenly that there was no movement at all on the airport, nothing coming, nothing going out. But then perhaps that was normal. Geneva was, after all, not Heathrow. It must have moments of peace. Or did this absence of noise, as noticeable as a scream in a nunnery, have sinister connotations?

Oh, Ferenc! Ferenc! Where are you?

If he doesn't come, what then? I will do it myself. Her mind rang that decision like a bell. If he does not come in the next five minutes, something quite clearly will have happened to him and he won't be coming at all. The thought steadied her by its sheer desperation. If Ferenc were dead, then there was only one thing to do—complete the mission and die gloriously in the doing, an Arab legend to ring down the ages!

In the cockpit the young pilot was revving up the port engine, testing the magnetos, watching the girl on the apron at the same time. Touch of madness in those eyes, he thought.

Up in the glass booth on the roof, a dispatcher was trying to get through to the little Apache on his radio. But the young pilot didn't have his headset on. The dispatcher turned to his assistant. "He hasn't got his radio on yet. Run down and tell him he might as well turn his engines off. The airport's closed."

The dispatcher kept his eye on the little airplane. He saw the girl on the apron look at her watch and then climb into the airplane and slam the door behind her.

Always one thing goes wrong. If I had not run into that girl, I would not have been delayed. If I had not been delayed, I would not have encountered André. If I had not encountered André, I would not have this Swiss flic on my ass. Ferenc was in the parking lot, ducking behind the cars, leading the man the wrong way, then doubling back to the Land Rover. If he could get out of this cul-de-sac. . . .

He got to the Land Rover with the Swiss cop at the other end of the parking lot looking the wrong way, leaped in and backed the car out, and spun it around. He had the coin and the parking ticket in his hand, and he handed them over with a smile to the attendant in the booth.

"*Merci, m'sieu,*" said the attendant. The barrier went up, and Ferenc drove the Land Rover out of the park and into the mainstream of the traffic. In his rear-view mirror he could see the Swiss flic running, waving his arms, shouting down the line of parked cars. Much good it would do him, thought Ferenc. The cop was afoot, and before he could get to a phone to alert the motorized cops, Ferenc would have vanished into the stream of traffic.

But that wasn't his problem now. He glanced at his watch. Three forty-five. The light-aircraft hangar was a mile—and three traffic lights—away. No time for traffic lights. He shot through the first one, missing an enormous truck by inches, and sped on.

The young pilot found himself at the other end of a .38 automatic. The gaze behind the gun was almost absentminded. "Taxi the plane to the grass runway," said the girl. She was very calm, the calmness beyond hope, her mood a mixture of exultation and despair. To the young man it was horrifying, this calm.

"I can't . . . taxi . . . without instructions from the tower," gulped the young man.

"I will kill you in thirty seconds if you do not gun those engines," said Nicole. Then, almost casually, showing her medals. "I am a member of the Young Palestine League."

The young man was half twisted around in his seat, facing Nicole in the back seat of the little plane. Through the window behind her head he could see the assistant dispatcher appear on the apron, waving at him and shouting.

"Ten seconds," said Nicole viciously.

The young man turned back to the instrument panel and gunned the engines and released the brakes. The plane moved off sharply. "Faster," said Nicole. She'd seen the man come out from the hangar, waving his arms. Something was up. She didn't know what it was, but instinct told her it was the explosive moment beyond which there was nothing. "Faster," she repeated. The plane picked up speed.

The assistant dispatcher turned and ran back to the hangar. Up in the glass booth the dispatcher was already picking up his telephone to alert the main control tower. Airport police had already noted the little plane taxiing along at speed toward the grass light-plane runway, and they were sounding the alarm bells. A police car left the main terminal at speed, but it was a good mile and a half away.

At four Army turrets around the field, alarm lights began winking, and the marksmen at all those points took the safety off their guns and began looking about for the trouble spot. There was nothing to be seen except a small twin-engine light plane running along down the grass runway at the far end of the field.

Ferenc, weaving in and around cars and frequently on the left side of the road, had arrived at the light-plane hangar and drove right around it onto the field. He passed a young man running back toward the hangar. Out on the field he saw the little plane taxiing. Ferenc roared after it, over the apron, off the concrete, and down the grass runway.

"Stop the airplane," shouted Nicole over the engine sound.

Gratefully, the young pilot throttled down the engines and slammed on the brakes. The plane slid to a halt on the grass. The young man half turned in his seat, his mouth open, and calmly Nicole shot him dead.

In the Land Rover Ferenc saw the plane stop on the runway, its engines idling. What would I be doing, he thought in an icy calm of concentration, if I were Nicole and I didn't know the airport was closed. I would shoot the pilot and then I would, in anticipation of the plane's arrival, step out on the runway. Three hundred meters away now, the accelerator of the Land Rover on the floor, he saw the door of the little plane open and the girl, slim as a saber, dangerous as a cobra, step out, the rocket launcher in her hand. Oh, Nicole!

"Fire at will!" commanded the Colonel in charge of the Army special troops from his headquarters on the roof of the main terminal building. "Low. We want him alive." At 800 meters one sex is indistinguishable from another, even through binoculars. Terror is unisexual. Four sharpshooters at four different control towers around the perimeter took aim. But 800 meters is a long way to call your shots, high or low. Or to hit anything at all. Especially with that wind . . .

Nicole stood on the grass runway a few feet from the plane, eyes to the northeast, where the plane should be coming from. A bullet threw up dirt and grass twenty feet to her left, the *ssssss* of its flight unmistakable to a trained terrorist. She heard it and ignored it, eyes on her watch. Five minutes after four. Just like an Arab airplane to be late, she thought bitterly.

In his control tower the sharpshooter corrected his sights for windage and aimed again.

Another bullet from a different marksman plowed into the ground almost at Nicole's feet, spitting dirt and grass. She glanced at it idly, absently, her mind exploding with one word: Ferenc. Then she heard the scream of the jet as it came in from the northeast. Aaah, good. The bullets would not miss forever. She put the rocket launcher to her shoulder.

The Land Rover was doing sixty, its top speed, only 200 meters away now. Ferenc saw the launcher go to Nicole's shoulder. Oh, God, no, no, no, no, it's the wrong airplane! Oh, Nicole! Her back was to him, and he was screaming at the top of his lungs—but he could hardly compete with the scream of a jet plane. . . .

Nicole pressed the button that energized the missile guidance system. A Grail takes a moment or two to warm up. Then a buzzer located in the launch grip stock informs the gunner the missile is ready to fire. A lot happened in those few moments.
Ferenc sounded his horn, and just for a single second Nicole was distracted from her target, something that should never happen to a terrorist. A single anguished glance at her lover. But for that interruption she would have noticed that the approaching jet was not the airliner she was gunning for but a Swiss fighter sent into action by the general alert. She took aim blindly. The Land Rover braked violently next to the Apache, and Ferenc hurled himself out of it toward Nicole.
The bullet hit.

The marksman had corrected this time not only for windage and drift but for optics—that is, the shimmering of light over a long distance which makes a target at 800 meters seem actually much higher than it is—and he had overcorrected. The bullet took Nicole in the lung—much higher than the marksman had planned—and it pulled her arm and shoulder back and turned the rocket launcher toward the sky just as she squeezed the trigger. The rocket went, not northeast, but almost straight up.

Blood was pouring from her mouth as Ferenc caught her in his arms. Her eyes were shining with triumph. She had no strength for thoughts, only feelings. She felt a lightness as if her ebbing life were turning into air. Her eyes were normous with elation. She had not expected ever to see him again, and she was deeply grateful. Triumph and Ferenc, too!

A Grail rocket is powered by a two-stage propellant engine whose first stage is designed to protect the life of the marksman. The missile leaps out of the launcher propelled by a small first-stage charge to a distance of about six meters. Then the second stage sends it at supersonic speed toward what it is aimed at, and when it gets within range, its ultrared sensing device locks itself automatically to the heat source of the target engine and guides itself in.

But the Swiss fighter had sheared off back to where it came from, and there was no engine in that closed airport for the rocket to home on. The rocket groped blindly in space, and finding nothing, curved down toward the only heat source within range.

"Stop firing," commanded the Colonel. But the four marksmen had already stopped, all of them gazing at the two terrorists locked in embrace 800 meters away.

Her victory, thought Ferenc, looking deep into the triumphant eyes. I'm not going to take it from her. She's won as much as any terrorist ever wins. He kissed the gushing lips.

The supersonic heat-seeking device homed in on the little Apache engine, and the airplane blew up, showering flaming gasoline for thirty meters in all directions, covering the lovers in a ball of orange flame precisely like the one Nicole had long dreamed of as the proper end of her revolutionary mission.

# *Epilogue*

André poured the wine, Mistinguett, from his own vineyard in the Loire, into Colonel Frère's glass, watching the redness of it bubble into the glass. Like a fireball when an airplane is consumed in its own fuel.

"You are making a very great mistake," said Colonel Frère in the tones of a man simply putting his objection on the record. He had no hope of changing André's mind. "You might have been Deputy Foreign Minister within a few years."

"Diplomacy is out-of-date," said André. "It's about as functional as a crossbow. We have reached the bloody end of measured accommodation, which is what diplomacy is all about. Do you like that wine? My own."

They were lunching at the Maison Blois, a tiny Left Bank spot that served only trout. "The idea that only white wine is good with fish is a superstition largely propagated by the English," André observed. "The English don't really like to drink wine, you know. They write about wine. They worship it. They hoard it. They do everything but enjoy it."

"*Très bon,*" said Colonel Frère noncommittally. He would have preferred a dry white wine, but it was André's luncheon. And his wine. André was in a heretical mood, thought the Colonel. Red wine with fish? Resigning from the French Foreign Office?

"Power comes from the muzzle of a gun these days," continued André. "In such a time, diplomacy is a mockery."

"You know diplomacy better than I do," observed Colonel Frère —diplomatically. "But I should have guessed that the time was coming very shortly—even in the Middle East—when one can no longer sit on the bayonets. Then the diplomats will resume where they left off. They always do."

"Not this time," said André. "We are at the beginning of another Dark Age, my friend. It's going to go on for a very long time. I should have enjoyed the middle of the Middle Ages—or the end of it. But the beginning must have been horrifying for everyone. We are at the beginning."

The two men ate in silence for a moment.

"You're too gloomy," said Colonel Frère. "I realize the death of your great friend, Ferenc, was a shock. But it could have been very much worse, the affair at Geneva. An airliner full of people! You know that your old colleague Fourchet had engineered a change of schedule so that—if things had worked out—they would have shot down a Pan American plane full of jolly American vacationers on their way to a safari in Africa. The Chinese planned to pin it on the Russians. The plan went awry, and I suspect Fourchet will pay dearly. It would have worked if they hadn't closed the airport."

"Who was the mastermind who thought of that?" asked André.

"Oh, there weren't any masterminds," said the Colonel. "There never are. It was a mistake, pure and simple. In place of closing the airport to takeoffs, someone pushed the wrong button and closed it altogether. They would have reopened it in another five minutes. That is the trouble with trying to run a terror operation on schedule. The rest of us—shall I call us the terrorized?—are off schedule most of the time." He sipped the Mistinguett appreciatively. Not quite enough strength, he thought, but very kind to the sauce.

"What are you going to do down there at your château besides raise grapes?" he asked.

"Survive," said André cynically. "It will take some doing in the next decade. I've been reading Koestler. Do you like Koestler? Koestler says it's quite wrong to think of mankind as aggressive. He says man commits his greatest crimes—war, terror, the like—not because of any inbuilt aggressive tendencies but out of *devotion* to the leader or to the country or the cause."

Colonel Frère consumed a mouthful of trout cooked in its own juices augmented by a little champagne, washed it down with Mistinguett, and reflected.

"From what we have found out about that girl, Nicole, she was very devoted to the Palestine cause. She killed three people. . . ."

"Four," said André. "Don't forget the fellow in the woods."

"Four then," said Colonel Frère. "But only in a spirit of the most intense idealism."

"Oh, yes," said André skeptically. "We are rapidly approaching the spiritual fervor of the Inquisition when they tore people's bodies apart for their own good. That's why I'm taking refuge in my vineyards."

"She was also very intelligent," said the Colonel mildly.

"Oh, they all are," said André ironically. "Almost invariably these days when you read of a young girl holding up a bank or blowing up an airplane, you find she was the brightest member of her class at university. The barbarians of the new Dark Age are more than intelligent, they are the most intelligent young people." He laughed. "That is why you must not sneer at survival as a career. It will take a lot of doing. It won't be very long before Nicole and her friends will have their hands on the odd hydrogen bomb, just as they now have the odd rocket—and then it won't matter if it's not aimed very well. It will make the most enormous, intensely devoted, wholly ideological hole in the ground."

The two men ate in silence with intense appreciation, chewing on each other's thoughts as well as the trout.

Colonel Frère dug into his pocket and handed André the well-thumbed leather-covered notebook. "A farewell present for you, André. Your cousin François Duvillard's diary. We found it in the glove compartment of the Land Rover, which is how it survived the holocaust. I spent all last night reading it. Very interesting."

The Colonel took the notebook back and opened it at a page he had turned down. "There is a passage here that your cousin wrote about the massacre at Fiumicino Airport in Rome that is enormously relevant."

André read:

The Rome massacre has shaken the established community by its senselessness. At Munich the athletes were at least Israelis. At Lod, they were visitors to Israel. But at Rome the phosphorous bombs burned alive totally innocent strangers who were not even going to Israel and had no relationship with Israel at all. This is part of a pattern of wantonness that has by no means reached its end. Terror will now begin to curve back and become inversely meaningful. The terrorists slaughtered first their enemies, then at Rome innocent bystanders. At Khartoum they killed their friends and fellow Arabs. There remains only the final and inevitable step when the terrorists blow themselves up—for terror is inevitably a form of suicide.

The observation—so simple, so lucid, so mocking—shook André, for it forecast the Geneva self-destruction months in advance. Even more startling was Duvillard's evident enjoyment of his conclusions.

The two men looked at each other soberly and sipped their wine.

"So you see," said Colonel Frère, "it wouldn't be quite accurate to say there were no winners at Geneva. François Duvillard was the winner."

"Posthumous revenge," said André dryly. "He'd have appreciated the irony."

"Oh, François Duvillard was a remarkable man, all right. Did you know that he also set up that triple killing at the Café des Pyramides? He found out that those three Arab gunmen would be at that café at that hour from Robert Pinay and passed it along to the Israeli counterterror people. It saved the life of the Israeli Ambassador, but one can't imagine that's why he did it because he was betraying the Israelis as well. Also, the Russians, the French, the Palestinians, and his own family. Where did his allegiance lie in the end?"

"To himself," said André. "He hated commitment, my remarkable cousin. He considered loyalty to an ideology or to a nation or to the group the most dangerous subversion of all—and isn't it?"

"You're beginning to sound quite a lot like your cousin," said Colonel Frère.